ROUGH SEAS

A TOM GRANT NOVEL

SAMANTHA ADAIR

Publishing Assistance by

Michelle Morrow, www.chellreads.com

ROUGH SEAS

1

TOM

Mashed pumpkin and sloppy peas hits Tom's cheek. He opens one eye as the giggling nine month old baby girl digs in her bowl for more ammunition. "I thought we were friends."

Isabella snorts from where she leans on the kitchen worktop. "What did I tell you about feeding a baby while dressed in a designer suit?"

"You didn't. But also…I wasn't planning on feeding her. Your phone rang and here I am."

Isabella grabs the spoon out of Tom's hand. "Go clean up. I'll finish." She sits in Tom's vacated chair and baby talks to Sylvie. "You'll be late for the dinner and Martha will shoot you."

"Well, she's coming here so I can't be late." Tom grabs a paper towel and wipes his face. "How did you get out of going anyway? You're training up. You should have to deal with this shit too."

Isabella rubs noses with Sylvie, who giggles and tries to grab at her hair. "I have *covert practice* lectures tomorrow. For eight hours. I would *rather* be eating five star food at a boring dinner party. But I need to get up at the crack of dawn." She gives him a smirk. "And, maybe I don't scrub up as nice in a dinner suit."

Tom swallows the grunt sitting in his throat as Mischa walks out from the bathroom. She spins on the spot to show off her dress, in turn making Tom want to push her back into the bedroom and forbid her from going anywhere.

"Who is actually taking you to the ballet? You never mentioned." *I need to vet him.*

Mischa's cheeks deepen in colour as she picks her daughter up out of the highchair, holding the pumpkin covered baby at arm's length. "I did not?" she asks in her soft Russian accent.

"No, you did *not*." Tom crosses his arms over his chest and watches as she avoids the question. *He won't be good enough.*

Mischa kisses Sylvie's plump cheek. "Thank you for looking after Sylvie."

"No problem," Isabella stands and tickles under Sylvie's chin before walking into the kitchen and inspecting Tom's face. She sweeps her thumb across the side of his mouth. "You have a bit right here."

"Do I?"

She stands on her tip toes and kisses his mouth. "No."

Can't I stay home and do this? He holds her face with both hands and kisses her. "Maybe you can throw a dress on and go too?"

"Martha asked *you* to go. Not me. Anyway, I have to study, and Edward might drop in for a cup of tea. Remember?"

Edward? "Wait, what?"

Mischa sucks in a sharp breath and scurries to Tom and Isabella's bedroom door. "I will change this one while you two argue."

Tom grunts out loud this time as Mischa disappears into the room. "Do you have to keep inviting him over here?"

Isabella opens the fridge and sticks her head inside. "This is the third time in the three months he's lived in this block, Tom. That's not *all the time*." She emerges with a bottle of water.

"Okay, but two of those times have been in the past week."

"He knocked on the door needing milk and I asked him in for a cup of tea. It's hardly inviting him over here. I was being neighbourly."

Tom huffs and leans on the back of his armchair, facing the kitchen. "Okay, fine. As long as he doesn't sit in my chair."

Isabella throws herself onto the sofa and puts her feet up on the coffee table. "Are you jealous?"

"Me? Jealous? Of...of him?" *Ludicrous.* Tom forces a snort and sits in the armchair. "No."

"Will you relax? It's a cup of tea."

"He *would* drink tea." *Prat.*

"Relax. I have loads of study to do. I can't be drinking tea all night."

"I know. You have a month on campus from tomorrow."

Isabella walks to Tom and plonks onto his lap. "You gonna miss me?"

"I can visit."

"You can. But give me a warning so I can make sure my on-campus boyfriends aren't hiding under the bed."

"It's fine." Tom brushes his mouth against hers. "I know you'll just be drinking tea."

"And studying."

"Right." He kisses her lips, and she runs her hands up the back of his neck and into his hair.

A throat clears softly behind them and Tom grins against Isabella's mouth. "Stop it, Iz. You're making Mischa uncomfortable."

Isabella pulls away and giggles before smiling at a point behind Tom. She holds her hands out and claps once. "Come to your favourite." Isabella walks to Mischa and takes Sylvie.

Mischa sits on the couch and grins at Tom. "Are you still having argument?"

Tom scoffs and stands as the buzzer goes off for the front doors. "We weren't arguing." He pushes the button. "It's open." He walks to the front door and unclicks it for Martha. "Also, you avoided the question before… who are you going to the ballet with?"

"Me!" James struts into the flat, dressed in a suit that actually fits.

Tom clenches his jaw. "You?" He turns to Mischa. "Him?"

"He helped me move to flat last week." Mischa kisses both of Sylvie's cheeks and picks up her clutch.

Tom's eyes widen. "Why is today the first I'm hearing about this?"

"Ah, 'cause you aren't her dad?" James shrugs.

Mischa and Isabella giggle at the same time and Tom eyes the pair of them. "James?" He keeps his eyes on the girls.

"Yeah?"

"A word?" He stalks into the hall and leans against the wall, waiting for James to join him.

James wanders out with his hands jammed in the pockets of his trousers. He grins at Tom, stops in front of him and rocks back on his heels. "What's up?"

"You helped Mischa move into her flat?"

"Yep."

"And somehow you decided that meant she wanted you to ask her on a date?"

James holds a finger up. "It's not a date."

"You're both dressed in fancy clothes and going to the ballet, James."

"Yes but—"

"Are you taking her for dinner?"

"Well, yeah I mean…"

"So it's a date." Tom holds both palms up and purses his lips. *I rest my case.*

"It's not a date. It's two friends going to the ballet."

"Do you like ballet?"

"Yeah…" James clears his throat. "Love it."

Tom grabs James' shoulder, spins him around and pushes him against the wall. "Lie." He leans in and squints at James.

"Tom, chill. I'm not gonna pull a move on her."

Tom's pulse ratchets and he glares at James. "She's been through hell. Has a nine month old baby and doesn't need snot nosed gits like you trying to get into her knickers."

"Who said I was trying to get into her knickers?"

"I'm not an idiot."

"Okay, listen." James pushes himself off the wall and scurries from where Tom has him pinned. "I'm taking her to the ballet. I promise to stay away from her knickers. Yeah?"

"And her bra."

James smirks. "And her bra."

"In fact just keep your slimy hands to yourself, maybe?"

James rolls his eyes.

"Her husband was shot dead in front of her a year ago. Just…" Pain spikes through Tom's chest. *Because of me.*

"I promise to be a perfect gentleman."

Tom snorts. "Like you know how."

"What are you two bickering about now?" Martha's voice floats down the hallway from the top of the stairwell to the foyer.

Tom looks up to see her decked out in a glittery dress and she's wearing... *makeup?* "Jesus, Martha. What happened?"

"What do you mean?"

"Are you wearing..." Tom leans forward as she walks towards them. "Lipstick?"

Martha glares at Tom. "Is that a problem?"

"No. It's... you know…unexpected." *Weird. It's weird.*

"It's a black tie event Tom."

"Yes. It's just…" *Weird.*

Martha tuts and walks past both of them into the flat.

Tom frowns at her retreating back and James chuckles. "Date night with Mum?"

Tom slams his palm into James' chest and bunches his shirt in his fist. "If you touch Mischa in any way, *any way.* I'll shoot you in the head."

"No, you won't."

Tom curls his lip.

"I mean… I won't touch her. But you also won't shoot me in the head." James winks and saunters back into the flat. He pokes his head out a second later. "Does she have a curfew too?" He grins and disappears inside as Tom stalks after him, gritting his teeth.

James holds his hand out and Mischa takes it, scooping her coat up before they walk into the hall.

"Bless. So cute," Isabella whispers.

James turns with his hand resting on the doorknob. "Don't

worry, sir, I'll have her home at a reasonable hour." He winks and shuts the door.

"Oh Tom, relax. It's James. Not some creep from Tinder." Isabella bounces Sylvie on her knee and Martha sits beside them and smiles at the baby.

"Exactly. It's James." Tom shrugs his dinner jacket on and runs his finger around the stiff collar of his shirt. "Tell me again why we're going to this thing?"

"Because we needed representation. And I was requested."

"And I'm going because?"

"Because James would have annoyed me. I can tolerate you."

"You know it's the twenty-first century. You could have gone stag."

Martha looks up from Sylvie and nods. "I expect your best behaviour."

"I'm not fourteen, Martha."

"You were better behaved at fourteen... marginally." Martha flicks her head towards the door. "Shall we?" She walks into the hall.

"I won't be late." Tom slides his hand up the back of Isabella's neck, into her hair and kisses her.

"Take your time. I'm drinking tea and studying." She winks and grins at Tom.

Tom grimaces. "Maybe I'll be late after all."

"Tom!"

Tom rolls his eyes. "Keep your wig on." He wanders to the door as Martha turns and raises her brow at him.

"Last chance to let me stay home and watch football."

"I need you at this dinner. Don't make it difficult."

Tom sighs and walks with her. "Why?"

"Why what?"

They walk outside to the waiting car and Tom slides in after Martha. "Why do you need me?"

"Because Lawrence will be there hobnobbing for his promotion. He will one hundred percent want to talk to me and if you're there he'll clear off quickly."

"Are you kidding me?"

"No. Also…I haven't seen you much since you got back from Russia."

"So?"

Martha shrugs and looks out the window.

"You're going soft in your declining years, Martha."

Martha snorts softly. "Just behave tonight."

———

A PIANIST IN TAILS SITS AT A GRAND PIANO, PLAYING FOR THE banquet. People mill around eating hors d'oeuvres and sipping expensive champagne. Tom grimaces at all the uniforms and stuffy dinner suits before glaring at his mineral water. *Bland.* He looks up at the fancy spirits on the shelf behind the bar before cracking his neck side to side and turning his back on them.

"I do hope you aren't planning on being a fool."

"I am not. Although I'm still trying to work out why I'm here."

"Haven't we gone through this?" Martha sips her brandy and surveys the room.

"Not really. I mean… I can't be the only bloke you could ask. And furthermore, you know I hate these things." He runs his fingers around his collar, pulling it away from his neck. "And I can't even have a drink to take the edge off." *I mean, I could…*

"Don't even think about it or I'll kneecap you."

I know. "Hmmm."

"Oh, Christ." Martha sips her brandy and nods in response to a crusty old man in a suit on the other side of the bar.

"Hey isn't that—"

"Yes, Tom. It is."

"Didn't you go on a few dinner dates way back—"

"Yes, Tom."

Tom smirks as Martha huffs and walks to the former Royal Navy Admiral, who takes her hand and kisses her knuckles. Tom leans on the bar and catches Martha's eye. He winks and almost hears her grumble from where he stands. He gulps water and chuckles to himself.

"Well, aren't you a tasty treat?"

Tom takes a breath, forgetting he has water in his mouth and inhales it the wrong way. He sputters and grabs a napkin. He looks at the woman next to him in her silver sequined gown and heavy makeup and slaps his chest. "Ah. Mrs Lawrence." *Mutton dressed as lamb.*

"You know who I am?"

"Only from photographs in the social pages."

She steps into Tom and drags a finger down the front of his shirt. "Is that right?"

"Yep." His voice squeaks and he clears his throat before gulping more water.

"And what's your name, handsome?"

"Tom Grant." He sticks a hand out to put some distance between them. Instead of shaking it she takes it and rubs her face against his fingers.

Jesus. He jerks his hand back and flattens it against his chest.

"Call me Daphne." She grins and tosses her blonde hair over her shoulder. "So where's your date?"

Tom nods towards Martha still speaking to the stuffy old Admiral. "She's the glittery one resembling a black widow." *Just as deadly.*

"How fortuitous."

"What?"

"You like your women a little older." She steps closer again and nudges her knee and thigh between Tom's own.

"Absolutely." He holds her gaze a moment before stepping away from Daphne and her exploring thigh. "She's my... *superior.*"

"Superior? You like to be told what to do, Tom?"

"Depends who's doing the telling…Daphne." He grins and throws a glance over his shoulder, making eye contact with Martha. *Save me.* She smirks and turns her back on him. *Really?*

"Tom?"

He spins and peers at Daphne as she puts her empty glass on the bar top and pulls a room keycard out of her clutch. "Sorry, what?"

She slides the card along the bar top and winks. "Four twelve."

"Oh you… I don't know that—".

"Daphne." Admiral Peter Moore sidles up behind her and glares at Tom.

God, I need a drink. Tom swallows the thirst in his throat.

"Grant."

"Pete." Tom grins, knowing the irritation it will cause. "Sorry. *Admiral.* So fancy."

Moore holds Tom's glare but speaks to the barman. "Bourbon on the rocks and a Verve."

"I'm on the water, thanks, Pete."

"It's not for you."

"No shit."

Daphne smiles directly at him while Moore hands her the Verve, his other hand rests in the small of Daphne's back for a moment. Tom looks at Moore's hand and back up into the Admiral's face. Pete drops his hand and gives Tom a smug smile.

Filthy perv.

"Thank you, Peter. So kind." Daphne sips her champagne.

Tom slides her room card back across to her. "Well."

She steps into Tom and puts her mouth to his ear. "Like I said, four-twelve." She saunters away without a backward glance, leaving the card on the bar top.

"She's rather direct, isn't she?"

"Yes. At times."

"How would you know exactly, Pete?"

Moore watches Daphne walk away. "Still harbouring a killer?"

"I don't know Pete. How's that hooker and cocaine problem of yours?" Tom raises his eyebrows. "And your wife? She's with you tonight? Such a lovely lady."

"Don't fuck with me, Grant."

"Or what? I must say you're looking sharp in your uniform. Shiny medals. About to get another one to add to the collection I believe?" *Goes to show...*

"Something you'll never experience, Grant."

"Agreed. Though I guess that's where we differ, Pete. I prefer not to decorate myself like a Harrods Christmas tree." Tom reaches across and dusts Moore's ribbon bar. "Perfect."

"Fuck you, Grant." He nods to Martha as she appears next to Tom. "Admiral Cole." He turns on his heel and marches away.

Martha rolls her eyes and gestures Tom to their table.

"Must you antagonise him?" Martha sits and realigns her cutlery.

Tom throws himself into the seat next to Martha. "He's a dick."

"A dick who can arrange to hold Isabella for questioning for hours on end if he so chooses."

"He won't."

"I believe you are out of ammunition with which to keep him at bay now, Tom."

"Tell me. Is there any evidence we were anywhere near Jack when he died?"

"Of course not."

"Then he's barking up the wrong tree. Isn't he? Not to mention we didn't actually kill him. And I'm sure there will be ample opportunity to catch him doing something else he shouldn't. Old perv can't help himself."

"Didn't I tell you to behave this evening?"

"Don't remember." Tom picks up his water and faces the front of the room.

"Well, well." A heavy hand lands on Tom's shoulder. "Fancy suit."

Tom grits his teeth and continues to stare at the front of the room. "Commodore Lawrence. Always a pleasure."

"Admiral Cole." Lawrence nods to Martha as he pulls out the chair next to Tom and sits.

Fuck's sake. "Can we help you?"

"Well, you *do* owe me. But I won't be cashing in today. You can relax."

"Commodore Lawrence," Martha starts. "To what do we owe the pleasure?"

"I'm networking."

Tom narrows his eyes and bites his tongue. "I'm far too busy for chit chat."

"I can see that."

"I also don't care about anything you have to say."

"Drink Commodore?" Martha gestures to the drinks waiter.

"What the hell are you doing?" Tom hisses.

"Stop being insolent."

Tom pulls in a long breath and pinches the bridge of his nose. "You and I are having words about this. *Admiral*." Tom smirks, knowing how much Martha hates being addressed by her former rank.

"I look forward to it."

"Thank you, Admiral Cole. I do love a tipple." He grins at Tom. "Don't we all?"

Tom slumps back in his chair and throws his hands out, gesturing for Lawrence to speak.

"I can't talk to a former sailor under my command without there being an ulterior motive?"

"Of course you can. However, we despise each other. Can't you choose someone else to *network* with?"

"Ah, Grant, I have to associate with the riff raff or people will think I am an elitist. It's important to be a man of the people." He winks and nudges Tom with his elbow. "Actually,

I'm more interested in speaking with Admiral Cole. She has the... connections I require."

Martha rolls her eyes.

"Ah, your promotion is looming, is it not?" *Of course they would promote someone like you.*

"You are as smart as they say you are, Grant. Pity we hate each other. I could use you."

Tom grunts and sips his water, trying to ignore the fact it does nothing to quench the thirst sitting in his throat.

"What is it you think I can help you with?" Martha swirls her brandy.

"Oh nothing much…I just thought I'd remind you of our joint venture some months ago…extracting assets trapped in Russia. Wonderful outcome I thought…" He sips while keeping his eyes on Martha. "I'm sure you both agree."

"An order, I understand, you were not altogether happy to receive?" Martha smiles.

Tom folds his arms over his chest. "Why does that not surprise me?"

"A daring and courageous mission was flown, on my direct orders and under my scrutiny. We flew into hostile territory, using subterfuge to mask the real reason for the flight. And a sister agency was saved considerable embarrassment. A resounding success under any measure I would say."

Martha nods. "And yet, I understand your initial response was *they can rot in hell.* Isn't that correct?"

Lawrence clears his throat and leans forward. "You owe me,

Cole. In fact…" He looks at Tom. "You *both* owe me. And I'll be collecting." He stands and adjusts his jacket. "Formal nominations are next week. Can I expect a phone call or two in my favour, *Admiral* Cole?"

"*Former* Rear Admiral Cole," Martha corrects him. "I don't know how much sway you think I have any more."

"Less than me." He turns on his heel and strides away.

"What does he mean by that?"

"Again, he's flexing."

Tom stands. "Let's go."

Martha grabs his wrist and yanks him into his seat. "Sit down and shut up."

2

ABBIE

Abbie stands at the bar and surveys the room. *Table seven...* Her gaze lands on her assigned table and she smiles into her red wine. *Well, won't this be fun.* She saunters across the room, sits in front of her name card, and waits for the person sitting next to her to glance up from where he's tearing his name card into tiny pieces. *He's thirsty.*

"Hey, Grant."

Tom flicks his eyes up and they widen. "Abs."

"Surprise." *How does one get better looking as one gets older?*

"You're here. And... on this table?"

"Yes. I'm no longer enlisted; they shove me over here with the extras." She sips her wine and punches his arm lightly. "Stop squirming."

"I'm not squirming."

"You're squirming, Tom." The older woman sitting next to Tom puts her hand on his shoulder and stands. "I'll be back. If the food arrives, I want the beef." She walks off, leaving Tom peering after her and chewing on his bottom lip.

"Why are they doing alternating servings at a five star dinner anyway?" Abbie sips her wine and turns in her seat to face Tom.

"Because all these pompous gits would be too difficult to take orders from."

"Ha! Fair."

Tom looks around the room, his eyes jumping from one place to another.

"Who's your date?"

"Martha. She's my boss."

"And where's Isabella? You know…assuming she hasn't kicked your sorry arse to the curb yet?"

Tom fixes her with a deadpan expression. "At home with the baby."

No way. "Baby?"

Toms' eye twinkles. "Yeah, you know. Small person…wears nappies. Can't feed themselves yet?"

"Thanks for the education, Grant. I had no idea…Wow."

"It's not mine."

"What?"

"She's babysitting, Abs. It isn't *our* baby." Tom smiles as Abbie punches him in the arm.

"God, Grant. You had me concerned for a minute."

"Concerned?"

"Yeah. You. In charge of a baby. It's rather frightening."

"Huh. Well, while I may agree with you... I'm offended."
He pushes a hand to his chest.

"You are not."

"No I'm not. You're right. The concept is frightening."

"So your boss asked you to accompany her?"

"Something like that." He grimaces. "I'd rather be at home
sticking pins in my eyes. But here I am."

Abbie grins. "Here you are. Relax. I promise not to accost
you in the broom cupboard." *But gee it'd be fun.*

"I wasn't... worried..." Tom shakes his head as his plate and
Martha's are set down. He swaps the plates.

"Didn't she say she wanted—"

"You should eat your steak before it goes cold." Tom nods
towards her plate.

"Still a smart arse I see."

"Don't know what you're talking about." Tom grins as he
chews.

You haven't changed.

Abbie scrapes at the pureed cauliflower and beetroot on her
plate and licks her fork. *Retirement home food.*

"Who combines cauliflower and beetroot in a mushy mess
under a perfectly good piece of rump?" Tom scrunches his nose
and puts his fork down.

"If I remember correctly Grant, a half price curry was your

lifeblood most Friday nights back in the day. Don't pretend you're all gourmet now."

"Doesn't count when you're drunk."

Abbie snorts and tips the last of her wine down her throat. She opens her phone and checks the time. *20:46.* She faces the phone away from Tom and types.

Got your room key? On my way.

A moment later her phone pings.

Three minutes.

Abbie smiles into her chest and stands.

"Hot date?"

Her stomach drops and she peers at Tom. "Excuse me?"

"Nothing. You stood up very suddenly. Like, you've got somewhere better to be."

"Oh." Abbie laughs. "No… nature calls."

Tom's mouth quirks at each corner and he nods. "Of course."

"It's true."

"Well, off you go then, don't want to get caught short."

"Nice to see you, Grant."

"You aren't coming back after your visit to the ladies?"

Abbie swallows. "No. I mean…yes." Heat crawls up her neck and she giggles. "Wine's going to my head. Back soon."

She takes off before Tom has a chance to ask any more questions. *Never could get one past him.*

As she weaves through tables and diners a hand grabs her around the wrist.

"You're certainly in a hurry."

Abbie gasps and swallows. "Mrs Lawrence. How are you?"

"Just grand, Darling. Why don't you take a seat? My husband has wandered off somewhere that's obviously far more pressing than his dinner."

"Well, you know how it is. With important status, comes important… meetings."

"Must be my fault for being attracted to powerful men." Daphne winks and sips her champagne. "Or maybe I told him something he didn't like?" She shrugs.

"I'd love to stay but heading to the Ladies. Lovely to see you again."

"And you Darling, good luck in your… future endeavours." Daphne's eyes flash for a second before her face softens into a smile.

"Thank you Mrs Lawrence. If you'll excuse me…" Abbie backs up a couple of steps before turning and scurrying away. *Bitch.*

She pushes open the heavy doors and stumbles into the hallway.

"The Ladies is inside, on the other side of the banquet hall."

Abbie slaps her hand to her mouth and looks into Tom's

face, grinning at her while he stands against the opposite wall. "Grant… what are you…"

"I was bored… and you walked in the complete opposite direction to the facilities."

"Well I…"

"So I thought I'd entertain myself with a spot of espionage."

"Espionage?" Abbie chuckles. "I went the wrong way. It's hardly worth leaving your steak over."

"True. You know what *is* worth not finishing dinner for?"

"Enlighten me?"

"A quick screw in a fancy hotel room."

Abbie tosses her hair over her shoulder and wills her cheeks to cool down. "Is that an invitation, Grant?"

"No."

"What a shame."

"Flattered." Tom pushes himself off the wall and strolls past Abbie, stopping beside her.

"Have fun, and don't forget to reapply your lipstick." He winks at her before walking back into the banquet hall without another glance back.

Abbie slumps against the wall and takes a few breaths to slow her heart rate. *Smart arse.*

———

ABBIE SLIDES THE CARD INTO THE LOCK FOR ROOM FOUR TWO six and walks in, slotting the key card back into her clutch.

"I said three minutes, Perkins."

"You did. Sorry, sir…I mean…"

"I do deplore tardiness." Matthew Lawrence turns from where he gazes out the window and Abbie bites her bottom lip. His perfectly styled silver hair and piercing blue eyes make her breath catch in her throat.

"I wish you'd worn something a little less sexy tonight, Perkins. It makes this a lot more difficult."

Abbie grins and walks across the room, dropping one spaghetti strap from her shoulder as she moves. "Well if you like it so much I can leave it on." She stops in front of Lawrence and hovers her mouth within a millimetre of his.

He pushes his mouth against hers and kisses her, cupping her face in his hands. The familiar flutter in her belly erupts and she grabs at his shirt, untucking it from his trousers. He slides a hand down her neck and to her chest, dipping inside her dress. Tingles shimmy up her body and she pushes her lips harder against his.

Lawrence pulls away. "Stop."

"What?"

"We can't."

"Excuse me?"

"This has to stop. Tonight. Now. It's over, Perkins." He straightens his shirt cuffs.

Abbie flares her nostrils and slaps her hand onto the middle of Lawrence's chest and leaves it there. "What the hell do you think you're doing?" The tingles fade and are replaced by a raging flame in the pit of her gut.

Lawrence grabs her wrist and holds her hand away from him. "I can't see you anymore."

"Because?"

"I'm about to be promoted. I can't have this carrying on, potentially being exposed."

"Exposed? What happened to leaving your wife?"

"Perkins—"

"No!" Abbie's heart hammers against her ribcage and she narrows her eyes. "I paid for this hotel room. I used *my* credit card so there was no record of you. Everything is always about you. You don't get to corner me here and tell me it's over for no reason."

"I gave you a reason."

"Your promotion? You said you'd leave her after that. You said you'd make it easier to be with me. Were you lying?"

"I thought—"

"You *thought?* What exactly were you thinking?"

"I thought I could leave her. But... the timing isn't good. Surely you understand?"

"Do you love her?" Abbie whispers.

"What?"

"Do you love your wife?"

"She's my wife."

"Do you love me?"

"I..." Lawrence stops and scratches his forehead.

"After everything I've done for you?"

"It was never… this isn't about love, Perkins."

"Abbie!"

Lawrence jolts and looks at her. "What?"

"My fucking name is Abbie. Not Perkins. I'm not on your ship, *Sir*. I'm in a hotel room, standing in front of you with half my dress hanging off. My goddamn name is Abbie." Her nose tingles and she rubs the back of her hand across it. "You owe me more than this, and you know it!"

"Lower your voice for God's sake." Lawrence scrubs the back of his neck and loosens the collar of his shirt. "I don't know what you're getting so worked up over. This was nothing more than two consenting adults having some fun."

"Is that a fact?"

"Yes." Lawrence straightens up and adjusts his tie. "Now stop acting ridiculous. It's time to go. You aren't in my league. You know that as well as I do."

What the fuck? Abbie bites her tongue and reaches across, smoothing Lawrence's tie. "I'm so sorry. You're right. What was I thinking?"

"I... well yes. You got carried away, Perkins, It's understandable."

Abbie keeps running her hand down his tie, to his belt and pushes her hand into his trousers. She grabs and squeezes. "You picked the wrong Petty Officer to mess with, *Commodore*."

Lawrence doubles over and yanks her hand away. "What the fuck are you doing, Perkins?"

"Abbie!"

She grabs his face and squeezes his jaw. She pulls her dress strap back onto her shoulder and shakes her hair down her back.

"Perk... Abbie. Wait."

Abbie stands at the door to the room with her back to him. "Sir?"

A hand slides up the back of her neck, grabs hold, and squeezes. "If you fuck this up for me, I will end you," he hisses in her ear. "Am I making myself clear?"

Abbie smirks at the door in front of her. "Crystal."

———

ABBIE SITS ON SOME CONCRETE STEPS AND LOOKS OVER THE Thames. She wipes the back of her hand over her eyes, knowing black mascara is going everywhere. *I'm such an idiot.*

She opens her phone and hovers her thumb over Matthew Lawrence's number before looking up at the inky sky. "Don't be a fool," she whispers to herself before a fresh flood of tears wells in her eyes. She drops her phone on the step next to her, covers her face in her hands.

"Abs?"

Shit.

Tom sits next to her on the cold concrete step. "Jesus Grant don't look at me. I'm a mess." She swipes under both eyes with her index fingers, and they come away covered in watery black smudges.

Tom picks her phone up from where she dropped it and hands it to her. "Toilet break didn't go well?" He gives her a soft smile.

"No. Not really." She sniffles again and shakes her shoulders out. "I'm fine."

"You know I know you're telling lies. But that's fine. Martha has been bailed up by some old Admiral who I'm fairly certain served with Nelson. I have time." He brings his knees up and rests his forearms on them. "You know, if you squint your eyes and tilt your head a little you could pretend you were in some glitzy city and not on the bank of the Thames in the freezing cold."

Abbie giggles and rubs her arms. "I'm warm enough." *My blood's boiling at least.*

Tom snorts, takes his jacket off and drapes it over her shoulders. "I need it back before I leave… It's all fancy and shit."

Abbie pulls the jacket around her and nudges Tom with her shoulder. "Thanks."

"So, what happened?"

"Got dumped."

"Ouch."

"But that's not the worst part."

"It's not?"

"No. I've been an idiot. For the past year and a half. He strung me along." She looks up at the sky again and takes a breath. "Made me promises. And I believed him. Did things I regret."

"Sailor?"

Abbie pauses and watches the lights dance off the surface of the water. "Yeah. He's on *Arrochar*. She's berthed at St Katharine's at the moment." Abbie shrugs. "Some big Royal event or another."

Tom grunts. "Remind me to take a wide berth. No pun intended." His phone rings and he takes it out of the jacket still around Abbie's shoulders. "Martha." He pauses and rolls his eyes at Abbie. "I'm down by the Thames." He shifts and looks back over his shoulder.

"God, don't let her see me like this. I bet she never cries."

Tom ends the call and shoves the phone back in his jacket. "What's that?"

"She's not coming down here is she?"

"No. I need to go meet her at the car. Why do you care if she sees you?"

Abbie's face heats up. "No reason. Just... don't like women seeing me cry."

Tom stands and Abbie does the same. "You aren't weak, Abs."

No. I'm fucking not. Abbie slides his jacket off her shoulders and gives it to him.

"Keep it. You'll freeze."

"I'm fine. I'm going to head home."

"You want a lift?"

"No. I need to wander."

"We could stop and get a curry."

Abbie laughs. "And what would Isabella think if you went and got curry with another woman?"

"She wouldn't care. Though she would make me sleep on the sofa on account of the curry breath."

"I bet." Abbie smiles. "Thanks Grant. But I'm fine."

Tom flings his jacket over his shoulder. "You're lying but... okay. And for the record Abs... he's the fool."

Abbie's nose tingles again and she nods back towards the roadside. "Don't keep your boss waiting."

Tom winks at her before running up the steps two at a time and disappearing. *I do miss that tush.*

Abbie wanders along the bank of the river towards the tube station. A female shrieks behind her and she looks back at the hotel. Lawrence and his wife are getting into a Rolls Royce. Daphne is laughing and swatting him with her clutch. She stumbles as she gets in.

"This isn't over. *Sir.*"

3

TOM

Tom gets into the backseat of the car waiting for him and nods to Justin, the driver. He peers out the window at Martha. *And she tells me to hurry up.* She inches away from Nelson's contemporary. Her knuckles are white around her handbag straps and her smile looks more like a grimace. Tom snorts, noting the discomfort in her posture.

"You should go and save her." The driver grins at Tom through the rear-view mirror.

"Yes Justin, I should but… this is payback."

"For?"

"She left me floundering with a fifty-year-old boiler trying to get into my trousers earlier."

Justin laughs. "You two are hilarious."

Tom continues watching Martha and smirking to himself

before noticing Moore making his way down the steps. "Well, now I'm certainly not going to her rescue."

Shouting and a car door slamming a few parked cars ahead shatters the calm of the night.

Tom looks through the front windscreen as Daphne storms across the road towards the entrance to the hotel. Lawrence power walks to her and grabs her by the elbow. He yanks her into him and says something in her ear. Daphne swings her handbag and hits him across the face with it.

Tom winces. "That hurt."

Lawrence stumbles and Daphne continues to steamroll up the steps and into the foyer while Lawrence gets into the rear of a black car, and it takes off.

"Well I can't say that wasn't entertaining."

Justin twists in his seat to face Tom. "Has Isabella ever hit you with her handbag?"

"Isabella? Carrying a handbag?"

"You're right. Absurd."

"I wouldn't mind getting home to her sometime in the next millennium."

Justin holds up both hands. "Talk to the boss."

Tom huffs as Martha stomps across the road. "Speaking of…"

Martha opens the door and gets into the car. "Let's go. I'm sure he's a vampire and if we don't get away quick enough he'll chase us down."

"You're the one who went on dinner dates with him."

"He used to be attractive."

"He always had that bald patch at the back of his head, Martha."

"Yes well, I'm too short to notice such things." She gives Tom a wry grin.

Tom blanches and looks back at the hotel. Moore is speaking on his phone and swaying slightly. "Moore looks a bit worse for wear."

"He's a mess." Martha shakes her head. "Let's go, Justin."

Yes, let's.

"Ma'am."

Justin pulls away from the curb. Tom watches Moore turn and go back inside the hotel. *Hopefully he passes out with his head in the toilet.* Tom chuckles to himself, leans back against the seat and closes his eyes.

"Something funny, Tom?"

"Nope. I'm drunk."

"Hilarious. So tell me. Who's the blonde woman?"

Tom's eyes peel open. "Blonde? Daphne Lawrence. She tried to give me her room key. Thanks for the help by the way."

"No, not her. I knew *she* was making you uncomfortable. It was rather amusing."

"Glad you got a laugh."

"The younger one at our table?"

"Oh. Abbie Perkins. Former sailor. I think she was there to get an award."

"You think?"

"I wasn't paying attention."

"You're always paying attention."

"Not to pointless ceremonial bullshit."

"You seemed to know her well?"

"Same ship."

"Ahuh."

Tom rolls his eyes. "We were friends."

"Were?"

"Are." Tom shrugs as his cheeks warm. "I haven't seen her since I left. She used to keep me out of trouble."

"You were *always* in trouble."

"More trouble. She kept me out of the way when I wasn't feeling peopley." *And I owe her a million times over.*

"Hung over, you mean."

"That too."

"She was crying."

Tom frowns. "How did you know?"

"I saw her leaving the hotel. She was beside herself."

"Yeah…she got some…bad news."

"That's no good." Martha smoothes her crease free dress. "Do you think Admiral Moore has collapsed with his head in the loo yet?"

Tom snorts. "Here's hoping."

"Idiot should have got in his waiting car and left."

Tom's mind goes back to Daphne storming towards the hotel, and Moore's hand in the small of Daphne's back at the dinner party. "I'd say he has other plans." *Ugh.*

"What's that Tom?"

Tom grimaces. "Nothing. Forget it."

"Isabella goes away tomorrow does she not?"

Tom turns and raises his eyebrow. "She does."

"Are you okay with this yet?"

"She's an adult Martha. She can go away for a month if she so desires."

"That's not what I meant, and you know it."

"I have no idea what you're on about."

"Isabella joining the agency."

"She's an adult. Like I said."

Martha says nothing and Tom refuses to look at her, although he can feel the holes burning in his cheek.

"Tell me, Tom. Apart from Isabella, does anyone know you better than me?"

"Nope."

"So stop lying."

"I'm fine with it."

"Honestly. I don't know why I bother."

"Me neither." The car turns into Tom's street and he spies James walking out the front of the building. "Ah look at that. You can give James a ride home. How lucky." Tom grins at Martha. "Pull over here please, Justin."

"Right you are." He pulls the car into the curb.

Tom opens the door. "So I'm out of the firing line for any more of these dinners now?"

Martha rolls her eyes. "Yes Tom. You're off the hook."

"Should I shout out to James?"

"No."

Tom grins and the car pulls away the moment his door slams shut.

Grouch.

———————

TOM OPENS THE DOOR TO THE FLAT AND POKES HIS HEAD INTO the dark lounge. He clicks the door shut behind him.

"Tom?"

Tom squints through the darkness at the foldout in the lounge. "Mish?"

"Yes. Be careful, I wheeled cot out here. Do not trip."

Tom moves to the armchair and sits, pulling his tie loose. "How was your date?"

"It was not date." Mischa reaches to the side table and snaps the lamp on.

Tom blinks against the sudden light. "Did James tell you to say that?"

"No."

Tom narrows his eyes.

Mischa winces. "Yes.

"So it *was* a date?"

"Tell me, Tom. If it was…does that make me bad person?"

"Why would you think so?"

"Because of Sascha," she whispers. "Am I selfish?"

Tom goes to her and sits at the end of the foldout. "No. It doesn't make you a bad person."

"I like James. He is smart and funny... and kind."

"Wait, smart?"

Mischa giggles. "Yes. And…kind, Tom. He is kind."

"Listen to me, Mischa." Tom grabs her hand and squeezes. "You're allowed to be happy. And I know how hard it is to accept. But you're allowed to lead a happy life. It doesn't mean you forget him. It means you honour him."

Mischa drops Tom's hand and lunges forward, hugging him. "Thank you, Tom."

"Do I wish it wasn't James? Sure…" Mischa sits back and giggles again. "But... as much as it pains me to say it. He *is* kind and funny. I'm still on the fence with smart." The last of Tom's words are tainted with a yawn.

"Go." Mischa nods towards the bedroom. "You look so tired."

Tom stands. "Sleep tight.

He wanders to the bedroom. Isabella is tangled in the duvet and she's hugging his pillow. *I should really let her sleep...*

Tom grins, pulls his clothes off and crawls under the covers. He slides his head onto his pillow and kisses Isabella's mouth. She pulls a deep breath in through her nose and opens her eyes.

"Hmmm…hey…" she mumbles against his face.

"Sorry." He pulls his pillow out of the way and Isabella slides her hands down his body. "Didn't mean to wake you."

"Yes you did." She reaches his waist and stops. "Don't be naughty, there's a baby in the room."

"Sylvie's out with Mischa."

"Is that so?"

Tom pushes his mouth to hers again. "Yep." He runs his hands under her singlet top. She raises her arms and Tom pulls it off over her head.

"I'm very sleepy." She teases dropping her hands and stroking her fingers along his lower abs. "And I have to get up at four am."

He holds his breath and shifts his body over her, pushing his leg between hers. "Okay, you should sleep." He drops his mouth to her neck and drags his lips down past the dip in her throat and the middle of her chest. He continues over her scarred stomach, across the rose tattoo and reaches her hip. He stops and looks up at her and she sighs dramatically.

"Well, fine. I guess I can stay awake for a little while."

"Only a little while?" He hooks a finger under the lace edging of her knickers and pulls the silky material across.

Her breath catches and he grins.

Thought so.

4

TOM

Isabella drags her backpack out and drops it against the wall "Shhh... you'll wake Mischa." Isabella holds a finger to her lips.

Tom looks at Mischa. Sound asleep with Sylvie in the bed with her. He nods to the hall. "Come on then." He grabs her bag and takes it into the hall.

She lifts her arms above her head, stretches and yawns. "I could have done with another hour."

"You shouldn't have stayed awake so late."

"I was sleeping peacefully until you came home."

"Sorry."

Isabella buries her face in his chest and wraps her arms around him. "Don't be."

"It's only one month."

"Are you telling me? Or yourself?" Isabella grins, steps back and heaves the backpack onto her shoulder.

"I was just saying…you know in general."

"I'll be perfectly safe, Tom."

"I know."

"And I can see you on weekends."

"You can."

"I have to go, the car will be wait—Oh, my God!"

Tom looks up and his heart rate soars. "Abs. What the hell?"

Abbie stands at the top of the stairs in a mac she has let fall open. The front of her hoodie is covered in blood.

"Thank God you still live here. I wasn't sure." She wipes a hand across her forehead, leaving a blood smear on her skin. "I'm sorry. I didn't know where else to go and I—"

"Abs. Stop." Tom goes to her. "You're covered in blood."

"Yes."

"Why?"

"I…I don't. It doesn't make sense."

"Come inside." Isabella opens the flat door and waves them towards her.

"Iz, you need to go. The car will be waiting for you."

"But…" She puts her both hands on Abbie's shoulders. "Are you okay?"

"No," Abbie whispers.

Isabella looks up at Tom with wide eyes.

He leans over and kisses her. "I'll call you. You have to go." He flicks his head towards the stairs. "I'll help her."

"I love you."

"Love you too. Be safe."

Isabella looks at Abbie again and presses her hand to her chest. "Bye."

Tom watches Isabella disappear down the stairs before steering Abbie into his flat and sitting her on the armchair.

"What is happening?" Mischa's voice is soft and sleepy.

"Sorry, Mish. Why don't you take Sylvie into the bedroom?"

"You are girl from ship." She hugs Sylvie against her. "Are you hurt?"

"It's fine Mish. Go sleep or look after Sylvie or whatever, yeah?" He nods at her, and she scurries to the bedroom.

He sits on the end of the fold out. "What happened, Abs?"

"He wanted to see me. And I went. But he wasn't..." She takes a breath and shakes her head.

"Abs. I have no idea what you're talking about." He looks at the front of her bloody hoodie; her hands smeared with the same. "All I know is that you're covered in blood, sitting in my lounge. You don't appear to be hurt?"

She shakes her head.

"Is someone else?"

"Yes."

"Okay..." Tom raises both palms upwards and leans towards her. "You're going to have to fill in some blanks for me here."

"He texted me. At two am, told me to meet him."

"Your...bloke?"

"Yes."

"Go on…"

"Said he was wrong and needed to see me. But when I got there…there was a knife and…" She swallows. "I tried to do CPR…"

"On who?"

"His wife," Abbie whispers. "I wasn't sure if she was alive…I tried to help her…"

"He's married?"

Abbie looks up at Tom and pulls a breath through her nose. "It's Matthew Lawrence."

Silence hangs between the pair of them as Tom gives her a slow blink. "Pardon?"

"For nearly two years."

"Jesus Abs." Tom runs his face with both hands.

"I know. I know. Don't judge me on that right now, okay?"

Tom sighs. "So who's blood is this?"

"Hers."

"Daphne?"

"Yes."

Tom stands and paces around the coffee table. "Where is he?"

"With her. I ran."

Tom stops and peers at Abbie. "Start at the beginning."

Abbie takes a shaky breath. "He asked me to meet him at the hotel again. We had a room for the night, but he told me to go to a room on the floor above. I wasn't going to go but… I was angry and wanted to tear shreds off him."

"What time was that?"

"Just after two thirty."

"Go on."

"I get to the room and the door is open a sliver. So I figure he's in there waiting for me. I walk in and turn the light…" She takes a breath and shakes her head. "Turn the light on and Daphne was lying on the floor, still in that silver dress she was wearing earlier. There was blood on her chest and a knife on the floor next to her." Abbie stares straight ahead. The tears stop now, and her face is blank.

Tom sits in front of her again and grabs her hands. "Then what?"

"I…umm…I ran to her—"

"Abs!"

"I know… I wasn't thinking. I leaned over her to listen to her breathing. But she wasn't. So I started doing CPR. But the wound in her chest just kept spilling with blood every time I pumped. It was pointless. She was…she was already dead." Abbie's voice is flat, and her face is emotionless.

"And then you came here?"

Abbie shakes her head. "No. I was leaning over her, willing her to breathe even though I knew she wouldn't when I heard Matt's voice behind me."

"What did he say?"

"He shouted at me. He screamed at me. *What have you done? What have you done?* I stood up, covered in her blood, and tried to tell him I didn't do anything, but he pushed me to the side and ran to…her. He lifted her against him and glared at me. He stared at me the whole time, holding her dead body against himself."

Tom pulls her into him and rubs her back. "It's okay. We'll figure it out."

"I knew how it looked; so I ran. I didn't know what to do so I walked for a while but then came here. What am I going to do, Tom?" She grabs at his shirt with both hands and bunches it in her fists. "I didn't kill her. I swear I didn't."

"It happened in a hotel, Abs. They have cameras. We'll figure it out."

"Okay." She sniffles again and stands.

"Why don't you go shower. I'll get some of Iz's clothes for you."

"What about that poor girl in your room?"

"Oh, Mish. She's fine. She's seen worse, believe it or not." He gives her a smile and nods to the bathroom.

He knocks on his bedroom door as the shower turns on. "Mish?"

"Come in." Mischa is folding the last of Sylvie's clothing and putting it into her overnight bag. "I will go."

"You don't have to leave. I'm sorry about this. Abbie's had…a rough night." He opens the wardrobe and grabs a set of Isabella's sweats.

"It is okay. Is your friend hurt?"

"She isn't hurt."

"Do you want me to cook food for her?"

"No, thank you Mish. She just needs to figure some stuff out."

She picks Sylvie up and holds her against her hip. "We will leave you alone. Thank you, Tom."

Tom pecks Sylvie on the head. "See you soon."

"Of course." Mischa walks out.

He rests his head against the bathroom door. "Abs?"

"You can come in, I'm behind the shower curtain."

He opens the door and drops the clothes on the vanity. "Sweats for you. Take your time."

"Tom?"

"Yeah?"

"Thank you."

"I'm sure I owe you a few favours."

"One or two."

"You're a goddamn mess, Grant."

Tom opened one eye and squinted against the bright light slicing through his brain. "Abs?" His voice croaked as though he hadn't used it in months. He sat up and looked around. "Where are we?"

"Some bed and breakfast in Portsmouth."

"Huh?"

"You were legless. I couldn't take you back to the ship. You'd have been crucified."

Panic hit his lungs. "Fuck. Where's Chris?"

"He went back."

"Jesus." Tom rubbed his temples and swung his legs over the side of the flowery bed. "Abs?"

"Grant."

"Did we…"

"Ha. No. Even if you'd have wanted to, there's no way." She leaned into him, her nose millimetres from his. "I can't keep covering for you."

"Why do you?"

"Because someone has to. You're impossible."

Tom pulled her against him and kissed her. "Thanks, Abs."

His phone sounds and he picks it up as he flicks the kettle on. *Bucket of coffee, thanks.* "Martha."

"I know it's early, but we have a situation."

"Well, you should have told the old coot you weren't interested."

"Very funny. Can you come in?"

"Now?" He looks at the closed bathroom door, with steam snaking out from under it.

"Yes, I didn't call at five am for a gossip."

"Well, I'm kinda busy at the—"

"Wonderful. I'll see you in half an hour." The phone goes dead as the kettle boils.

"Tom?"

Tom grabs another mug and pours coffee for Abbie as she sits on a stool at the worktop. "Have some coffee. I need to duck out."

"At five am?"

"Yeah... I'll shower, go and be back by seven. Don't open the door to anyone, okay?"

"Okay."

"And sleep."

"I'll try."

He closes the bathroom door behind him and pushes his fingers into his temples.

What a shit fight.

————

THE WAREHOUSE IS QUIET WHEN HE WALKS IN. THERE'S NO ONE there, but Martha's office door is open halfway and light streams into the empty office space. He pushes the door open all the way to see Martha reading through her half glasses at her desk. She flicks her eyes to his and gestures him to the chair in front of her.

Tom sits and waits.

"Daphne Lawrence was murdered early this morning."

Tom's blood slows to a crawl and tingles cascade down his neck.

"Did you hear me?"

"Yes."

Martha looks him square in the eye. "Where's Abigail Perkins?"

Tom holds her stare and resists the urge to swallow. "Why are you asking me?"

Martha folds her hands in front of her on the desk and doesn't answer.

Leaning back in the chair, Tom crosses an ankle over his knee and intertwines his fingers behind his head.

Seconds tick by and Tom's patience wears thin. "This won't work on me."

"What?"

"You're leaving me hanging, hoping I'll say something. Like an interrogation." He leans forward and stares hard into her eyes. "Is that what this is?"

"Don't be ridiculous."

"Right." He stands. "I'll be off then."

"Sit."

Tom turns back to face her but doesn't sit. "What do you want me to say?"

"Answer my question."

"She's in my flat, asleep on the foldout in a pair of Isabella's sweats. Her blood soaked clothing is in a black trash bag in my kitchen."

"Sit."

Tom grabs the chair and straddles it.

"Did she kill Daphne?"

"She says she didn't."

"Do you believe her?"

"She was having an affair with Matthew Lawrence. He broke it off with her during the dinner. That's why you saw her crying."

"I see."

"She turned up at my place as Isabella was leaving at four this morning. Covered in blood and dazed."

Martha taps her desk with an index finger and leans back in her chair. "Is she capable of this?"

"Yes."

"So I'll ask you again. Do you believe her?"

"Why does it matter what I think?"

"Because I will back you and your actions, Tom. So I need to know what you believe."

"Give me twenty four hours to work out this mess with her."

"Done."

Tom stands and walks to the door of the office. "You know what'd be nice?"

"What?"

"To be able to go and play golf, watch football and be normal."

"You don't play golf."

"No. Stupid game. I'll call you." He turns to leave.

"Yes. You will."

5

ABBIE

Abbie lies awake staring at the sliver of early morning light across the ceiling from the crack in the curtains. She closes her eyes and sees Daphne's body on the floor of the hotel room. She smells the blood mixed with expensive perfume. Her eyes snap open and she sits up.

"What was I thinking, coming here?" She grabs her trainers and burrows her feet into them, keeping the laces tied. *I can't have Tom tangled up in this.*

She runs to the door and opens it.

"Going out?"

"Jesus! Tom!" Abbie stumbles backwards and grasps at her chest. "You scared the shit out of me."

"Get inside. I brought you coffee and a bacon sarnie."

"You said you weren't getting home until seven."

"I said *by* seven. And what difference does that make? Why were you leaving?"

"I… I wasn't… I just panicked." *As if he'll buy that.*

"Sit." He flings the sandwich at her. "Eat."

"What happened? Where did you go?" She opens the paper bag and takes a bite.

Tom gulps from his coffee and puts the cup on the coffee table.

"Tom?"

"Were you about to do a runner, Abs?"

Shit. She looks at her sandwich and picks at the bacon. "Yes."

"How do you expect me to help you if you run?"

"I shouldn't have come here. What I'm asking of you is too much."

"Technically you haven't asked anything of me yet. But if you haven't done anything wrong, what's there to run from?"

Too much. I'm fucked. Abbie snaps her eyes to Tom and drops the sandwich. "If?"

They both eye each other and Tom rubs his chin and down his neck. "Did you kill Daphne Lawrence?"

Abbie holds his gaze without blinking. "No."

Tom sits upright and drains the last of his coffee. "We have work to do."

"Work?"

"You're the prime suspect, Abs."

Abbie's gut jerks. "I know."

"So you need to think. Was anyone else there?"

"Apart from Matt?"

"Yes."

"Not that I remember. It was two am. Normal people sleep at two am."

Tom's phone sounds and he grabs it without looking at the screen. "Yep?... I figured as much... what?... " He looks at Abbie and his jaw tenses. "Why?... Later. I'm busy right now... I said later." He hangs up and leans his elbows on his knees. "Royal Navy Police have assumed jurisdiction of the murder."

No! "What? Why? She's a civilian. It happened in a hotel, not a ship or Navy land." *This is very bad.*

"A civilian who was married to a high ranking Officer. No doubt strings have been pulled. Tight." Tom stands and walks to the window. He peers through the open curtains, chewing on his bottom lip.

"You're making me nervous, Tom."

"I'm thinking."

"About?"

"There has to be a reason."

"For her murder?"

"For pulling strings."

There is. "Oh." Abbie twists her fingers in her lap. *I'm screwed.*

"I need to go back in."

"To do what?"

"I don't know."

"What do you do, anyway?" *How much can you actually find out?*

Tom turns from the window and sits on the sofa. "Well… we aren't Navy. We aren't anything. In fact, our agency doesn't even have an official identifier. We don't exist as far as the outside world is aware."

Oh.My.God. "Why?"

"Because sometimes things need to be handled in secret."

"So, you're a spy?"

"Sometimes. Other times we provide close personal protection, investigate in the shadows." He looks up. "Look after VIPs visiting the country… all sorts of things. And I want you to understand something at this point, Abs."

"What?"

"I shouldn't have told you any of that."

"Why did you?"

"You came here needing my help and you trust me."

"Yes."

"If you betray my trust in you… I'll cut you loose and set them on you. Do you understand?"

Abbie stares into his green eyes. *He's never spoken to me like that before.* "I…"

"Abbie?"

"I understand."

"So if you didn't kill Daphne… who did?"

"I don't know."

He stands. "Let's find out."

6

TOM

James looks up from his screen as Tom walks into the warehouse.

"James."

"Hey. How was dinner?"

"A blast. How was the ballet?" James' fingers tighten over the mouse and Tom grins. "That good?"

"I didn't touch her."

"Didn't give her a sly kiss goodnight?"

"I—"

"I'm not here to bust your balls. She likes you."

"She does?"

"Yes. So all I'm going to say is this." He perches on James' desk. "I don't have any siblings. I have no one apart from…"

"Mum?" James grins.

Tom slaps his hand into James' chest and bunches his shirt

in his fist. "If you hurt her. I will rip both your arms off and beat you with them. Do I make myself clear?"

"Yes. But I won't hurt her."

"That's right. You won't." Tom lets go of James' shirt but stays sitting on the desk.

"Was there something else?"

"Yes. I need you to search Abigail Perkins for me."

"Why?"

"Because I want some light bedtime reading, James."

"Leave it with me."

"If you find something, come and get me out of there. Understand?"

"Geez, Tom. Am I going to end up knee deep in shit?"

"No." Tom stands. "Waist deep maybe." He grins to himself as James mutters under his breath. "Don't worry James. I'll get you a snorkel." He opens Martha's door and walks in without knocking.

"Ah. Tom. Take a seat."

Tom stops inside the office door and grits his teeth. The back of Lawrence's head ignites his veins and he clenches his fists. "Commodore."

"Grant." Lawrence doesn't turn around.

Tom pulls the chair next to Lawrence further away and sits. "Deepest condolences."

"Very heartfelt, Grant."

"Why is he here?"

"I told you. You were requested."

Tom's neck pounds. "By *him?*"

Lawrence looks at Tom. "Yes. By me. I have questions you need to answer."

"Have you heard of the term *when hell freezes over?*"

"Tom." Martha slaps a glass of water in front of him and sits. Her eyes drill into his and he hears the unspoken warning.

He slumps against the back of the chair and slaps both palms on his thighs. "Go on."

"As you are aware, my wife was killed early this morning."

"Let's skip the recap. What do you want?"

"Abigail Perkins."

"What makes you think I can help you with that?"

"You two were thick as thieves."

"Your point?"

"Stands to reason she would go to you now."

"Now?"

"After stabbing my wife to death."

"*She* killed your wife?"

"I walked in to find her leaning over my wife, covered in blood." Lawrence turns in his seat and glares at Tom. "You tell me."

A knock at the door draws everyone's attention. Martha huffs. "Yes?"

James opens the door. "Um… Could I see Tom for a sec?"

Tom stands. "I've never been happier to see you." He saunters out of the office before Martha or Lawrence can say a word.

James grabs Tom's arm and pulls him to the computer. "You need to see this." He gestures to his chair for Tom to sit.

Tom peers at the screen. "What am I looking at?"

"Well, I searched Abigail… her file is currently printing for you, not much on her, but… there was one incident I found interesting, so I delved deeper and well…" He nods at the screen.

Tom clicks through a number of surveillance photographs. They depict Abbie having dinner with a man in Middle Eastern headwear six months prior. Tom swallows and tries to act natural. "They're having dinner, James."

"Do you realise who that is?"

"A man who knows a good red wine when he sees it?"

James rolls his eyes. "Amir Saleh."

Tom looks at James and raises both palms.

"He's an Iranian Revolutionary Guard who also happens to control the oil trade in and out of Iran."

"Right… I still don't see the big deal."

"Don't you remember a while back there was an embargo on Iranian oil due to some dispute over our ships in the Gulf allied with the US?"

"Yes."

James taps the monitor. "This guy. He was right in the middle of it."

Tom looks at the photographs again. "And Lawrence's direct competitor for promotion was implicated in the collusion before the oil trade was restored. I remember it was all over the news."

"Exactly."

"Can you get me information on the Saleh bloke?"

"Yeah. Easy."

James starts to flick through his screen and another picture flashes past. Tom slams his hand down over James'. "Stop."

"What?"

"Go back."

James flicks his screen back and stands, stretching his arms.

Tom stares at the screen. His gut plummets and he swallows the bile in his throat. "Print it." Abbie is handing an envelope to a smiling Amir Saleh. *What the fuck?*

"So, this Abigail Perkins..."

"What about her?"

"She is?"

"In trouble. Bring in the photos of Abigail drinking red." Tom rips the printout of Abbie off the printer and stalks to Martha's door. He barges in and slams the printout face down on her mahogany desk.

"What's this?"

"Please tell Commodore Lawrence we are done for today." He drills his eyes into Martha's. *Do not argue with me.*

"Commodore Lawrence, allow me to have someone see you out." Martha keeps her eyes on Tom as she speaks.

"Taking orders off subordinates now, Admiral? How telling."

Tom turns to glare at Lawrence. "We aren't in the Navy, *Matthew.* So take your rank and fuck off."

"Give me Abigail Perkins."

"I don't have her."

"Commodore, please. I'll keep you informed." Martha's voice takes on a hard edge.

"We aren't finished." The office door slams, and Tom moves his hand off the printout and sits.

"What on earth is going on, Tom?"

Tom gestures to the paper. "Have a look."

Martha picks up the printout and squints at it. "Amir Saleh."

"Yes."

"And Abigail Perkins."

"Yes."

"What's this about?"

A knock at the door sounds. "Come in, James," Tom calls without turning around.

James scurries in and slaps a stack of paper on the desk.

"And these are?" Martha picks up the stack and looks through it. Her nostrils flare but she says nothing.

"Umm... should I..."

Tom gestures to the chair Lawrence vacated. "Have a seat."

"When were these photographs taken?"

James sits forward in his chair. "Around the time Commodore Phillips was suspended."

"For colluding with the Iranians... apparently." Martha keeps her eyes on the papers.

"Yes, I believe so."

Tom says nothing, staring at Martha.

Martha sits back in her chair and takes her glasses off. She rubs her lenses with a tissue. "So, we have a dead Commodore's wife, fancy dinners with an Iranian oil trader and a former sailor, who is currently a suspect for murder, apparently slipping him... something."

"I need to speak to her." Tom stands.

"Yes. You do. And Tom?"

Tom stops at the door and waits.

"If she's involved in sharing secrets and collusion... we can't help her. We will report her."

"I know."

———

TOM BARGES INTO HIS FLAT AND SLAPS A FOLDER ON THE COFFEE table.

Abbie looks at it and back at him. "What's that?"

"Open it."

Abbie slides the folder in front of her and flips it open. She spreads the photographs across the table and covers her nose and mouth with both hands. "Damn."

"What the fuck, Abs?"

"Who took these?"

"Answer my question."

Abbie stands and flares her nostrils. "Who took these photos?"

"No idea."

Abbie holds Tom's stare and says nothing.

"You want to tell me what you're involved in? Before I make a phone call, and have you arrested?"

"Grant, no. Please. I didn't. I was…"

Tom says nothing.

"Matthew asked if I would wine and dine his friend, visiting on business. Even though his friend didn't drink."

Tom raises a brow. "Are you *that* stupid?"

"I trusted Matt, so I did it. Apparently his friend likes blondes." Abbie shrugs and gives a half smile. "He said if I helped him get connections in all the right places, he'd leave his wife after the promotion, and we could be together… legitimately."

"Jesus Christ, Abs. You are *not* that fucking stupid."

"Apparently I am. I'm currently being screwed; in case you haven't noticed."

"Are you seriously sassing me right now?"

Abbie slams herself into the armchair and glares at the ceiling.

"What are you giving him in this photo?" Tom holds up the picture of Abbie slipping the unknown man an envelope.

"An invitation."

"To what?"

"I don't know… some banquet?"

"You met with an Iranian businessman… and slipped him an envelope without knowing what was inside?"

"Yes, but Matt—"

Tom slams a hand on the coffee table and Abbie jumps. "I don't give a fuck what *Matt* said. How could you be so goddamn naive?"

"I trusted him! And... it wasn't *just* me." Abbie stands and paces the lounge, hugging her arms around herself.

"What?"

"There was at least one other sailor involved."

"Who?"

"I don't know. Matt never told me. He was doing behind the scenes stuff and when I asked what he was doing and who it was Matt said it wasn't my concern."

Tom presses his fingers into his temples and takes a deep breath. "Just so you know Abs, my brain is currently exploding with your stupidity right now."

"Don't. I feel stupid enough without you pointing it out. Am I fucked?"

Tom picks up his phone and presses James' number as Abbie sits on the sofa and holds her head in her hands.

"Tom."

"Hey. Listen... those photos of Abigail Perkins."

"Yeah?"

"Can you see when they were uploaded?"

"Yeah hang on..."

Tom listens to James click away on his keyboard and watches Abbie.

"Around two this morning."

"I see. And... who uploaded them?"

"Scrubbed. I'll have to do some hacking."

"Do it." Tom hangs up and waits for Abbie to look at him.

"What was that about?"

"You're being set up. And it has to be Lawrence."

Abbie snorts. "Well, if it is, you'll never pin him. He's too smart."

"We'll see. I'll call Martha and fill her in. We need to figure out who this mystery sailor is that's working with Lawrence. Start thinking."

"Okay."

———

TOM STARES OUT HIS KITCHEN WINDOW AT HIS HARLEY PARKED below. *Where I'd rather be...*

A loud knock echoes through the flat. Tom's head snaps towards the door and he holds a hand up to Abbie in a stop motion.

He presses a finger to his lips, and she nods. He peeks through the peephole and relief lifts the weight off his shoulders when he sees the top of Martha's head.

He opens the door. "Hey." A large box is next to her, bringing back memories that prickle at Tom's neck. *Uniform box.* "What's that?"

"Uniform."

Bingo. "Because?"

"You'll need it." She walks past him into the flat and stands in front of Abbie. "Martha Cole." She doesn't offer her hand.

Abbie looks at Tom and he nods as he slides the box into the flat with his foot.

"Abigail Perkins."

"In a pickle, Ms Perkins?" Martha sits in Tom's armchair.

"Yes."

Tom sits next to Abbie. "You've come up with a plan, I assume?"

Martha takes a breath. "You're going to pose as a Commander on *Arrochar*."

Tom's hands clench into fists and his blood stands still. "Pardon?"

"We need to find the sailor working with Lawrence."

Tom's jaw aches the harder he clenches it, and he stares at Martha. "No."

"Tom, I really think—"

"No."

Martha bunches her lips and stares at Tom.

Tom clutches the sofa cushion either side of his legs. "Are you fucking kidding me? What if I'm recognised?"

"I have a backstory for you. Tom, listen—"

"No. *You* listen." He springs off the sofa and paces in front of the coffee table. "I refuse... *refuse* to get back on that ship. Or any ship. And... *back in uniform?* As a *commissioned* officer? Have you lost your mind? Have you forgotten the mess I was when I left that life?"

"I have not."

"And now you're asking me to just waltz back in there... as a *Commander* for Christ's sake?"

"It's the only way. You aren't in the Navy anymore, Tom."

"Thank you for the clarification, Martha. I'll just have a quick conversation with my subconscious and let him know that the uniform and ship mean nothing and I should just pretend it's Wonka's Chocolate Factory. Shall I?"

"Tom—"

"Ignore the sounds and smells and memories on that ship. Pretend I'm in a candy garden full of little orange men mixing chocolate, loving life."

"You are speaking absolute nonsense."

"Exactly. And you know what?"

"What?"

"So are you." He stares at Martha. "If you think I am going anywhere near that ship, you are in some make believe world. Plus I'm only thirty seven."

"So we say you're forty two."

"I'm not sure if that's an insult or not."

"How much does Abbie mean to you?"

Tom looks at Abbie. "She's a friend. A close friend." *Who would do anything for me?*

"And out of all the people in the world she could have come to this morning she comes to you."

"I shouldn't have. It was... *stupid.*" Abbie gives Tom a pointed look.

He bites the inside of his mouth.

"So obviously there's a level of trust and history there meaning something more than just *friend*. And I know you well enough to know you're going to help her."

"I don't need to be covert on a ship to help."

"Yes, Tom. You do."

Heat envelopes Tom and he shrugs his jacket off to air his shirt.

"Tom, calm down."

Tom stops pacing and peers at Martha. "Don't tell me to calm down. What you're asking of me is huge. Don't you dare tell me to fucking calm down."

"You'll have a staff officer to assist you."

"Who?"

"James."

Tom blinks. "Am I in the middle of some elaborate prank right now?"

"No."

"James? James is going to bumble through this job with me. You really have gone senile, haven't you? Should I be looking at retirement villages for you? Is there a particular Zimmer frame you have your eye on?"

"Tom." Abbie puts her hand on his arm.

Martha flares her nostrils and stares at Tom. He glares back and tries to lower his heart rate with deep steady breaths. It doesn't work.

Tom holds her stare a moment longer before spinning and stalking out of the flat. *I feel sick.*

———

"Wow." Isabella lets out a long breath down the phone line and Tom closes his eyes, imagining it hitting him on the neck.

"Yep. She swears she didn't kill her, and that she knows nothing about the Iranian collusion."

"Do you believe her?"

Tom stands in front of the statue of Queen Victoria in Kensington Gardens and stamps his foot against the gutter. He stares up at the statue and blows air out of his mouth. "I don't know, Iz. I want to. I really want to."

"But?"

"But… she's feisty and emotional and completely capable of stabbing someone to death."

"You say that like it's a bad thing."

Tom catches the smirk at the end of Isabella's words and smiles. "I miss you already."

"God, I miss you too. You should see the room I'm in. It's like being in prison."

"Well, if Moore had his way…"

"Where are we with that? Should I be looking over my shoulder?"

"I have no idea. Lawrence and his dead wife have kind of taken priority. But I'll sort it. I told you not to worry."

Tom walks and waits for Isabella to say something.

"Iz?"

"What else is going on?"

"What do you mean?"

"I can hear it in your voice… there's more than Abbie making you anxious."

"I'm not anxious."

"Please… you're probably balling your hand into a fist as we speak."

Tom glances down at his fist and unclenches it. "Wrong…"

"Liar."

Tom chuckles and sits on the edge of the grass. "I have to go covert."

"For how long?"

"Not sure."

"What doing?"

"I'm the new Commander on *Arrochar*."

Isabella giggles. "Hilarious. What are you *really* doing?"

"And James is my staff officer."

"Tom. Stop. You can't get back on a ship… as a sailor…"

"No. It won't be pretty."

"Tell Martha no."

"I did."

"And?"

"We argued and I asked her if she had her eye on a particular Zimmer frame."

"Oh my God."

"So yeah… it went outstandingly well."

"Are you gonna be okay?"

"I'm not going to drink if that's what you're asking."

"I wasn't…"

"Iz."

"Okay I kind of was. This is going to be stressful."

"You don't say."

"At least James will be with you."

"Yes. I'm counting my blessings. We can listen to The Spice Girls after lights out. Fun."

"Tom, listen to me… should I come back?"

"What for?"

"I have a bad feeling about this."

"I'll be fine. It's a job. I'm not actually enlisted. I can leave whenever I want."

"And Abbie?"

"She needs to stay in our flat. Are you okay with that?"

"Of course. She needs your help. If she's innocent."

"Right."

"You should really figure that out first."

"I don't think she would lie to me. She would have run if she had something to hide." *Like she was about to when I came home. Fuck.*

"Okay, well I trust your judgement."

"That's dangerous, Iz." Tom grins and stands.

Half an hour later, he stops outside his door and scratches
Pebbles under the chin.

"Ah, Tom," Lorna's crackly voice is behind him. "I thought
I heard you."

"Did you?" He smiles and hands Pebbles over.

"Of course, dear. How else would I know you were in the
hall?"

Peeping through the peephole, sly old fox. "Fair point." He
slides the key into his door and opens it. "Nice to see you,
Lorna."

"And you, always."

Abbie turns the TV off as Tom flops into his armchair. She
nods at the box. "Are you gonna open it?"

Tom sits and stares at the box, making no attempt to get up.
"Yep." His gut sends waves of anxiety ricocheting through his
body. *Not a good start.* Sweat beads line Tom's top lip and he
goes to the kitchen for water.

Abbie twists to face him. "I'll sort it. I'll iron a shirt and…
whatever."

"You don't have to do that, Abs."

"Let me."

Tom downs the water, hoping Abbie doesn't notice the
tremble in his hand as he holds the glass. *Calm the fuck down.*
The water doesn't quench his thirst the way he craves but he
fills it again and drinks more, so he doesn't have to speak.

"Tom?"

Tom turns and Abbie is leaning on the worktop, waiting for him to answer her. "What if you can't find him?"

"Then it's just a nice little holiday for me… in hell."

"Grant. Don't do it. I'll turn myself in. I didn't kill her. They can't prove I did."

"You were covered in her blood. You were found leaning over her dead body."

"Yes."

"It doesn't bode well for you, Abs."

"But… I can't expect you to do this."

"It's done. And I suspect it wouldn't be any different if you had come to me or not. At least this way I know where you are and you're safe."

"Are you going to be okay?"

"No. Not at all."

7

ABBIE

Abbie lies awake, listening to the shower and Tom slamming bottles and objects around inside it. *He's freaking out.* She sits up and flicks the TV on. *Antiques Roadshow.* She settles back on the foldout, hugging her pillow to her chest in an effort to calm her heartbeat.

Tom walked into the room carrying Chinese takeout and a bottle of whisky.

"What's on?" He nodded at the TV, pulling plastic containers and chopsticks out of the plastic bag.

"Antiques Roadshow." Abbie flips onto her back and squints at Tom. "I thought shore leave meant we could explore the town and have a real meal in a real restaurant."

"You've been to Scotland a million times, Abs."

"Yeah but... we could go and look at stuff together."

*Tom stopped unloading the food and looked at her.
"Together?"*

*"I just mean..." She blew her fringe out of her face and
shook her head. "Forget it."*

*Tom moved next to her on the bed and pulled her against
him. "Let's not make this complicated."*

"I wasn't. I just thought..."

"I'm a mess, Abs. Best we stay friends."

"Friends?" She smirked and reached for the rice.

"Friends with benefits. Lots of benefits."

Abbie gasped and threw a chopstick at him.

*He grinned and used it to stab a dim sim. "And... when we
aren't enjoying each other's... company... we have each other's
backs. Yes?"*

"Always, Grant."

Tom nodded once. "Always."

"Always," Abbie whispers as the bathroom door flings open.

Tom walks into the lounge in grey tracks and no shirt, towel
drying his hair. "What's on?"

"Antiques Roadshow."

He peeks out from the towel and smirks.

"What are you smirking at?"

"Antiques Roadshow is like an aphrodisiac for you."

"I swear Grant, if I had a chopstick, I'd stab you with... it."
Abbie winces.

"Probably not your best choice of words right now, huh?"

He grins. "I'm off to bed. I have to be at that god damned ship at the crack of dawn…"

She sits up as though stabbed through the middle. "Don't do it."

Tom turns at the bedroom door and rests his head back against it. "I have to, Abs. They'll come after you if I don't."

Her heart squeezes. "Got my back, huh?"

"Always." He holds her gaze a moment before disappearing into the bedroom.

Abbie stares at the closed bedroom door for too long before shaking her head and lying down. She tries to watch as an old lady hopefully hands over a box covered in silk to an expert. Her mind drifts back to Scotland and her stomach flutters.

"Oh my god, it really is an aphrodisiac." She flicks the TV off and stares at the pale moonlight lining the edge of the curtains. Energy floods her veins and sleep is a pointless endeavour. She sits up and looks at the front door. *I need to disappear.* She looks at Tom's door.

Always.

She flicks the covers off and pads across the lounge barefoot. She walks to the bedroom door and presses her palm against it. *Don't be stupid, just leave.*

She rests her forehead next to her hand and squeezes her eyes shut.

The door flings open and Abbie stumbles against Tom's bare chest. "Shit." She steps back and winces. "What are you doing?"

Tom tilts his head and frowns. "I feel I should be asking that question." He grabs a shirt and puts it on.

"I…" She looks around the tiny hallway. "I was just…"

Tom walks into her and puts a hand on her shoulder. "I was getting some water. Want some?"

"Okay," she whispers and follows him into the kitchen.

He slides a glass of water in front of her and leans on the worktop. "Are you alright?"

"I feel so alone. I'm sorry. I wasn't going to come in."

"I know."

She looks at him. "You sound so sure." She smiles and sips the water.

"Do you remember when I started seeing Claire?"

Abbie nods. "Yes. You told me we couldn't be special friends anymore."

"I think my exact words were '*the fucking has to stop*'."

"Well yes, I was trying to be polite."

Tom smiles. "But when I told you… you never tried again."

"Of course not."

"So… I know you wouldn't have come in just now."

"I'm so lost. I don't even know which way is up."

Tom drinks from his glass, watching Abbie. He puts the glass in the sink and leans against the worktop. "Well, I think we both know that neither of us are sleeping anytime soon."

"True."

"So, let's watch and see what trash some old duck brings in

to waste everyone's time with." Tom walks into the lounge and lies on the sofa.

Abbie sits on the foldout and a flood of affection and guilt envelops her. "Thanks, Grant."

"Always."

8

TOM

Tom grabs hold of Chris's lapels and shakes him. "Wake up. It's not funny anymore."

He shakes harder, knowing it won't make a difference. Tom's heart jumps to his throat and tries in vain to escape. He squeezes his eyes shut, but when he opens them Chris is gone. Tom is shaking the pillow. He throws it aside and searches the bunk.

"Chris?"

"Grant?" A voice booms behind him.

Tom turns. Lawrence stands at the entrance to the berth. He's laughing and swirling whisky in a glass. "Stupid kid." He leaves and Tom pushes himself against the wall. The room closes in...

"Grant?"

Tom gasps a breath and opens his eyes. He's on his stomach,

gripping the sofa cushion. He shakes his head and sits up. *Fuck.*
He swipes a hand down his neck, over his throat and realises
he's sweating. "Jesus Christ," he whispers.

Abbie sits next to Tom on the sofa. "Are you alright?"

"I'm fine."

"You were breathing erratically and squirming."

"I just..."

Abbie grips his arm. "Don't get on the ship, Grant. It's a
really bad idea and you know it."

"Do you want to sit in a filthy cell somewhere while they try
to prove you killed Daphne and sold information to the
Iranians?"

"I didn't do those things."

"Then, I go on the ship." Tom checks the clock on the
kitchen wall. "I have to meet Martha in full uniform at seven.
Best get moving." He stands and walks to the bathroom.

"Grant?"

"Yeah?" Tom turns to look at her, and Abbie says nothing.
"Abs?"

She shakes her head. "Nothing. I'll make you coffee."

He walks into the bathroom and shuts the door, leaning
against it to get his bearings. "I'm not even on the fucking ship
yet." He peels his sweaty shirt off and throws it in the basket.
"Fuck. This."

Twenty five minutes later, after sitting in the shower,
wanting to stay there, he walks out to find his perfectly ironed
dress shirt hanging on the door handle of his bedroom. He knots

his towel tighter around his waist and looks to the kitchen worktop where the iron is sitting, unplugged next to a fresh cup of coffee.

"Thanks, Abs." He pokes his head into the lounge to find the room empty. His gut twists and he marches into the middle of the lounge and looks around. "You have got to be kidding me..." He looks to his bedroom; the door is half open. His heart leaps into his throat and he slams into the room. *Fuck.*

He throws sweats on and goes back to the kitchen. He picks up the iron and it's still warm. A slip of paper flutters to the floor and he picks it up.

"I'm so sorry"

9

ABBIE

"**D**ammit Abs!" He storms into the hall looking around.

"Ah, Tom. Good morning."

Not now. "Yeah hi, Ed. Can't really chat now."

"Up bright and early aren't y—"

Tom slams his door shut and grabs his phone. He pushes Abbie's number. "Pick up, pick up, pick up."

The foldout vibrates and he clenches his jaw. He ends the call and yanks Abbie's phone out from under the pillow. He throws it onto the sofa, hard and it bounces onto the floor. "Fuck!"

He knots his fingers through his hair and takes a slow, hard breath.

His phone rings. "What?" he grunts.

"Change of plan. Meet me at the warehouse. Be in full

uniform, we are going to brief Lawrence here instead of St Katharine's. I think it's safer."

"Abbie's gone."

"Excuse me?"

"She's fucking disappeared and left her phone behind."

"Calm down."

Tom's blood pressure spikes and he squeezes the phone. "No problem, Martha. I'll get right on that."

"Get dressed and get in here. And have your damn shirt ironed."

"It *is* ironed."

"To dress standard?"

Tom rolls his eyes. "Abs ironed it before she legged it."

"How kind."

"I need to find her."

"You need to get your backside in my office."

"I can't just—"

"Now!"

The phone goes dead, and Tom taps it against his forehead to stop himself hurling it across the room.

The phone rings again and Tom slumps into his armchair. "What now?"

"Hey."

"Iz. Hey."

"What's happened?"

"What do you mean?"

"You sound stressed."

Tom sighs and leans over his knees, massaging his temple. "Abs ran."

"What? When?"

"About forty-five minutes ago."

"Why?"

"Good question."

"That won't help her."

"Maybe *I* shouldn't help her." The simmering rage in his veins bubbles.

"You know you will. You know she's innocent. I can tell."

"She has to be. If I don't prove it... who will?"

"Maybe that's what she's run off to do?"

"She's always been hot headed."

"Hmmm... reminds me of someone."

"I have to be on that fucking ship today."

"I know. That's why I called. Are you okay?"

"Yes... no... I don't know, Iz. I really don't."

"One thing at a time. Get through today. Maybe once you're there it'll be okay. You coped well enough when we came home from Russia."

"That was a life or death situation. Would I rather be stuck in Russia or spend fifty odd hours on a ship, knowing I can get off it at the end?"

"Well, that's a fair point."

"But this time... I'm in a goddamn uniform and people are gonna call me *Sir.*" He grimaces. "Not to mention James will be yapping at me like an excited puppy."

"Give him the benefit of the doubt."

"It's a nightmare on all fronts."

"I have faith in you." A loud, long beep sounds in the background of her call. "I have to go. Speak soon?"

"Yeah. Thanks for calling. I didn't know how much I needed your voice until I heard it."

"Love you." She ends the call.

TOM STANDS IN FRONT OF THE MIRROR AND LOOKS HIMSELF UP and down. Trousers, belt, the shiniest shoes in history. *Nothing to it.* He looks at the shirt on the hanger. He walks back and forth in front of the bed, clenching and unclenching his hands. *Get a grip.* He lets out a huff and pulls the shirt on. He refuses to look in the mirror as he buttons it up, but the tremble starting in his fingers says everything. He yanks the loose belt open and tucks the shirt in without looking up. He buckles the belt and stares at the ceiling for a few seconds before turning to the mirror.

Prickles cascade down the back of his neck and his stomach swells with waves of nausea. He swallows and fiddles with the cuffs of his shirt. The phone on the bed rings and it nearly sends him through the ceiling.

"Calm the fuck down." He checks the screen and rolls his eyes. "Martha."

"Have you heard from Abbie?"

"No."

"So what other reason would there be for you to not be in my office?"

"Because I'm trying to get dressed. And it's making me sick."

Martha doesn't respond but he hears her breathe out.

"Do you hear me? I'm not even on the fucking tub yet and I want to vomit."

"I was harsh this morning. I'm sorry."

"Wait. What?"

"I underestimated how hard this is going to be for you. I should know better."

Tom sits on the end of his bed and chews on his lip. "Forget it. I'm carrying on like a child."

"No. You're displaying completely legitimate trauma."

"Stop." He stands and grabs the jacket laying on the bed. "Please tell me you have more than this damn number three dress."

"I have working dress here for you… two sets."

"Thanks."

"Come in. I'll push Lawrence back til nine. We can have coffee."

"I'm fine."

"No, Tom. You're not."

10

ABBIE

Keeping her hood on and her eyes to the floor, Abbie walks through the doors to Spar. She grabs a few protein bars and a flavoured milk. Her heart flutters as though a thousand butterflies are trapped within it as she throws a couple of five-pound notes on the counter for her breakfast and leaves without saying a word. She walks down a side street, careful once again to keep her head down and hood up. A filthy alleyway provides the cover she is looking for and she perches on an upturned crate to eat.

Grant's gonna rip my head off when he finds me.

"He *will* find me," she whispers.

A disturbance among a pile of rubbish bags behind her reveals two rats who scuttle into a hole in the wall. She grimaces and shoves the last of the bar in her mouth, standing up. *Brass rats.*

Back out on the street she sneaks a peek at a clock in a store window and calculates how long it will take her to get to her destination. *Too long on foot.* She hails a cab and slides into the back seat.

"Hampstead, please. High street and I'll direct you."

"Right you are." The driver pulls away from the curb and Abbie curls herself towards the window, avoiding his eyes in the rearview mirror. "You're out and about early."

"Don't like to waste the day."

"No, not these days. Too much to do, eh?"

Shut up. "Yeah."

"My late wife, God rest her soul, she used to have friends that lived around Hampstead. Not too shabby. Not too shabby at all."

"Right."

"'Course, we could never afford to live there. I would have, though. I would have given her the world, my wife."

"That's sweet."

Twenty minutes later she gives the cabbie a sizable tip and slams the door without saying goodbye. She dashes across the road and down a narrow side street before walking out to a street she knows well but shouldn't. Ducking behind a bush she peeks around and decides the street is suitably deserted before stepping out. As she goes to run across the road a black car with dark tinted windows pulls to a smooth stop. *Shit.* She stumbles backwards up onto the pavement and hides behind the same bush. *He's still fucking home.* Her heart pounds and sweat dribbles down her temples. The close call does nothing to ease the tension in her shoulders and she crouches lower, waiting for movement across the road. *Did he see me?*

Her eyes track the terrace house to the top floor where the bedroom and office are located. The front door opens and her pulse races faster. Matthew Lawrence steps out in his dress uniform and locks the door behind him. Abbie grits her teeth and swallows the bitter taste rising in her throat.

Matthew looks across the road in the direction Abbie is crouched. She leans further behind the thickest branches. He brushes down the front of his jacket and gets into the back seat. The car takes off and brown leaves on the street dance in its wake. Abbie waits until the car turns the corner before she paces across the road, her eyes darting from houses to cars to empty windows. The street appears deserted and Abbie hopes all is as it seems this time. She pulls a key out of her bra and slides it into the lock. *No clothing, no identification and no more cash but I kept the essentials...*

The door swings open, and Abbie takes one more look into the street before slipping inside the empty house. She flips open the alarm pad and keys in the code, watching the keypad turn green. *Arrogant fool.*

Taking the stairs two at a time she runs up to Matthew's office and goes straight to the safe hidden inside the trapdoor to the floor cavity. *Nine, oh, seven, six, nine.* Abbie grimaces as she enters Daphne's birthday into the safe keypad - the same code for the alarm. *Idiot.* It clicks open just as the thud of a car door outside draws her attention and she peeks out the window. The black car Matthew left in is back.

"Shit, shit, shit." She slams the trap door shut with her foot and runs from the room. She gets to the hallway as the front door opens. *God.* There's nowhere else to go but the master bedroom. She dashes into the room and throws herself under the bed, the sage green valance hides her from view, and she waits. Memories of being in the bed she hides beneath play at the edges of her mind and she shakes her head.

"Odd," Matthew's voice floats up the stairs. Footsteps climb the staircase, getting louder and closer until she spies a pair of shiny black shoes walk past the room to the study. He mutters words Abbie can't decipher as she hears the sound of the trap-door and safe being accessed. She winces.

A phone rings.

"Why does he need a doctor?... No I have work to do, that's why I hired you, is it not?... Just let me know what they say. Nuisance of an old man…"

Abbie closes her eyes as her heart thumps against the floorboards.

The shiny shoes move to the bedroom and the bed sags as Matt sits. "Marriage certificate, birth certificate."

Abbie squeezes her hand over her mouth. His shoes are so close she can practically see her face in the patent leather.

"The sooner this shit show is over the better." The shiny shoes walk from the room, moments later the keypad to the alarm is pressed.

Abbie holds her breath and waits until she hears the front door close. "Thirty seconds." She peeks around the curtains and sees the car move away before sprinting down the stairs and disabling the alarm. She slumps against the wall beside the entrance to the lounge and takes a few breaths to calm her nerves.

She scuttles back to the study and opens the safe. She fossicks through paperwork to find the file she's after. The green folder is at the very bottom and she plucks it out.

She pushes a hand against her chest, her fingers brushing over the gold chain around her neck. She closes her eyes a moment and relives the moment Matthew gave it to her for Christmas the year before. She unclasps it and drops it into the safe. "Maybe I'll end you instead."

She walks downstairs and sits on the bottom step of the staircase and thumbs through the papers in her hand. She looks for anything with Commodore Phillips' name on it. *He's the only one who can help.* Maps of oil rigs and credit card statements and records of Commodore Phillips' court matter and sentence details. "Why would you keep this? Entitled fool."

She goes to stand up before noticing a bunch of photographs at the bottom of the pile. Photographs of Commodore Phillips shaking hands with Amir Saleh. *Useful.* The last photograph stops her heart. Admiral Moore having dinner with Daphne Lawrence, his hand sitting very high on her thigh as she leans into him, her nose brushing his cheek.

"Oh, wow."

She folds the papers in half and shoves them down the front of her sweats. She covers her hand with her sleeve and opens the front door before remembering the alarm. As she starts to key in the code her eyes land on the phone in the lounge. She bites her bottom lip before blowing a breath out and scurrying to the phone. She picks it up and dials Tom's number. It rings twice before she hangs up.

Guess who.

11

TOM

Tom walks into the warehouse holding his dress jacket in one hand and his helmet in the other.

"Tom," Penny says, waddling from behind her desk. "Wow… you look…"

Tom raises a brow and presses his mouth into a thin line. "Look what, Pen?"

"Ah… crisp."

He grunts and keeps walking towards Martha's office.

"You rode your bike in full Officer's uniform?" Her voice is behind him.

Tom stops and grimaces. "Yes Martha. I folded the jacket in my saddle bag." He holds it up. "Look, it's not even creased."

"What about your shirt under that leather bike jacket?"

He looks down at himself. "It'll be fine. But are we here to talk about wrinkles in my pretend uniform?"

"It's not pretend. It's real."

"Okay sorry, in my *covert* apparel?"

Martha rolls her eyes and gestures into her office. "Come in. Sit down. I made you some coffee."

"A vat?"

"A mug. Make do."

"Thanks."

"Is there anyone on that ship that will know who you are?"

Tom thinks back to their rescue months earlier in Russia. "The medic."

Martha nods. "Okay, I'll get him transferred for a secondment."

"No. Don't."

Martha looks up.

"He may come in handy. He's friendly."

"Are you sure? It's a big risk, Tom."

"I'm sure."

"Voodoo magic?"

"Something like that."

Tom sips the coffee and tracks Martha as she walks around her desk and sits. She folds her hands in front of her and looks at Tom.

Tom lowers his mug. "Say whatever it is you want to say."

"If I could think of another way for you to infiltrate that ship I would."

"I told you I'm fine."

"You were a mess when I called you earlier."

"And look at me now. Drinking coffee, having a right lark. Is there a field of buttercups I could go frolic in?"

Martha sighs and takes her glasses off. "I'll send James in. He can do it."

Tom coughs as his coffee goes down the wrong way. "Are you kidding?"

"No. I'm not."

"As a Commander?" *Definitely going senile.*

"Lord, no. A sailor. He can talk to people, find things out."

"No. This has to be done right. It's not a game." He clenches his fist as heat rises up his body. "He needs supervision."

Martha leans forward over her hands and squints at Tom. "Out with it."

"Out with what?"

"You are an extremely loyal and trustworthy person, to a fault... despite being a complete pain in the neck."

Tom snorts.

"So for you to put yourself in the last place on earth you want to be... she's more than *just* important to you. So... out with it."

"I'm not... there's nothing..." Tom takes a breath. "Stop staring at me like that."

Martha's eyes flick to the bottom corner of her computer screen. "We have an hour before Lawrence arrives."

"We used to... "

Martha pinches the bridge of her nose. "You were intimate?"

Tom shrugs. "Yeah… not like candles and baths full of rose petals but…"

"Please stop."

"You asked."

"So why are you doing this for her? It's not just because she took her top off for you."

"It wasn't just her top."

Martha glares at Tom.

"I'm using humour to… ward off my crushing anxiety about the situation."

"I'm not sure it's working."

"It isn't."

"Right, so… what else does she have on you?"

Tom shakes his head and looks around the room, avoiding Martha's stare but knowing she won't move a muscle until he addresses her question.

Seconds tick by and Tom takes another gulp of coffee while Martha cracks her knuckles and gives the time on her computer screen an exaggerated glance.

"Do you remember the Storehouse Twelve fire?"

Martha's eyes snap to attention, and she purses her mouth. "Portsmouth. Yes. Unsolved."

"It won't get solved."

"Because?"

"They'll never figure out it was… me."

Martha wrinkles the paper up on the desk in front of her, never breaking eye contact with Tom.

"Abbie got me out of there and gave me an alibi and to this day has never told a soul what I did."

"Why?" Martha's voice is husky, and she sits back in her chair, covering her mouth with her hand.

"Because she's loyal."

"No. Why did you do it?"

Tom stumbled into the dockyard and swigged the last of his whisky before throwing the bottle into a nearby skip, full of discarded building materials and oil soaked rags. He sat against a storehouse and wiped his nose along his sleeve. Tears fell freely down his cheeks, and he didn't bother to wipe them away.

"Grant?"

"Leave me alone."

"You know that's not going to happen."

"They didn't listen to me, Abs. And they didn't help him. They let it happen. They just let him... they didn't..."

Abbie pulled him against her chest and wrapped both arms around him. "I know."

Tom slumped against her, pressing his thumb and forefinger into his eyes. "No, but... we were eleven. I've known him since we were eleven. It's all my fault. He followed me into this life." Tom scrambled to his feet and stumbled against the wall.

"Let's go. You need to sleep."

"I need to be alone."

"Grant, for fuck's sake."

"Just leave me Abs. I'm a lost cause. It's all fucked."

Abbie grabbed his arm and pulled him back and he fell into her. *"You aren't a lost cause. But you're plastered and completely useless right now. Come on, you can stay at my place."*

Tom yanked his arm back and stumbled backwards. *"No. I said fuck off. I'm fine."*

"You're a pain in my arse, Grant." She stormed off and disappeared behind the building.

Tom kicked at the gravel under his boot and fell on his backside. He grunted and laid back, staring at the sky. It was a clear night, and the dark sky held a thousand stars.

"How did this happen?"

He reached into his pocket and pulled out a silver lighter engraved with the letters CM. He lit it and stared into the lone flame, dancing against the black sky. A scuttle behind him drew his attention to the skip, shoved between two buildings.

"Rats. Maybe they're in officer's uniform..."

He got to his feet and shuffled towards the skip. He peered over the edge. *"Come out little rats...Bring your hat and fancy jacket."* He chuckled to himself and fell against the skip. He lit the lighter again and looked up at the stars. *"C'mon MacMillan... one more prank?"* He dangled his arm into the skip and lit an old burger wrapper. It shrivelled up and a spark landed on a neighbouring cardboard box it smouldered and Tom rested his head on his arm and watched it. *"Let's give the brass rats what they deserve."*

A gust of wind picked up and thunder rolled somewhere in

the distance. It had been the driest summer in years but maybe now rain was on its way.

He put the lighter back in his pocket as another gust swept dry leaves and rubbish from the ground around him. A whoosh drew his attention back to the skip and the metre high flame crackling and spreading through the rubbish. His chest caved in.

"Fuck." A couple of leaves fluttered through the very top of the flame and were carried by the breeze to the roof of the storehouse, settling in the guttering. "Fuck!" He stumbled backwards as the gutter erupted in flames.

"Holy shit, Grant. What did you do?" Abbie was behind him, she grabbed his shoulders and glared into his face. "Grant?"

"I... it was cold... and... but I didn't... I wasn't trying to..."

"You fucking idiot. C'mon. Let's get out of here."

"But—"

"C'mon!"

"That was you?" Her voice is hushed, as though she needs all her strength just to speak.

Tom swallows and blows a breath out. "It was an accident."

They lock eyes for a second longer before Martha nods and sits back. "We should work out how to tell Lawrence our plans."

"He doesn't know?" Tom's eyebrows jump to his hairline.

"No. I thought we could inform him together."

"He's gonna have a damn conniption."

"Yes."

"This will be a hoot."

"Hmm."

A loud knock fills the room. Tom grins as Martha stands and straightens her clothes. "He's early." She places her hand on his shoulder as she walks past and squeezes before letting go.

Tom knows all the words she wants to say were in that one gesture and he's thankful for her being there.

"Admiral." Lawrence's gruff voice invades Tom's ears before a lengthy silence.

Tom smirks into his shirt.

"What the actual fuck is he wearing?"

Tom stands. "Commodore."

"I'll ask again. What the fuck are you wearing, Grant?"

Tom looks down at himself and back up to Lawrence. "Well, I mean… it's been a while so correct me if I'm wrong, but it *appears* to be Officer number three dress."

Lawrence looks past Tom to Martha. "What's this about, Admiral?"

"I've cleared an operation with the Secretary. Tom will be going onto *Arrochar*, while the substantive Commander takes some *leave*." Martha gestures for Lawrence to take a seat.

Lawrence stares at Martha, the only movement he makes is to breathe and sit in the chair. "Why?"

"Well, we need to find this Perkins girl, do we not?"

"We do."

Tom pipes up. "No-one knows her better than the sailors on that ship."

"Wrong, Grant." Lawrence glares at him. "You do."

"True. Though we have established I don't know where she is."

Lawrence glares at Tom, his left eye twitching.

Tom grins at him. "Problem?"

"I am not having *you* parading around in an Officer's uniform. It's an insult to the rank and the Royal Navy as a whole. No. I won't have it." He crosses his arms.

"No offence taken," Tom says. "Just in case you were wondering."

"I don't care if you take offence or not. Rank and respect are things you earn, Grant. It's not a game of dress up."

"Quite right. Which begs the question… how did you end up where you are today?"

Lawrence's head snaps and he leans towards Tom. "Shut your insolent mouth."

Tom grins and winks. "Okay."

"Gentlemen?"

"You can forget this whole charade, Admiral. It's not happening."

"As a matter of fact… *Commodore*…" Martha holds up the operational orders. "As you can see, the Secretary has signed the front page. Therefore… I'm afraid you have no recourse." She puts the papers down without offering to show them to him further. "Sorry about that."

"This is outrageous."

"Now, if you're quite finished?" Martha raises a brow and glares at Lawrence.

He slams himself back into the chair and lets out a heavy, loud huff.

"Wonderful. Now, as I was saying. Tom will be in command for all intents and purposes on that ship while Commander Peacock takes a well-earned two weeks leave."

"Two weeks?"

"Yes. That should be plenty of time."

Tom sits silently, hoping the eruption of his heartbeat at the mention of two weeks can't be heard outside the thump pumping through his ears. *That's a damn lifetime on a ship.*

"*Arrochar* is meant to leave port in four days."

"Well, she's staying for an extra week or so. I'm sure she will appreciate the rest, Commodore. Considering she was only set to sail back to Portsmouth for maintenance?"

"Yes. Well… Still, I think…" Lawrence pulls a tissue from the box on Martha's desk and spits into it before polishing the rim of his dress hat.

"Commodore?"

He blows a breath out, his face deepening in colour to a nice puce. "Nothing. Go on."

"Wonderful. So this morning you will introduce Tom to the crew and make sure they believe he is who we say he is. You'll treat him with respect and make sure the crew understands he's in charge. Do I make myself clear?"

"Me? But—"

"It's all in the orders." Martha taps the file. "The ones signed off by the Secretary, if I may remind you?"

"No need," Lawrence says through gritted teeth.

"Lovely. Well… I'll see if James is ready to go. If you'll excuse me, gentlemen." She walks out, giving Tom a side eye as she leaves.

But I don't want to behave. Tom waits until the door clicks, and he looks at Lawrence. "That must have been painful, huh?"

"What, Grant?" Lawrence stares straight ahead, not turning to look at Tom.

"Being told what to do by a *Former* Admiral. And a woman no less. For you that must have been excruciating, no?"

"Fuck you, Grant."

12

TOM

Tom stares out from under the brim of his dress hat. He strides towards the ship, attempting to exude confidence while his heart beats at a million miles a minute and his lungs squeeze shut.

"Ah, Tom?"

"What?" He stops and James bumps into him.

"You're just… You're walking really fast."

"I'm walking like an adult, James. You should try it sometime."

"No. You're walking like someone who has all this pent up energy and you're gonna explode."

Tom peers at James, hating him for being insightful. *Since when?*

"I'm just… saying…"

"I want to get this shit show over and done with. So are you going to be a pain in my arse? Or are you going to shut your mouth and say yes sir, no sir?"

"I… well I'll play the part."

"Wonderful."

"But are you… I mean are you okay?"

Tom squints. "Why would you ask me that?"

"Well, it's just… Martha said—"

"*Martha* said?" Tom steps into James, making him stumble backwards. "And what exactly did Martha say?"

"Just that you… you know… won't like being on the ship and I should be… accessible in case you need… something." James straightens his hat. "More or less."

"More or less?"

"She said your last experience on a ship wasn't great and…" James pushes past Tom and gestures. "Let's get this over with. Like you said."

Tom grabs James by the collar and yanks him back. "Let me make something very clear. I'm fine. Do you understand?"

James tilts his head. "No. You are *not* fine. But… continue."

"Are you pulling sass on me?"

James huffs. "I'm trying to be a friend. A mate. You know… someone you can count on. So for once, maybe you can deal with the fact there's something you can't handle on your own and let me help you?"

Tom blinks.

James takes a breath and winces. "So… we're cool?"

"We will never be… *cool*, James."

James nods and looks at his shoes.

"But... thanks." Tom cracks his neck and marches towards the ship. "Are you coming?" he calls over his shoulder.

"Yep. Right here."

"Great. Like a parrot on my..." Tom spies the sailors, all lined up on the deck waiting to be lied to. Tom swallows as his gut plunges beneath the pier. Heat travels up his neck, his back automatically stiffens and his fists clench at his sides. *Never again.*

"Tom?"

"Yeah," he wheezes. "Where's Lawrence?"

"Right here. *Commander.*"

The contempt dripping off Lawrence's words is enough to bring Tom back to himself and he grimaces. "Well, don't you have introductions to make?" Tom sweeps a hand towards the gangway to the ship.

"Let me make myself very clear, Grant. I have no choice in this debacle."

"No." Tom smirks. "You don't."

"And if you so much as step one pinky toe out of line, I will have you flamed. Do you understand?"

"Tell me, *Sir.* What makes you think you have any power in this operation? You know... considering you weren't even consulted? Nor included? You're simply here now to play a part in this whole charade." Tom straightens Lawrence's lapels, patting him once on the chest. "Make sure you look presentable for your big moment."

Lawrence's face deepens in colour and his nostrils flare. "I'll have you, Grant."

"I'll pencil it in my diary." Tom holds Lawrence's stare until the Commodore grunts and storms onto the ship.

And here we go...

———

TOM SITS BEHIND THE DESK AND REACHES A HAND TO EITHER corner, blowing a slow breath out. *Jesus.* The groans of the ship as it gently pulls against its ropes and the subtle movement do nothing to calm Tom's anxiety. He glances out the porthole and the sky is filled with grey clouds, perfectly mirroring his mood. *Those clouds are ready to unleash.* He clenches and unclenches his fists.

"Tom?" James stands at the door. "Alright?"

Tom gestures for James to come in. "Close the door."

James sits across from him, his eyes roaming the office. "Fancy."

"It's an extension of the Commander's dick." Tom glares at the mahogany desk and the leather chairs, studded with brass buttons.

"Right." James twiddles his thumbs and looks at Tom.

"I want off this ship sooner rather than later. You get involved and talk to people, yes?"

"Yes."

"I want names and information. I want to know who was closest to Lawrence and who's acting shady. All of it."

"You sound like you're in a spy movie."

"We practically are. This whole thing is a fucking mess."

Cheers, Abs.

"What are you going to do if someone recognises you? It's easy for me... I was suspended and now I'm back." He puts the word back in quote marks. "But you..."

"I've been stationed overseas, supervising bases and operations offshore and that's how I earned my promotion. It's ridiculous but..." Tom sits back and shrugs. "Whatever."

"Lawrence looked like he swallowed a lemon when he was introducing you on deck earlier."

"Yeah well, he knows there's someone on this ship that could sink him, no pun intended. And he knows he has no power to interfere with this operation."

"I wonder if he knows Admiral Moore is my Unckie Pete."

"He knows. He's no fool, at least not when it comes to knowing where he stands in a power play."

James grins at Tom.

"What, James?"

"You look so uncomfortable in uniform."

"Thanks for the vote of confidence." Tom pulls at his starched collar and grimaces. *You're not wrong though.* "Don't you have somewhere to infiltrate?"

"Right. Yes." James jumps from the chair. "I'll umm..." He gives Tom a quizzical glance. "Are you gonna be okay?"

"I'm going to be fucking fantastic."

"So that's a no?"

"Get out, James."

James goes to salute and stops, biting his lip. "Am I meant to... "

"Get the fuck out will you?"

James marches out the door, closing it behind him.

Tom lets out another slow, long breath and flicks his eyes around the room. Mahogany furniture, leather chairs, an empty liquor cabinet. *Pathetic.* He looks beyond the chairs to his private bathroom and bunk, wider and better than anything he has ever slept in on a ship before. *Brass rats.* He reaches into his pocket and pulls out a silver lighter with CM engraved on it. *It's always with me in uniform.*

"Who'd have thunk it," he whispers.

He looks to the leather chairs and his heart jolts with the memory of the one and only time he ever sat there while serving.

"I warned you," Tom hissed through his clenched teeth. "You didn't listen. What was it? Some kind of joke to you? A game? He was a god damn human being." He leapt from the chair and clawed his fingers through his hair.

Commander Lawrence rubbed his forehead. "No, Grant. Stop jumping to irrational conclusions. One mess at a time."

"Mess?" Tom peered at his commanding officer. "Did you call this a mess?" His throat ached.

Lawrence's staff officer takes a step forward and Lawrence waves him back. "Go and wait for the Admiral to get here will you? I want a word with Grant."

The staff officer saluted and marched from the room.

Tom looked out the porthole and suppressed the ache in his throat, he couldn't be sure if it was sobs or thirst. Probably both.

"Grant. Sit."

"Fuck you."

"I beg your pardon?"

Tom turned and faced his Commander. "I said, fuck you. Sir."

"Who do you think you're speaking to?"

"I know exactly who I'm speaking to."

Lawrence strode across the room to Tom and stood toe to toe with him. "This needs to be cleaned up and sorted out. I won't have you causing a problem."

"Well, unfortunately for you, Sir. I intend to cause huge problems. You were told about his mental state. I told the medic, I told his CO. I fucking told everyone and what did you all do? Nothing. I'll say it again. You did nothing!" Tom gritted his teeth. "Sir."

Lawrence swallowed but kept eye contact with Tom.

"So don't bother trying to clean this mess up, as you put it. It's too late for that. You screwed up and I'm going to make you pay."

"How do you propose to do that, Grant?"

"Admiral Sampson will listen to me. And if he doesn't I'll burn this whole place down."

"Excuse me?" A smile danced across Lawrence's lips.

"Figuratively."

"Well, Grant. I think it's best if you get off this ship. Take some shore leave. Approved by me. Starting now."

"I think I'll wait until—"

"Get off my fucking ship, sailor!"

A LOUD KNOCK AT THE DOOR BRINGS TOM BACK TO THE present. "Come in."

The friendly face of the ship's medic peers around the door and smiles at Tom.

"Lieutenant Campbell." *Let's hope you're still friendly.*

"*Commander* Grant. I believe I've told you to call me Mike?"

"Okay fine but only if you drop the commander bullshit."

Mike chuckles and walks in, sitting across from Tom. "You sent for me?"

"I'm going to read you in on this covert operation. Which isn't really covert because I'm being me. But anyway…"

"The Lawrence murder?"

"Yeah… amongst other... " Tom pauses and looks Mike in the eye. "Things." He picks up the operational orders from the table and hands them to Mike. "Read these and we can chat."

Tom wanders around the office while Mike reads the orders.

His chest tightens and he rubs a hand over his thumping heartbeat.

Mike lets out a slow whistle. "I knew he was up to no good. Lawrence is a bastard of a man. Not many sailors on this ship liked working under him either as a Commander or above."

"When you say, not many…?"

"There are always a few that brown nose their way up the ranks. You should know that?"

"Yes."

Mike nods. "And others who are hustled into doing things they don't want to. Though Abigail Perkins surprises me. That doesn't seem to fit."

Tom clenches his teeth and Mike's gaze slides to Tom's jaw. "Maybe I could encourage certain people to come and… introduce themselves?"

"Yes, that would be ideal. If you don't mind."

Mike slaps the operational orders onto the table. "Consider it done. What else do I need to know?"

Tom smiles. "First of all, if anyone asks... I've been working abroad for a number of years and now I'm back. Rescued from Russia actually."

"Ah of course." Mike smiles. "I did note your service record was miraculously updated and you are no longer *discharged.*"

"You looked at my records?"

"I have some... concerns about your wellbeing." Mike isn't smiling anymore.

"I'll be fine."

"I'll be checking in on you. And I want you to meet with me at least once a week while you're here."

"Aren't I the one that's supposed to be giving orders?"

"If you were an actual Commander maybe." Mike grins. "I know what they put you through and I know how you responded. Let's leave it at that and keep our standing appointment for once a week. Yes?"

Tom grimaces but nods. *I'll only be here for two weeks.*

"And if you're thirsty… drink water."

"Thanks for the tip."

Mike bows his head and leaves.

Tom wanders to the porthole and looks out. Navy personnel mill around the docks and members of the public hang about to look at the ship in port. Tom focuses on the kids, their excitement and smiles at the big ship right in front of them. He shakes his head. *Don't do it, kids.*

He spies his phone on the desk and goes to check it, hoping Isabella has a break and calls him. A missed call from Martha and one from a number he doesn't recognise. He hits redial.

You've contacted the Lawrence residence. Daphne and I are unable to take your ca—

Abbie, you idiot.

13

ABBIE

A bbie sits in the very back of the train next to the window. *At least I can watch the scenery fly by.* She lifts her legs and rests her knees against the seatback in front of her. She pulls the papers from her waistband as she scrunches her body in the seat. Peering around the carriage she notes only three other people but none near her. *Perfect.*

"Lass?"

Four other people.

Abbie peeks out from her hood and a grey haired, lavender adorned woman stands next to her seat. "Yes?"

The woman holds out a five pound note. "Here, get yourself a warm drink."

"What? Oh... no. Thank you, I'm okay."

"Please. I like to do a good deed every day. You look hungry."

My God, she thinks I'm homeless. "No, honestly I'm—"

"Please."

Abbie smiles and takes the five pounds. "You're very kind."

The woman smiles, continues along the aisle, and sits in a seat two in front of Abbie. The woman pulls a gaudy pink phone out of her bag and unlocks the screen. *One, nine, four, nine.*

Abbie rolls her eyes and looks at her papers. The very first page snaps her to attention. She hunches over her knees to read.

A Swiss bank account statement with her name on it. *But, how…*

She rifles through the stack and finds affidavits with her forged signature, copies of her identification papers, more surveillance photographs of her eating dinner with Amir - at least seven or eight times. *But I only dined with him twice…*

Abbie pulled her hair out and flicked the hairband onto the dresser. "I'm fairly sure he thought I was a prostitute, Matt."

Matt scrambled to pick up her hairband and shoved it in his pocket. "For God's sake Abbie, don't leave your things lying around. She gets home on Sunday."

Abbie spun around and slapped a hand in the middle of Matt's chest and kissed him. His hands travelled down her arms to her waist as he manoeuvred her towards the bed.

Abbie pulled away and waggled a finger in front of him "Uh uh… you tell me why the hell you made me have dinner with that slimy creep."

"I told you." Matt kissed her neck. "He just wanted to have dinner in an exclusive restaurant with a beautiful woman.

Simply for wealthy, connected appearances... and so I asked the most beautiful woman I know." His lips travelled up her neck to her mouth.

She relented and fell onto the bed, pulling him by the tie with her. "Flattery will get you everywhere."

"Everywhere?"

"Everywhere."

Abbie claws her fingers through her hair under the hood and shakes her head to dissolve Matt's face. *How stupid can one girl be?*

The train lurches to a stop and movement in the carriage draws her eye to the vestibule.

A train guard steps onto the carriage and Abbie's heart, already jumping out of her chest, plummets to her gut.

Time to be homeless again.

She folds the papers and shoves them back down her sweats, before crumpling into the seat and pretending to be asleep. No sooner has she closed her eyes, but a warm hand is on her shoulder. She opens one eye and it's the woman that gave her the five pound note. She holds out an Oyster travel card.

"Take it, Lass."

"Oh, no I couldn't."

"It's my daughter's card. She isn't with me today." She smiles and gestures for her to take it. "You need one. Don't you?"

"Well... yes but—"

"Go on then. Quickly."

Abbie leans across and takes the card. "I… thank you."

"Not at all." The woman sits next to Abbie. "Marjorie's my name."

"Oh. I'm… Sally."

"And what brings you out this way, Sally?"

"It's nice out here. Don't you think?" *Please go away.*

"Well, it's a matter of opinion I suppose. I come here to visit my brother."

"He lives here?"

"Sort of."

Curiosity gets the better of Abbie and she sits up. "Sort of?"

"Tickets?" The guard stands beside them with his eyebrows raised. They both show their cards, and he nods and moves on his way.

Abbie tries to hand the card back to Marjorie, but she shakes her head. "No Lass. You keep it. I can get Helen another one."

"Thank you." She tucks the ticket into her pocket. "So… your brother?"

"Well." Marjorie bows her head. "He's in the MTCT."

Abbie's breathing hastens. "The military jail?" *Shit.*

"Yes. He got caught…" She smiles and pats Abbie's arm before standing. "Well, anyway. I'll leave you to your thoughts." Marjorie picks up her handbag and her phone slides out, falling beneath Abbie's seat. She doesn't notice and walks back to her seat.

Abbie flicks her eyes up to Marjorie and back to the phone. "Excuse me?"

Marjorie turns to her. "Yes?"

"Nothing." Guilt covers Abbie in a heavy cloak, and she bites her lip. "Just... thank you."

"You're welcome, Lass." Marjorie opens a paperback and starts to read.

Abbie bends down and grabs the phone, slipping it into her pocket alongside the card Marjorie gifted her.

I am the worst person in the world.

Another forty-five minutes pass and the train pulls into Colchester station. Abbie waits until Marjorie gets off the train before following. She paces out of the station and dips around the side of the building before she pulls the phone out and dials. Her eyes dart around the street as she waits for her call to be answered.

"Yes?" Tom's voice is abrupt and no nonsense.

"Grant."

Tom says nothing.

"Grant?"

"Shit."

"What?"

"I broke a pen. Fuck."

"Right, um—"

"Where the *fuck* are you? And if you tell me you're still hiding somewhere in Lawrence's house I'll throttle you."

"You got my missed call."

Tom stays silent.

"No, I'm not still there. I just got off a train."

"How lovely. Day trip? Cream tea somewhere? You must be having a wonderful time."

"Stop with the sarcasm. I'm having the worst day of my life."

"Funny, I'm also having a mediocre day. But please… do go on, I can't wait to hear about your adventures."

"Grant, stop!"

A loud thud reverberates down the phone line and Abbie winces, knowing Tom has just punched something.

"Don't you *fucking* dare. You come to me, asking for help. I help you and… I admit… in the back of my mind I'm still skeptical you're telling me the whole truth… You *run*, I get on this fucking ship to get to the bottom of the Iranian bullshit, while, might I add, I'm also waiting to hear of Daphne's autopsy results and evidence from *that* shit fight. Don't you *dare* call me and tell me to *stop*. I'm wearing a fucking commander's get up and I'm sweating like a pig. Don't."

"Calm down, or you'll burst that vein in your temple."

"I swear to every deity, Abbie… I will throttle you."

Abbie sniffles as her nose tingles.

Tom sighs. "Where are you?"

"Colchester."

"Why?"

"I need to speak to Josh Phillips."

"Why?"

"Because."

Tom waits and Abbie doesn't elaborate. "That's your answer? *Because*?"

"I need you to get me on his legal visit list."

"Excuse me?"

"I need to speak to him."

"No way in hell. Get your arse back to my flat and stay there. Do you hear me?"

"I can't, Grant. I need to speak to Phillips. Please trust me."

"Did you just ask me to trust you?"

"Yes," she whispers.

"That's rich, Abs."

"I know. But I'm doing the right thing. You have to understand…"

"I don't *have* to understand. How can I possibly? Can you explain that to me?"

"Just get me on his visitor list. Please?"

"What did you find at Lawrence's?"

"Let me speak to Phillips. Then I'll call you."

Tom says nothing for a second before letting out a rough huff. "I'll see what I can do."

"I know you can make it happen."

"I said I'll see what I can do."

"Grant… I'm sorry."

"For which bit?"

"All of it."

"I'll call you on this number. You make sure you answer it."

"I will."

"You will." The phone goes dead.

She slides the phone into her pocket and stares at the cloudy sky. *How did I end up here?*

Fingers wrap around her elbow and jostle her slightly off balance. Her heart rate hits the extreme and she pulls away. "What the—"

"Shit. Sorry, thought you was someone else." A pimply, skinny kid of about nineteen in a nylon football tracksuit and beanie holds a hand up in apology.

"Well… I'm not." Abbie pulls her hood closer around her face.

The kid steps towards her and grins. He's missing some teeth and the others are decayed. "Do ya wanna be?"

"No. Get lost."

"But you're pretty."

"And you're off your face. I said fuck off." Abbie glares at the kid until he slinks away.

Abbie stands against the side of the station and waits for her heartbeat and breathing to even out. Her stomach growls and she gives herself a shake before walking up the road to find a greasy spoon.

Five pounds should get me some toast and tea.

14

TOM

Tom storms towards the mess and sailors walking towards him leap out of the way like discarded obstacles in a video game. He stands at the door and scans the room. "Moore!"

James looks from where he is laughing with a couple of other sailors. His complexion pales as he takes in the fury clearly painted on Tom's face. "Sir." James stands.

Tom flicks his head towards the corridor and takes a step back.

James scurries out and winces at Tom. "Are you about to murder me?"

"No."

"You look like you're about to murder me."

"Get yourself in my office."

"O... kay..."

"Just…" Tom massages his forehead. "Get into the MTCT system. Use my PC."

"What for?'

Tom clenches his jaw and practically snarls at James.

"Never mind, I'll… get started." James walks backwards and holds both palms out. "Are you coming?"

"Yes I'm—"

A loud crash and laughing draws Tom's attention back to the mess. A young sailor, sitting alone at the back of the room has both fists clenched on the table while another sailor is laughing and ruffling his hair.

Tom steps into the mess and leans against the wall.

"Cheers, Hampshire." The sailor standing up dusts his hands off and turns away from the table.

There's an empty tray with remnants of food half on top of Hampshire's unfinished lunch. Tom's left eye twitches and he steps in the path of the smirking sailor.

"Name?"

The sailor looks Tom up and down and squares his shoulders. "Pike."

"Pike what?"

"Sir."

"And what are you doing with your lunch tray?"

"Oh, well it's an arrangement we have. Hampshire takes care of my lunch tray. He's good like that." Pike smirks and holds Tom's glare.

"How very interesting."

"It is?"

"I've never heard of such an arrangement."

"Well, maybe you've been onshore for too long?"

Tom's jaw screams to be released and he grins. "Maybe." He glances over Pike's shoulder at Hampshire, stacking the two trays. "Hampshire?"

"Sir?"

"Leave those."

"Y... yes Sir." He takes his hands off the trays but stays at the table.

Tom looks back at Pike. "Go get those trays and clean them up will you, Pike?"

Pike's nostrils flare. "Sir." He turns and walks to the table.

"Oh and... I think a week of kitchen duty might be the ticket." Tom waits until Pike looks at him before winking. "Good job."

Hampshire edges from the table and stands against the wall.

"Hampshire?"

"Sir?"

"Come with me." Tom walks from the mess and waits for Hampshire who slinks out, as Pike grumbles and slams the trays against each other. "Two weeks then, Pike?" The noise stops and Tom grins at Hampshire. "What's your name?"

"Hamp—"

"Your given name."

"Liam."

"Come with me, Liam." Tom turns and strides down the

corridor. Five minutes later they emerge on the upper deck and Tom gestures for Liam to sit before sitting next to him. "How old are you Liam Hampshire?"

"Twenty."

"And you've been in the Royal Navy for…?"

"Two years active."

"What did you want before the Navy?"

"I love football. My dad used to take me to see the Seagulls every weekend. It was my favourite thing to do with him. But that changed after…" He shakes his head. "Anyway."

Tom gives him a moment as they both stare out at the water. "Brighton?"

Liam nods.

"So, what's Pike's problem?"

Liam shrugs before seeming to straighten. "I'm sorry, Sir. That was insolent."

"I've gotten through life to this point by being insolent. Carry on. What about Pike?"

"He's just… we don't get along."

"I noticed. Why not?"

"He's an arsehole." Liam presses his mouth closed. "Sir."

"Yes I figured that out for myself. And why is he expecting you to clean up after him?"

Liam gazes out at the water. "Like he said… we have an arrangement."

"That's a lie." Tom stands. "But I'll let you get away with it, for now."

Liam bows his head.

"Report to my office at oh eight hundred tomorrow."

"Why?"

"Are you questioning a direct order?"

"No Sir. Sorry. Yes Sir."

"Dismissed."

———

"ARE YOU IN?"

James looks up from the PC as Tom walks into the office and shuts the door. "Almost. What am I doing in here?"

"I need you to put Abigail Perkins on the legal visitor list for Commodore Joshua Phillips."

"Are you serious?"

"No. I just wanted to hang. We can watch YouTube videos of cats frightening themselves in mirrors and toddlers falling over while their parents film it."

"Okay. So you're serious." James peers at the screen. The tip of his tongue protrudes and runs along his top lip. "Joshua Phillips... suspicion of selling... are you sure? Does she really need to get tangled up in this?"

"She's already tangled up in it." Tom sits on a leather chair and steeples his fingers under his nose. "I trust Abbie. If she says she needs to speak with him... she needs to speak with him."

"So where is she?"

"Colchester."

"Well, shit Tom. I can't get her in until tomorrow at least."

"Just do it." Tom's voice comes out louder than he meant and immediately feels bad. *What the hell is happening to me?*

"Okay, calm your tatas. Sir."

Tom glares at James, but for some reason doesn't want to stab him as violently as usual. *Progress.*

"What took you so long to get back?"

"Mingling with the troops."

"Ha. Yeah right."

"Have you met Pike yet?"

"Yeah. Harrison Pike. He's a right twat."

"How so?"

"Just swans about like he's important. Like he's got some sort of privilege. I know the sort. Hell, I *am* the sort."

Tom chuckles. "True."

James looks up from the screen. "I've gotten loads better."

"Also true." Tom stands and looks over James' shoulder. "Done?"

"Done." James hits a key on the keyboard with a flourish and stretches his arms above his head. "But that Hampshire kid he was picking on... he's strange."

"How?"

"Just quiet. Almost frightened half the time. I don't know. He's just odd."

"He's not odd."

James quirks a brow. "Really?."

Something in Tom clicks and adrenaline spikes through his veins. "I said he's not odd. He's a kid. Maybe you should find out why Pike thinks it's okay to throw his half eaten lunch tray at him, instead of simply deciding he isn't worth the effort."

James stands and holds both hands up. "Okay… calm down. What's that about?"

Fair question. Tom cracks his neck side to side. "Nothing. Just… keep Pike in his place."

"I'll do my best." James nods at the PC. "I put her in as Melissa Brown." James clicks his tongue, and it awakens something deep in Tom's gut. "Tom?"

Tom blinks and shakes his head to dissolve the face floating in his mind's eye, the face clicking his tongue and waggling his eyebrows mischievously. *C'mon Grant. Let's cause havoc.*

Tom looks at James. "That's all."

"Right, well if you need—"

"I said that's all."

James huffs and marches from the office.

Tom sucks in a breath and rubs a hand over his chest as his lungs ache. *Jesus.* He drops into his chair and pushes the heels of his palms into his eyes. *Stop, stop, stop.*

Chris clicked his tongue and grinned. "Hey Tom"

"Hey." Tom threw himself on his bunk and buried his head under the pillow.

"Where have you been? You and Perkins wear yourselves out again?"

Tom poked his head out and Chris's grinning face looked up from the bottom bunk. "No. Just got another conduct infraction."

Chris clicked his tongue again. "Will you ever learn Grant?"

Tom groaned. "Can you stop that god damn tongue clicking thing? And what the fuck? You're just as bad."

"I learned from the best."

"I don't click my tongue like a jockey."

Chris climbed out of his bunk and swatted Tom across the head. "Let's go do weights or something."

"No." Tom stuck his head back under the pillow. The mattress next to him sank a little and he peeked out to find Chris resting his chin on his arms. "I said no."

"Seriously Grant. Please? Mitchell and Price are in there and..."

Tom rolled his eyes. "Fine."

Tom's phone sounds and he snaps his face up, blinking against the bright light of the office. "Martha." He grimaces as his voice comes out strained and raspy.

"What's wrong?"

Tom swallows and clears his throat. "Nothing. I was... working out."

"The fact you think I'd buy that is appalling."

"I was having a moment. But I'm fine now."

"A moment?"

"Yes. What can I do for you? I want to go have a shower and get out of this straight jacket."

"Uniform."

"Whatever."

"Have you made any progress?"

"It's been half a day - not even. Are you kidding?"

Martha doesn't say anything.

Tom squeezes his eyes shut. "Sorry. I'm… not myself."

Martha chuckles. "On the contrary Tom. You are being completely yourself."

Tom can't help but let out a smirk. "Fair."

"Are you alright?"

"Nope. But Abbie called me."

"And?"

"We're going to need to get her overnight accommodation and some clothes in Colchester."

"Why is she there?"

"Why do you think?"

Martha sighs. "This is a nightmare."

"No shit."

"And you trust—"

"With my life."

"Right. I'll find her somewhere to stay. I'll send you a code for her to get some money to buy clothing and food."

"Thank you. And what about the autopsy?"

"Nothing yet. You'll be the first person I call."

"Right."

"Tom?"

"I'm fine."

"Terrible liar." The phone goes dead.

———

Tom sits in the brass studded leather chair in his Navy issue sweats and calls the number Abbie is using.

"Grant."

"Alright?"

"I guess. You?"

"Yeah. Peachy."

"I'm sorry," she whispers.

Tom leans back into the chair and fixes his eyes on the light in the ceiling. "I'm going to send you a code. Find a Tesco cash point and select emergency cash. Withdraw three hundred quid. You need to get yourself appropriate clothing if you intend to pass yourself off as a solicitor. You'll go in under the name, Melissa Brown."

Abbie lets out a gasp. "You did it?"

"James did it. But yes."

"I knew you would."

"So, clothes. And Martha is arranging somewhere for you to stay the night."

"Stay?"

"You can't go in until ten thirty tomorrow."

"Right."

"And afterwards you get yourself back to my flat. Do you hear me?"

"I hear you."

"And you stay there."

"You're not fine. You're tense as hell."

"Thanks for the briefing, Abs. I just had a hot shower to relax."

"It didn't work."

Tom smiles. "Don't forget. Your name is Melissa Brown."

"I won't. Thanks, Grant."

15

ABBIE

The sky is still dark when Abbie wakes up in the Premier Inn Martha booked for her. She looks around the tiny room and stretches. She sits up and eyes the pants suit she bought the day before. *You're a classy lady, Melissa Brown.*

She swings her legs over the side of the bed and pulls on Isabella's sweats as adrenaline runs riot through her blood stream. *I can't mess this up.* She ties her laces and jogs out of the room. Moments later she is outside, blowing steam from her mouth as she runs along the deserted roads. Dawn colours the sky with pink and yellow, but she doesn't stop to admire the beauty. Running helps her relax. Most of the time.

"Abs. I won't stop chasing you until you talk to me."

Abbie stopped dead and turned to Tom. "What? I'm training."

"You've ignored me for a week."

"You said you couldn't see me anymore." She shrugged.

Tom pursed his mouth and stared at her.

"That's what you said."

"I said I wanted to see how things go with Claire, so I wouldn't sleep with you. Not that I wouldn't see you."

"Same thing."

"Not the same actually."

"I get it. Whatever." She turned and ran again. Tom kept up with her effortlessly.

"I can do this for hours, Abs."

She stopped again and thrust her arms out. "What do you want me to say?"

"I want you to talk to me."

"About?"

Tom blew a breath and looked around the empty road. "Anything, stuff, I don't know. We're mates are we not?"

"Yes."

"So?"

"I just need to get used to not ripping your clothes off you anymore. Is that a crime?" She smirked but hated that she could never stay mad at him.

"We agreed we were just... friends with benefits."

"We did."

"And as much of a bastard as I am... I won't cheat on Claire."

"As you shouldn't." Abbie bit her lip. *"And I admire you for being a good guy, to be fair."*

Tom grinned. *"So… no more cold shoulder?"*

"No."

Tom nodded once before taking off. *"Last one back buys a round."*

Abbie sits in the tiny room with a door behind her and one on the opposing wall, behind a desk cutting the room in half. A small window in the door opposite her shows people walking past every so often. She has been waiting for five minutes when the door opens and Commodore Joshua Phillips walks in and sits. The man in uniform behind him closes the door and they are alone.

Abbie has seen him a few times in the past, but they have never met. She hardly recognises him now. His once handsome and strong face is drawn and weathered. His eyes are empty as he raises them to meet hers. His salt and pepper hair seems thinner than the last time she saw him.

"Who are you?" Phillips squints at her.

"They didn't tell you?"

"They said my solicitor was here. *You* are not my solicitor."

"Is this room secure?"

Joshua smirks and stands. "The fact you need to ask? You aren't a solicitor. Don't waste my time." His voice still carries an air of authority, yet weakness flows through his baritone.

Abbie's neck pulses and she claws her nails on the desk. "No. Please. I can help you."

Joshua shakes his head; his back to her. "My trial starts in a month. Who the fuck are you to come in here now telling me you can help me?"

"I'm…" Abbie's mind goes blank and she gives her head a shake. *One chance.*

"Who.The.Fuck.Are.You?"

"Melissa Brown."

"Bullshit." He looks through the glass window on the door and nods to someone.

Abbie scrambles. "You're being set up."

He chuckles. "Well… there we are. I'm being set up. Master stroke." He knocks once on the door.

She fiddles with the papers in her lap and spreads some over the desk. "Give me five minutes. What have you got to lose?" Sweat dribbles down Abbie's back and she squirms in the chair.

He turns and peers at her.

"Nothing. Right?" She nods at the photographs. "Please?" She widens her eyes and pleads with every puppy dog feature she can muster.

The door opens and Joshua runs his tongue along his top lip, watching her. He puts a hand up to the guard. "Sorry… false alarm." He sits, his eyes never leaving Abbie's face. "For the moment." The door closes again and Joshua crosses his arms. "Five minutes."

Abbie pushes the photographs and forged bank statements towards him. She dips her head towards them and says nothing.

Joshua leans forward in his chair and picks them up. His

eyes drift over the bank statements and he looks between photographs of him and photographs of her, both with the same man and both clearly being photographed without their knowledge. He looks up again. "Who are you?" His voice is husky.

"Abigail Perkins. Former Petty Officer."

"Former?"

"I got out a month ago."

"Why are you in these photographs?"

"Because Commodore Matthew Lawrence used me."

Joshua's cheek tics at the mention of Lawrence. "He and I were friends."

"Were?"

"He hasn't made contact with me once since I've been in here. Not that I can blame him. In his position."

Abbie tilts her head, studying him. "Um. Sir…"

"Joshua."

"I'm sorry?"

"I'm not Sir. I'm Joshua Phillips. I'm no one of status." His jaw tightens and Abbie notes the tic again.

She pulls in a breath and nods. "Okay… Joshua. Do you know who put you here?"

"No. And despite the best efforts of my team—"

"It was Lawrence."

"Pardon me?"

"He put you here. And he's framing me as well."

"Those are some very serious allegations."

"His wife was murdered after an awards banquet a couple of nights ago."

Colour drains from Joshua's face. "Daphne?" His voice is strained.

"Yes. And it looks like I killed her."

"Why would you…?"

"I didn't. But I was sleeping with him… so..." Abbie bites her tongue to stop saying anything else. *For now.*

Joshua leans back in his seat, the hand holding a photograph trembles. "He killed her?"

"I don't know who killed her. He found me leaning over her and lost the plot. I ran."

"Has there been an autop… I mean do we know anything? I can't…" He leans forward and runs his hands over his head. "Daphne. Dead? I just…"

"I'm not sure. I've been hiding."

Joshua rubs his eyes with his thumb and index finger. "And you're telling me both you and I are being set up by him?"

"Yes."

"It seems far-fetched."

"It does." Abbie pushes the papers towards him again. "This isn't a coincidence. These photographs, we both have Swiss bank accounts. And I know I never opened one for myself. I bet you didn't either."

"No. I didn't."

"His promotion means everything to him."

"The promotion I was also being touted for."

"Yes."

"How did you get this stuff? I have some of the best barristers working on my team… how come they couldn't find it?"

"Because it was in a safe in Lawrence' house."

"I see. And how did you… happen upon it?"

"I broke in. I remember him saying once he doesn't trust technology, even though he's a wiz. I knew he'd have papers… records somewhere. He keeps flawless records of everything. And I knew he had a safe in his office."

"So you broke into his house and stole it."

"I *did* have a key… for when I'd go—"

"I can fill in the blanks."

"Yes. Of course. But… I broke in."

"Then this stuff is all useless. You acquired it illegally."

Abbie bites her lip and looks to her lap. "Yes. Essentially."

"Unless…"

Abbie looks up.

"Was there a thumb drive? External drive? Anything in the safe with it?"

"I… I don't know. I didn't have enough time to keep looking."

"You need to go back."

"What?" *Tom will literally kill me. Dead.*

Joshua has a new spark in his eye, and he stands up, pacing behind the desk. "You have to go back and find where all these files are being kept."

"But I—"

"No!"

Abbie gasps and pushes a hand to her chest.

"You don't come in here... show me this stuff and refuse to follow through."

"I wasn't... refusing... but..."

"But?" He sits across from her again, both palms down on the desk. "Get my team what they need. It will help both of us. That's why you came here isn't it? Essentially, you want to help yourself."

Shame cloaks Abbie and she nods. "Yes."

"Which is fair enough. But this way we both get exonerated."

"We do."

"Do you have anyone that can help you?"

Tom, sitting on a ship, dressed in a uniform, and glaring at her floats across her mind's eye. "Yes."

"Come back when you have it. Don't bother unless you find it. Do you understand?"

"I understand."

"I want that information. And it has to mysteriously be sent to my team. I don't see any other way."

"No. I don't think there is."

16

TOM

Tom listens to the robotic voice on the other end of the phone line for the seventh time in the last five minutes.

"The number you have called has been disconnected. Please check the numb—"

He frisbees the phone across the room and it slides along the floor. *Fuck's sake.*

"Morning, Boss Man." James plonks a tray of food in front of Tom. "I figured you didn't want to mingle with the rest of the boss men in the officer's mess."

Tom takes the fork James hands him and moves the scrambled eggs around on his tray. "Not so watery these days."

James shrugs and sits. "Maybe it's the first batch of the day."

"You'd know." Tom smirks as he chews on a corner of his toast.

"*Anyway*... why are you throwing phones around?"

"Practice."

"Huh?"

"So when I want to throw something small and heavy at you I won't miss."

James gestures to the tray of food. "I brought you breakfast and coffee."

The scrambled eggs lodge in Tom's throat as guilt dips his head. "You did." He swallows and nods. "I'm just pissed at Abs."

"Because?"

"I haven't heard from her."

"Since her meeting at Colchester?" James' eyes are wide and he leans forward on the desk.

"Exactly."

James lets out a low whistle. "Have you punched something?"

"What?"

"Well… you usually punch things when you're pissed off."

Tom squints at James. "I feel like you're getting to know way more about me than you should about me."

James snorts.

Tom glances at the time on his computer screen. "I've got a meeting in ten minutes."

"Sure yeah." James stands. "Holler if you need anything."

"James?"

"Yeah?"

"Thanks for breakfast."

James grins. "Don't mention it." He leaves without closing the door.

Tom picks the coffee up and gulps. The bitterness coats his throat, and he screws his face up. "Terrible." He plonks the mug on the desk and looks up to see Liam hovering at the door. "Liam."

"Yes, ah I can come back in eight minutes. Sorry I was... I finished eating and I thought I'd... I can wait."

"Liam."

"Sir?"

"Come in and shut the door."

Liam walks in and pushes the door closed behind him. He looks around the office and back to Tom.

Tom stands and gestures to the leather seats. Liam sits and Tom joins him, leaning back and relaxing in the chair, watching Liam.

Liam claws his fingers into his knees, his eyes darting everywhere avoiding Tom's face.

"Okay, you've squirmed long enough. Why do you think I asked you in here this morning?" Tom crosses an ankle over his knee.

"Am I in trouble, Sir?"

"Trouble? Why would you be in trouble?"

"I'm not sure. I mean... ah..." Liam shrugs before

squeezing his eyes shut and hissing a breath in through his teeth. "Sorry."

"For?"

"I was being insolent again."

"You apologise a lot. Has anyone ever told you that?"

"Everyone."

"And yet… you still do it?"

"It's just easier I guess."

"Easier than what?"

"I don't know. Maybe it gives me something to say." His voice trailed off into a whisper as he finished speaking. He looks at the cabinets on the wall behind Tom, his shoulders drop a little and he lets out a sigh.

"I'm sure you have a lot to say."

"Maybe."

"Why did you join up?"

Liam looks up from his lap. "What?"

"Why did you join the Royal Navy?"

"I… my brother is in."

"Where is he?"

"Middle east."

"So… you wanted to be like him?"

Liam adjusts his posture and bites his lip. "With all due respect Sir, why does it matter?"

Tom blinks and sees Chris sat in front of him, clicking his tongue.

"Sir?"

Tom blinks again and Liam returns. "Sorry. You're right. It's none of my business."

"Well, no it's just…"

"No. It's… none of my business." *You aren't him.*

Tom's phone rings from where it lies on the floor. He picks it up. "Judith."

"Autopsy results have come in."

"And?"

"And… It makes for rather interesting reading. Are you busy?"

Tom dips the phone from his ear. "You can go Liam. We'll continue this later." *Continue what later?*

Liam stands. "Sir."

"Tom?" Martha's voice is impatient.

"I'm here."

"Right. Well first thing you should know is that DNA was found inside her."

"Belonging to?"

A throat clears at the door to the office. "It's mine."

Tom spins and stares.

Liam is frozen a few feet from the door, staring at Admiral Peter Moore.

Martha puts her phone in her handbag next to him.

Tom notes the tremble in Liam's shoulders and leaps across the room.

"Thank you, Hampshire." He steers him into the corridor. "You alright?"

"Yes. Sorry."

"No apologies needed. I didn't know he was coming onboard today. Go on." Tom nods towards the end of the corridor and Liam scurries away.

Tom walks back in. Martha and Moore are each seated on a leather chair.

Tom gestures to the pair of them. "Make yourselves at home."

"It's my ship, Grant."

Tom rolls his eyes and sits. "Am I going to need popcorn for this?" He gives Martha an eyeballing as she pulls a folder from under her arm and puts it on the table.

"Autopsy report and photographs of the scene. Have a look and tell me what you see."

Tom holds a hand up. "Hang on… You can't expect me to not address the fact Pete's DNA was inside the dead woman." He raises an eyebrow at Moore. "Pete?"

Moore removes his hat and swipes a hand across his glistening forehead. "Grant, don't make this any more difficult than it needs to be."

"I'm sorry. What?"

"I said—"

"I heard what you said. Any *more* difficult?" Tom gives an exaggerated glance around the office and down at the uniform he is wearing. "It's pretty fucking difficult already, Pete. I'm not exactly sipping margaritas by the pool here."

The two glare at each other and Tom grinds his teeth.

"Tom." Martha's voice cuts through the tension lingering between the two men. "It's best we start with what we know and get to the… DNA in due course."

"You're the one who opened with that useful piece of information, Martha."

"Yes, I wanted your attention."

"Congratulations. Job done." He looks back to Moore. "Spill."

Moore clears his throat. "We were having an affair."

"I know."

"You know?"

"You knew what she was drinking at the banquet without having to ask, and your eyes lingered way too long on her retreating backside. I'm not an idiot."

Moore glares at Tom before slumping his shoulders. "No. You aren't. I've hated you for that fact for quite some time. But now I need you in my corner."

"Are you fucking kidding me? Do I not seem to have enough on my plate right now?"

"I know Abigail Perkins didn't kill Daphne. And I'll help you prove it. My DNA inside a married woman doesn't look good. I'm a suspect. Or I will be when they realise it's mine."

"How do you know Abbie didn't kill her?"

Moore slides the crime scene photographs from the folder and hands one to Tom of Daphne's dead body, her chest covered in blood. He then opens his phone and holds up a photograph of Daphne in the exact same position with no blood on her.

Tom looks between the two photographs. "How did you…?"

"I left the room to get more scotch. I was fucking getting out of the lift when I heard shouting. I was drunk—"

"Hammered."

"Excuse me?"

"I saw you as we left. You were hammered."

Martha shifts in her chair. "Yes. Slaughtered."

Moore sighs and scratches his hands through his thinning hair. "Fine. Very drunk. Anyway… by the time I got back to the room she was laying there on the floor in that position. I knew she was dead. Her lips had already paled and her body was different. I don't know how to explain it. But I didn't want to go near her and incriminate myself, so I took a photograph and left."

Tom snorts. "Incriminate yourself? Your *able seamen* are inside her and you're concerned that being found at the scene is incriminating?"

Moore stands and paces the office. "The point is. I didn't kill her."

"Says you."

Moore stops pacing and looks at Tom. "I didn't. And I know Perkins didn't either. So maybe we help each other?"

Martha clears her throat. "If I may, gentlemen?"

Tom slides his glare from Moore to Martha and folds his arms across his chest.

Martha holds his stare a moment before continuing. "Admiral Moore. I have a proposal for you."

"Yes?"

"We will assist you."

Tom curls his lip. "We?"

"We. And in return. You help clear Perkins *and* you drop your vendetta against Isabella Wirth."

Tom raises his eyebrows and looks at Moore. *This just got interesting.*

"She killed Jack Ford."

Tom stands. "No. She didn't. And those are the terms. Take them or leave them."

Silence hangs in the air as the two eye each other.

Moore relents first. "Fine."

Tom grins and sweeps a hand to the chairs. "Do take a seat. We have so much to discuss."

"I loathe you, Grant." Moore pushes past Tom and sits.

"The feeling's mutual. So don't feel too bad about it." Tom sits and crosses an ankle over his knee.

"Gentlemen?" Martha glares at both of them. "So if you didn't kill her and Perkins didn't. Who did?"

"Lawrence did it."

Tom slides the crime scene photographs across the table and peers at them. "He stabbed her after she was dead to frame Abbie."

"Yes. Nicely spotted. It's what the report says too."

"Abbie said she came in, saw her lying there and pumped her chest. Blood spilled from the wound only then."

"Because her heart had already stopped." Moore nods. "Note the angle of her neck."

Tom picks up a photograph. "Broken."

"As I said. There was shouting and a struggle. By the time I got back to the room she was on the floor and Lawrence was gone."

"So why didn't you come forward? This whole mess would be cleaned up by now. CCTV of the hallway, your evidence… Abbie's… I don't understand why we're here." Tom grits his teeth as heat surges up his neck.

"CCTV was down for maintenance." Moore uses quote marks as he says maintenance.

"You checked it?"

"I tried. They couldn't get into their own system."

"How perfect." Tom drops the photograph. "Doctored."

"Have you heard from Abigail, Tom?" Martha uncrosses her ankles and swaps them over.

"I can't get hold of her. The phone she was using has been disconnected."

"So we don't know how her meeting went or where she is?"

"No."

"Well we need to find her."

"Get me off this ship. I can't do it from here."

Martha holds up a hand. "You know we still need to sort out the Iranian issue."

Tom rolls his eyes and fixes them on the ceiling.

"Not to mention, we don't want to make Lawrence suspicious yet."

Tom huffs and stands. "He's not an idiot."

"He can't outrun this." Martha stands and slides her handbag over her forearm. "We'll leave you to it. I'll be in touch."

Moore picks up his hat and nods. "Grant."

"Pete."

Tom grins as Moore's jaw twitches.

Martha moves to follow Moore out and Tom puts his hand on her shoulder. "Wait a sec."

"Yes, Tom?"

"This could have been discussed over the phone."

"Possibly."

"So why did you and Moore come here?"

"No reason. I thought it would be more appropriate."

"You were checking on me."

"And why would I need to do that?"

"Because I'm one irritation away from losing my head."

Martha grins. "What's new?"

Tom jerks a brow but can't help giving her a half smile. "Can we trust Moore to leave Iz alone?"

Martha leans in and whispers. "Always have insurance." She pats Tom on the arm. "Chat soon."

Tom blows a breath out and slides his phone from his pocket. He pushes the number Abbie was using again, knowing it's useless.

"The number you have called has been disconnected. Please check the number before dialing again."

17

ABBIE

A bbie sorts through the third drawer of Matthew Lawrence's desk, careful to make sure it doesn't look disturbed. No thumb drives or external hard drives anywhere. She stands upright and sweeps her eyes around the office. *Where would be put something so valuable to him?* Her eyes land back on the desk, and the papers regarding Daphne's funeral in three days. She lowers herself into the desk chair and picks up the top sheet.

We welcome you to celebrate the life of a much loved and cherished wife and friend.

Abbie drops the paper. *You didn't love her.*

She wanders into the bedroom and trails her fingers across the post at the end of the bed. Meticulous as always; the bed is made perfectly. *Matt can't abide mess and clutter.* Abbie grins to herself and wonders how she can leave a message that she's been there. *But first... the thumb drive.* She sits on the bed and looks through the open walk in wardrobe to the ensuite beyond and chews on her lip. Everything in its place. Abbie hears Lawrence's voice in her head because *everything needs order. Or the world won't spin.* Her eyes drift to the shelves above the hanging racks and the boxes stored there.

Maybe?

She goes to the wardrobe and reaches up, dislodging a box and pulling it down. She is greeted with photographs and newspaper clippings featuring Lawrence at a banquet or awards ceremony, meeting the Queen, she sorts through old epaulettes, name badges. *Nothing.* She stands to replace that box and pull down another when the front door opens and keys jangle as they are tossed onto the hall table.

"Hey Charlie," Lawrence greets the cat.

Abbie's heart leaps into her mouth. *Shit!* She stands in the middle of the wardrobe, her feet frozen to the floor. *Why is he home in the middle of the day?* Her eyes dart around the tiny space and she grips the box in her hands. Footsteps echo along the floorboards downstairs. *He's going to the kitchen. Maybe I can...* The footsteps come back down the hall and stop.

Abbie's blood runs cold, and she swallows the vomit pooling at the base of her throat. She slides the box back on top of the shelves and waits. The silence is eerie and the prickles erupting on her skin do nothing to calm her. She dives into the long dresses and gowns hanging in front of her and presses herself against the wall of the wardrobe.

As though on cue, the footsteps climb the stairs.

"C'mon Charlie, let's have a think." Lawrence's voice grows louder as he reaches the top of the stairs. "The alarm malfunctioned two days ago, which is odd. And today again… it seems to be out."

Abbie squeezes her eyes closed and tries to breathe silently through her nose. Her shaky breaths thunder in her ears. The smell of Daphne's clothes envelopes her. The faint leftover perfume may as well be Daphne's ghost, encircling her and intensifying the tremble in her body. *She's here Matthew my love, she's hiding in my clothes.* Nausea creeps through her body.

"So, the only conclusion I can come up with is that the alarm was tampered with." Lawrence's voice is so close he could be standing right next to her. A mew emanates from the floor in the middle of the wardrobe. *That fucking cat.* Abbie holds her breath.

"But of course, no one else is here. Right, Charlie?"

Abbie presses her lips together and flattens her back harder against the wall. The dresses are packed so tightly along the hanger rail there's no way she can be seen. Daphne's vanity serves to protect the woman her husband was sleeping with. *Ironic.*

Silky fur and low vibrations from a content purr brush

against Abbie's ankles. If her blood was cold earlier it's positively freezing now.

The cat mews again.

Abbie bites her tongue.

The hangers clash together and light hits Abbie in the face as the dresses part. She lets her breath out in a loud, trembling huff before holding it again.

Matthew Lawrence stands in front of her. He slides his hand down his dead wife's dresses before letting it fall to his side. He peers at Abbie. His eyes are hard and icicles stab Abbie through the gut.

"Perkins." His nostrils flare.

Abbie says nothing, staring straight into Lawrence's rigid face.

"Charlie. Out." The cat scampers from around Abbie's feet and darts from the room.

The two stare at each other for an eternity. Neither moving.

"Abigail." Lawrence's face breaks into a soft, warm smile. "Abbie, my darling. I was so worried about you." He steps forward and cups her face in his hands.

Abbie lets out the breath screaming to escape her lungs and as her mouth opens Lawrence leans in and presses his lips against hers. Abbie doesn't move. Her palms, slick with sweat, press against the wall behind her.

Lawrence pulls his face a millimetre from hers and looks into her eyes. "Where have you been?" He sighs against her face, and she closes her eyes a moment, remembering how comforting and sweet his breath used to feel against her skin.

"I don't... understand." She opens her eyes again and slides her hands off the wall. She grabs both his wrists and pulls his hands away from her face.

"Don't understand what?"

"You... your wife. I..."

Lawrence tilts his head; concern creasing his brow. He takes Abbie's hand and leads her into the bedroom. "I'm sorry my darling. You must have thought so many things when I reacted the way I did." He steps back into the wardrobe and straightens Daphne's dresses.

"I... I didn't kill her." Abbie backs towards the door to the bedroom.

"Oh Sweetheart I know. You could never do something so... so cold and evil."

"What? But you... you screamed. You shouted at me. What have you done?"

"Yes... I was in shock..."

"That's what you said to me. What have *you* done?" Abbie keeps creeping towards the door.

Lawrence emerges from the wardrobe, grabs her hand, and pulls her into him. He buries his face in her neck and kisses along her collar bone. Abbie closes her eyes for a second as his lips send currents down to her gut and beyond.

"No!" She yanks her hand from his and stumbles backwards. "What are you doing?"

"I need you, Abbie. I'm going through hell. Please…"

"No. I can't. You broke it off. You're cold and heartless. Why… why after you find me in your house…"

"I've been looking for you since you ran. I need you. I never realised how much."

Abbie leans against the doorframe and squints at him. "You're a liar."

"No. I'm not. Don't run. Stay."

"You set me up. The same as Phillips."

Lawrence frowns and walks towards her. "Phillips is in jail because he broke the law."

"But… but you…"

His hands run down either side of her neck and he drops his forehead against hers. "Phillips will get what he deserves. And it's devastating. He was a friend."

Abbie closes her eyes. *Matthew Lawrence was a friend.* "I saw him."

Lawrence's eyes open and his hands tighten ever so slightly against her shoulders. "When?"

"Yesterday. In Colchester."

"Why?"

"I thought I could help him."

"Help him?"

"Yes."

Abbie watches Lawrence's face. It doesn't change. "Help him do what?"

"Did you know there are photographs of me having dinner

with Amir?"

Lawrence's Adam's apple bobs as he swallows. "Photographs you say?"

"Yes. Practically identical to the ones of Phillips having dinner with him."

Lawrence's eyes shift to a point above Abbie's head, and he runs his tongue along his top teeth. He walks to the bed and sits. "Phillips." He shakes his head.

"Phillips?"

"Yes. He wanted insurance. He must have had them taken."

"He didn't know about them."

"He's a liar Abbie. The man's in jail for selling information to a foreign government."

"Allegedly."

"He's in jail. People don't get arrested and charged with such a serious crime without *evidence*, my Darling." He pats the bed next to him. "Come sit. Let's work out how to distance you from all of this."

"No. I should go. I'm sorry I came into your house. It was wrong of me."

"I'm so glad you did. Don't go." Lawrence holds both arms out. "Stay with me?"

Abbie swallows and closes her eyes. *He's playing you.* She opens her eyes and Lawrence has dropped his hands onto his knees. "You're lying."

"No. I could never lie to you. Ever."

"You lied to your wife."

"To be with *you*." He pats the bed again. "I miss you."

Abbie takes a step forward before an image of Tom stepping in front of her clouds her vision. *Are you fucking kidding me, Abs?* She closes her eyes and shakes her head. "I can't."

"Just sit with me. We don't have to say anything." She squeezes her eyes shut tighter. "I'm so lonely and sad. You make everything better, Abbie. You always have."

Abbie wrapped her hands around the cast iron bars in the headboard, her legs knotted around Matts' waist. He dropped his mouth to hers and pulled her hips harder against him.

"You're everything, Abigail."

Abbie tilted her head towards the ceiling and moaned as colours exploded behind her closed lids. She tightened her grip on the headboard and slammed her hips upward as Matt's fingers dug into her back.

His face rested on her chest as he huffed hot air against her sweaty skin.

They stilled and Abbie trailed her fingers along the back of his neck and down his spine as he fell onto the mattress next to her.

She turned onto her side to face him. "Everything?"

He pulled her face to his and kissed her mouth. "Everything."

She opens her eyes to him, sitting on the bed. The same bed she used to be wrapped around him in. The same bed that smelt of his cologne and skin. His breath on her face…

She walks and stands in front of him. She runs a hand

through his hair. He leans into her, wrapping his arms around her waist and burying his face in her stomach.

"I thought I knew you, Matt."

"You do know me Abbie. No one knows me the way you do. No one." His hands slide up and under her jumper and around to her bra clasp. "You know every part of me." He snaps it open.

Abbie straddles his lap and brushes her thumbs across his cheeks. "You'd never hurt me. Would you?" *He wouldn't.*

"Never." His fingers drift down her back and familiar tingles produce goosebumps all over her body.

"Okay," she whispers against his mouth. "I trust you." She pushes the image of Tom's pinched face and pulsing temple away. *I'm sorry.*

He pulls her jumper off over her head and flings it on the floor. Her bra follows.

"I'm so glad you came back." He falls back on the bed, pulling Abbie with him.

"Me too."

18

TOM

Tom deadlifts one last time before dropping the bar at his feet.

"Heavy," James says, flopping down on a bench.

"Yep." Tom grabs his towel and wipes his face. "Tell me you have something worthwhile?"

"Still haven't heard from Perkins, huh?"

Tom glares at James.

"I checked the phone number she was using like you asked. And you're right. It's been disconnected. So whoever she stole it off reported—"

"I know how it works. She still should have fucking called me. From somewhere."

"Right. Well yes." James takes a breath. "I have something else for you."

Tom flaps his hand around and sits across from James.

"That dickhead, Pike." James nods once and stops talking.

"That's it?"

"It's day two. Gimme a break."

"What about him?"

"Shore leave. This weekend."

Tom raises both brows. "Again I say… that's it? Wow. Thanks Sherlock. You're fucking amazing."

James fixes Tom with fed up eyes and pursed lips.

Tom drops his head and scrubs both hands through his hair. *The line has finally been reached.* "I hate being here. I hate it." He gulps from a water bottle. "The smallest things are getting me tense, like a bell for dinner or sailors walking the corridors laughing and mucking about… whatever. I hate it." Tom's heartbeat comes alive and his muscles tense. "Things like that shouldn't bother me, James. I don't have control over it and I—"

"You hate it."

Tom presses his mouth together and stares at a spot past James on the other side of the room.

James purses his lips in a perfect imitation of Martha's cat's bum. "Wanna talk about… it?"

"With you?"

"Well… yeah?"

"No." *I need to shut my mouth.*

James nods and the silence lingers a moment longer.

"Aren't you meant to be telling me things?" Tom swishes the water in his bottle and peers at James.

"Okay so..." James leans forward. "Here's what I know. Pike is going to take part in a LAN party while he's on shore."

"LAN?"

"Yeah he's a gamer. So he sets up his PC and plays games with people over the internet. These LAN parties can go all night. I've played a few in my time."

"On account of the fact you're a nerd?" Tom gives a small grin.

"Yes. And also… I figured he knows his way around a computer. And he's cocky. So that makes me think he believes he's untouchable."

"Lawrence."

"It fits." James shrugs.

Tom takes another swig of water and studies James. "Well, I hate to say it but… you make a lot of sense."

"But there's more."

"Okay listen… we aren't on a game show. Just tell me the things."

"Sorry. I don't get to do the cloak and dagger stuff much. It's kind of fun."

Tom stares at James and waits.

"He also reckons he's going to be cashed up when he comes back."

"Cashed up?"

"Yeah. A normal person wouldn't say shit. But Pike's so far up himself I'm surprised he can see daylight at all. He's involved in something."

"And if he's protected by Lawrence… and being paid off for doing tech for him…"

"Well, yeah. Makes sense he's an arrogant git."

Tom bites his bottom lip and stands. "Send Pike to my office in an hour." He grabs his towel and flops it over his shoulder.

"Send him to you?"

"Yeah… one hour." Tom walks to the door and stops. "Good work, James."

"Yeah. Thanks."

———

TOM SITS BEHIND THE DESK AND STARES AT HIS PHONE. *RING!*

A knock draws his attention, and Pike is at the door with his hat under his arm. "Sir."

"Harrison Pike. Come in." Tom nods to the chair in front of the desk. "Sit."

Pike marches to the chair and sits ramrod straight, placing his hat on his lap. "You summoned me?"

"Summoned? I'm not a wizard, Pike."

"No sir."

Tom picks up a sheet of paper. "You have shore leave this weekend?"

"Yes, Sir."

"I'm cancelling it." Tom flicks his eyes to Pike and waits.

Pike's face pales before pink spots appear on both his cheeks. "Sir?"

"Cancelled."

"But…" Pike swallows and starts to run his fingers around the top of the hat on his lap. "I haven't seen my family in a long time."

"Your family?"

"Yes, Sir."

"What were your family plans?"

"Ah. Catching up."

Tom raises a brow.

Pike hooks a finger in his collar and pulls it from his neck.

"Is something wrong?"

"Well, it's just… I had plans."

"Cancel them." Tom leans forward and squints at Pike. "Unless of course, there's something you'd like to speak with me about? Convince me why these plans are imperative?"

Pike's nostrils flare. "Permission to stand up?"

"Granted."

Pike stands and paces the office. "I need the break, Sir."

"Because?"

Pike pauses and rubs a hand across his forehead. "My mum. She's sick."

Oh no you don't. "I'm sorry to hear that."

Pike looks up with a renewed determination in his eyes. "Yeah. So… I wanted to visit her."

"I'm not unreasonable." Tom nods and gestures for Pike to sit again. "I'll allow the leave."

Pike's shoulders relax and a smile comes across his face

though he tries to squash it. "Thank you Sir."

"But your behaviour towards other sailors needs improvement. Do you understand me?"

"I understand." Pike's smile turns into a smirk. "But Sir?"

"Yes?"

"Hampshire isn't a sailors bootstrap."

"Excuse me?"

Pike shrugs.

"You're entitled to your opinion. But, while I'm in charge of this ship, you leave him the fuck alone. Do you understand?" Tom's pulse spikes and he holds his breath a moment.

Pike peers at Tom with confusion spreading across his face. "I understand."

"Dismissed." *Get out.*

Pike stands and marches from the office while Tom watches his back, wanting to throw something at him. *Lying piece of shit.*

Tom springs from the chair. *Fresh air.* He paces through the ship and up onto the deck. He storms past the chopper hangar to the bow of the ship and leans against the railing.

"Should I jump? Try some backstroke?"

Tom looks to his left, knowing no one is there but still sees Chris grinning and wiggling his eyebrows up and down. He turns and stalks back to his office.

"Don't be daft, besides it's fucking freezing." Tom grabbed Chris in a headlock and dragged him back to the door into the cabins.

Chris wrestled him the whole way, laughing. "Steady on. I was just kidding."

"You kid too much." Tom let him go and they went inside.

"I do. But... you know I'm just kidding. Right?"

"I used to. But... I don't know anymore." Tom stops and leans against the wall. "Has it got any better?"

"What?"

"You know what."

Chris shrugged. "Not really. They harass me all day. Well... when you aren't around."

"I can't be around all the time. I have duties—"

"I know. Okay?"

Tom put his hand on Chris' shoulder and leaned to his eye level, waiting for him to look up. "If you stand up to them once, they'll leave you alone."

Chris huffed. "No they won't. Anyway, I'll stop the morbid jokes. Sorry to annoy you." He pushed past Tom.

"Hey." Tom grabbed his shirt and yanked him back. "I'm not annoyed. I'm... concerned."

Chris looked Tom right in the eye. "Don't be."

Tom wanders the ship, startling sailors and making small talk with brass wanna-be's. He stops short as he realises he's heading towards the berths. His gut pangs and the back of his neck prickles. The ship's hull groans, almost like a warning. *Point taken.*

"Commander! Lovely morning."

Tom jolts and shakes Lieutenant Campbell's hand. "Mike."

Mike smiles. "What are you doing down in the dungeons?"

"Just… having a wander. But…" He swallows the obstruction in his throat. "I'm done now." He sweeps a hand out and he and Mike walk.

"Interesting."

Tom looks sidelong at Mike. "What is?"

"That your wandering led you down to the berths."

Tom hastens his steps. "Not really." He shoves a hand into his trouser pocket and fiddles with the silver lighter lying inside.

"Coffee?"

"Pardon?"

"I know technically we weren't going to be having a chat until next week but… you look as though you need a coffee."

"I've got work to do."

"As do I. But I also have information for you as discussed. So maybe you can chat with me and I'll tell you?" Mike raises a brow and tilts his head to the side. "I have a hunch your pressing work would benefit?"

Tom can't stop the smile turning the corners of his mouth up. "You're a pain in the neck."

"Agreed."

They reach the Officer's mess and Tom is relieved to see it's empty. "I'm not used to people brown nosing to *me*."

Mike smiles and sets a mug down in front of Tom before sitting across from him. "I'm sure your responses shut them up pretty quickly."

"How dare you." Tom grins as he takes a mouthful. "But… yes."

Mike nods. "You've noticed Pike I believe?"

"You might say that."

"Rough life."

"Is this your information? He had a rough life?"

"His behaviour is… indicative of such."

"That may be so, but it doesn't excuse shit."

"I understand your dislike of him. I'm sure it brings up—"

Tom stands. "Was there anything else?" *Sneaky bastard.*

Mike smiles and stands to face Tom. "You gonna run from it forever? Or are you going to process it, deal with it and accept it wasn't your fault?"

"I've got things to do. Thanks for the chat." Tom spins and paces from the mess. He's halfway down the corridor when a hand grabs his shoulder.

"Tom."

Tom stops but doesn't turn around. "Leave it."

"You think you wandered down to the berths by accident?"

Tom clenches his jaw. "I'll see you Tuesday." He marches away as his pulse thunders in his ears. *You weren't there.*

He reaches the office and stumbles in. He closes the door before leaning against it and sliding to the floor. He pushes both thumbs into his temples and closes his eyes.

Two sailors used all their strength to push Tom out of the berth.

"Get the fuck off me!"

"Grant you need to go."

Tom ripped the hands off his chest and slammed one of the sailors against the wall. "Don't tell me what to do. Fuck off."

A hand slid around his shoulders and throat and yanked him backwards. He lost footing and crashed into the wall, and the person behind him. They fell to the floor in a mangled heap while Tom continued to try and get into the berth. Hands clawed at him and ripped his shirt.

"Grant!"

Everyone stopped.

Tom looked up into Commander Lawrence's face. "Get yourself into my office."

"I'm not leaving him here."

"You can't help him now. It's too late."

Tom thuds his head back against the door. "It's too late," he whispers.

The silence of the office cloaks him and he sits on the floor for eons, staring across the room at the porthole but not seeing it.

His phone sounds from where it sits on the desk and Tom heaves himself off the floor and shuffles to it. He looks at the number and his pulse increases rather than calming. He squeezes the phone and holds it to his ear.

"Yes?" His teeth grit so hard his molars ache.

"It's me." Abbie's voice is a harsh whisper.

"Why the fuck are you in his house?"

"I can explain."

19

ABBIE

Silence travels from the other end of the phone line, but it speaks a thousand words.

"Tom?"

"There is no reasonable explanation for you to be there. Get out now. Before he finds you."

Abbie winces. "About that…"

"Excuse me?" His voice takes on a dangerous tone and Abbie's spine tingles.

"Just let me speak. He's in the shower and I don't have a lot of—"

"What?" There's a loud crash. "Fuck!"

"Tom?"

"Oh... I'm terribly sorry... the vision of you playing Becky Homecky with Lawrence caused me to leap from my chair in disgust and hammer my knee into the drawers."

"I'm not playing Becky Home… what was it?"

"Get the fuck out of there Abbie. I swear I will blast the door in and drag you out by the scruff of the neck." Another crash.

"Did you just beat yourself up with another piece of furniture?"

"No. I kicked the chair. On purpose."

"I think we're wrong about Matt."

"Don't you *fucking* dare, Abs. I'm not sitting on this ship wanting to gnaw my fingernails to the quick for a fucking holiday."

"No. But I don't think you need to be on the ship. Matt is suspicious of Josh. And I hate to admit but he makes sense."

"I'm not listening to this bullshit. Get to my flat. Now. Why did you even go back there?"

"Josh wanted a thumb drive with everything on it. So I came back to search for it… Matt turned up and found me here. But… Tom, he's broken. He's so upset about his wife and he knows I didn't kill her—"

"I cannot believe this bullshit is coming out of your mouth. Are you fucking kidding me right now?"

Guilt hits Abbie between the eyes and she sighs. "I'm so confused," she whispers.

"I've had a visit from Moore. His DNA was inside her."

Abbie's heart lifts. "It is? So it was him?"

"No."

"But it had to be…"

"It wasn't. He wouldn't come to me for help unless he really needed it. It wasn't him."

"But—"

"Listen to me. He killed her. I know it. You aren't safe there. Get out."

"He wouldn't. I—"

"I'm not on a damn P and O cruise here, Abs! We cannot let Moore's name be made public in connection with this, or Lawrence will think he's won. That he can get away with anything."

"I know, but I trusted him for so long…"

"Do you trust me?"

"What kind of question is that?"

"Do you *trust* me?"

"Yes."

"Abbie?" A voice behind her makes her fumble the phone.

Her heartbeat leaps into her throat. "Ah right yes… so that's *extra* anchovies." Abbie closes her eyes.

"Anchov… Fucks sake, Abs." Another crash. "I'm your pizza boy now?"

"Great, yeah…"

Tom gives an exaggerated huff. "Six pm. Make sure you get to the box first."

"Six pm would be fab. Ta!" Abbie hangs up the phone and turns to the doorway of the lounge. "Hey."

"Ordering pizza? At one in the afternoon? For six tonight?"

"Yeah... I had a hankering. I don't want to wait on the phone later."

Lawrence watches her as he steps into the room and lowers himself into the armchair.

"Matt?" Abbie stands and walks to him, putting one knee on his lap. "Do you mind?"

He runs a hand up her leg to the top of her thigh. "Of course not." He pulls her into his lap and kisses her. "Anything for you, Sweetheart."

Abbie closes her eyes as his voice vibrates against her neck. *This shouldn't feel so comfortable.* Tom's voice shouts in her head, *he killed her!* She waits until he reaches her collarbone, and the tingles intensify before she pulls away. *I can't.*

"Abbie?"

She climbs off his lap and moves to the doorway of the kitchen. "It's just... I need some water."

She goes to the sink and fills a glass. When she turns around Lawrence is standing against the doorframe with his arms crossed. She sips and watches him. His phone rings in his pocket and he takes it out, never looking away from Abbie.

"Yes?... Well no I can't visit right now..." Lawrence frowns. "He doesn't even remember who I am. You're the nurse. You sort him out." He hangs up the phone and slides it back into his pocket.

"Is your father unwell?"

"Dementia. And the nurse I hired is a damn pain in the backside."

Abbie sips her water and tries to ignore the coldness of Lawrence's attitude towards his own father.

"What's going through that pretty little head of yours?"

Abbie's blood simmers as the patronising tone hits her with full force. "That maybe you're lying to me."

Lawrence's cheek twitches and he moves into the kitchen. "About?"

"Everything?"

Lawrence stands behind a dining chair and runs his hand over the velvet backrest. The fabric changes appearance with his touch.

"I really have no idea what to think anymore."

"Don't you trust me?"

Coming from Lawrence, it seems to sound different. *Hollow.* Abbie sits in the chair opposite the one Lawrence stands behind. "Who killed Daphne?"

He looks up. His face is drawn and his eyes are cloudy. "Well… I…" He pulls the chair out and sits. "It was Moore."

"Excuse me?" Abbie's insides squeeze and red mist forms at the edges of her vision. *That's not public.*

"Admiral Peter Moore."

"But, what makes you think it was him?" Her voice takes on a rasp and she swallows.

"They were having an affair. Remember?"

"Right." Abbie bites her lip. "But… you told me to go to that room. Why?"

Lawrence's swallows and knots his hands together on the

table. "It was the room Daphne and I had booked. I naturally assumed she would be in Moore's room. Not in ours. So sordid." He huffs and looks out the kitchen window.

A chill hits Abbie in the back of the neck. She stands. "You know… I wouldn't mind a shower myself."

Lawrence looks at her and smiles. "Of course, my Sweet. I need to do some preparations for the funeral." He waves his hand around, almost dismissively and wanders to the lounge.

Abbie stands in the silent kitchen and takes a few breaths. She shuffles to the door and peeks at the back of Lawrence's head as he sorts through papers spread out on the coffee table. Her throat insists on staying dry as she climbs the stairs towards the bathroom. She passes Charlie in the hall and glares at him until he scoots into the study with his tail in the air.

She stands in the middle of the landing, her eyes sweep past the bedroom, bathroom before noticing a holdall sitting on the edge of the desk in the study. *That wasn't there last time.* She leans towards the top of the staircase. Lawrence is talking on his phone, his voice muffles as he closes the lounge door.

She dashes to the study on the balls of her feet and stops, waiting to hear footsteps behind her. Silence. The cat is on the windowsill licking his paws, he glares at her with his yellow orbs, and she gives him a short sharp hiss. The cat flinches but stays put. She opens the holdall and finds folders, official letters, waiting for his signature, pens, envelopes, a spare dress hat with braiding and… wads of cash. Abbie picks one up and reads the paper band holding it together. *Matthias. Who is Matthias?*

"It may be in my other bag." His voice echoes off the staircase walls, as he climbs.

Abbie's breath hitches and she shoves everything inside the bag, before zipping it closed. She goes to run to the bathroom but Lawrence steps onto the landing just as she makes it to the study door. Lawrence stops walking and dips the phone from his ear. Abbie holds her breath.

"Did you forget where the bathroom is?" He gives her a dry smile.

"Ha! No… I was…" She looks behind her at Charlie licking his paws. "I was saying hello to Charlie."

"You hate Charlie."

"I don't… hate him. I… I wanted a soft cuddle." *What the actual hell am I talking about?* She smiles. "It's been a rough couple of days."

As though just remembering he was on a phone call, Lawrence jerks the phone back to his ear. "I'll call you back." His eyes stay fixed on Abbie's face.

"But I *would* like that shower." She goes to slide past him, and he curls an arm around her waist.

"Maybe we could finish what we started downstairs first?"

"Oh. Ummm…"

He moves his mouth to her neck. "More fun than a cuddle from the cat…"

"I should shower." She sidles away from him and moves towards the bathroom.

He watches her. "You seem… uptight."

"Not at all." She gives him a smile. "I guess I'm just trying to adjust to… everything."

Lawrence nods. "Of course."

Abbie shuts the door and leans against it. She covers her mouth with her hand and muffles a whimper.

A loud knock makes her jump, and she hits her head on a hook jutting out from the door. She grabs her head and stifles a profanity. "Yes?"

"Do you want a robe?"

"Oh. Thank you." She opens the door. He hands her a satin robe, and a pair of black lacy knickers.

"I still have *some* of your things." He looks into her eyes and Abbie struggles to hold his gaze, dropping her eyes to the floor.

"It'll all be okay, Sweet." He pulls the door shut.

Abbie rests her forehead against the door, pushing her nails against the white painted wood.

Why is it so hard to hate you?

20

ABBIE

Abbie steps out of the shower and wraps herself in a fluffy bath sheet. The room is full of steam and she sits on the edge of the bath for a moment and closes her eyes.

"Seriously, Abs. It's a wonder you don't end up poached in there."

Abbie smiled as she pulled the shower curtain across. "Are you just jealous you aren't in here with me?"

"And suffer third degree burns? No thanks." Tom leaned towards the mirror and flossed his teeth.

"Are you sure about that?"

Tom turned and leaned against the sink. "Are you trying to sound seductive?"

"Is it working?"

"No."

"Hmm." She whipped the curtain closed. "That's a shame."

Seconds later the curtain opened, and Tom grabbed her hand, pulling her into him. "Okay fine. I have fifteen minutes."

"You always give in."

"Not always."

"Name one time."

"Not when I'm right." He slid his hands over the wet skin on her back and he rested them behind her neck, his thumbs caressed her cheeks.

"When are you ever right?" She closed her eyes and let him kiss her.

"I'm always right," he whispered against her mouth.

She opens her eyes and stands. She grabs a smaller towel and rubs her hair, looking back and forth between the tracksuit she had on before, and the robe and knickers. *Can't run far in a satin robe and French knickers…*

The television is on in the lounge when Abbie emerges from the bathroom, she looks in the bedroom and it's empty. She sidles towards the study, having decided in the shower to take the money and run. She gets to the study door, but the holdall isn't on the desk. She digs her fingernails into her palms and slowly turns to the staircase. *Shit.*

Standing at the lounge door she peers in, and Lawrence is on the phone, but he isn't talking. She waits and after a few more seconds he hangs up and leans back in his chair. She notices the holdall, open on the coffee table in front of him. She takes a deep breath and skips into the lounge.

"Hey. Ugh! That feels so much better." She flips her damp hair around and perches on the sofa, next to Lawrence's chair. "I was kind of waiting for you to come join me." She leans on the arm rest and raises a brow at him.

He steeples his fingers under his nose and gives her a half smile. "Is that a fact?"

"Absolutely."

"You aren't in the robe."

"No well… it felt a bit early for a robe. But maybe later…" She slides off the sofa and falls to her knees, sliding her hands up his thighs.

"Maybe." His smile grows but remains stilted. He places his hands over the top of hers, gently pushes them from his lap and stands. "Coffee?"

Abbie frowns, watching him walk to the kitchen. "Sure." She follows and leans against the doorframe.

Lawrence moves around the kitchen, fussing with cups and his coffee machine.

"Are you okay?"

"I'm burying my wife tomorrow," he replies without looking up from the milk frother.

Abbie looks at the floor. "Of course. I'm sorry."

"Sugar? I can't remember."

"No. Thank you."

Lawrence nods and pours milk into the cup. He slides it to the other side of the island worktop and gestures to it. "Drink up."

She sips the scalding coffee and gasps as her lip burns.

"Alright?" Lawrence watches her, amusement tinges the corners of his eyes, though he doesn't smile.

"Just… hot."

"Apologies."

Abbie puts down the cup. "What's wrong?"

Lawrence sits on the other side of the worktop and sips his own coffee. "Ah, just right." He looks at her. "What makes you think something's wrong?"

"You're being… strange."

He takes a long sip of his coffee, peering at her over the rim of the cup. Abbie runs a finger around the rim of her own cup and gives him another smile.

"Are you paranoid?"

"Paranoid?"

"Yes."

"About?"

"Why don't you tell me?"

Abbie smiles. "Maybe I need a nap. It's been a tiring day."

"A shower and now a nap?" Lawrence gulps the last of his coffee and turns to put the cup in the sink. "Are you suddenly a middle aged woman, Sweet?" he asks without turning around.

Abbie forces a chuckle. "No. Just exhausted. Do you mind?"

He turns and smiles again and instead of filling her with warmth it sends cold water cascading down her spine. "And why would I mind?"

Abbie changes tack and leans on the worktop. "Because I didn't ask you to come with me?"

"Is that an invitation?"

No. "Yes."

"I need to make some calls. So… why don't you run along? I'll join you if I get through my work."

"You make it sound like an appointment."

"Did I?" He walks into the lounge.

———

THE DOORBELL CHIMES AS ABBIE REACHES THE BOTTOM OF THE staircase at six pm. She didn't sleep a wink. Lawrence never joined her, and he walks into the foyer as she reaches the door.

"It'll be the pizza. I'll sort it." She spies a set of keys on the hall table, next to a letter opener and picks them up.

"Maybe I'll pay for this one."

"No really. It's fine. Let me do something for you." She flicks her head towards the lounge. "Go relax, yeah?"

Lawrence gives a look that goes straight through her. "I'll give you this one." He walks into the lounge and shuts the door behind him.

Abbie stares after him. *Definitely not paranoid.*

She opens the door to a rosy cheeked, plump woman smiling at her. "Hi hi! Pizza for Abbie?"

Abbie steps onto the front doorstep and pulls the door to, behind her. "Yes…"

The plump woman giggles a weird giggle and hands her a pizza box. "Hot from Martha's Kitchen." She raises a pencilled eyebrow. "All paid for."

Abbie takes the box. "Thanks."

"Receipt's in the box." The woman narrows her eyes at Abbie. "Perhaps check it to make sure it's right?"

Get to the box first. She opens the box to a wad of cash, a mobile phone, a key and a note encased in cling wrap on top of the pizza. She shoves them into her pocket and smiles at the woman. "Thank you."

"Enjoy your meal." She winks and trots down the garden path.

Abbie walks into the kitchen and slaps the pizza on the table. "Just need the loo. Get started and I'll be right back." She walks to Lawrence and kisses him, running her hands down his neck. "And after maybe we can have that dessert we almost started earlier?"

Lawrence smiles, but his eyes don't change. "Looking forward to it."

Abbie skips to the powder room off the hall. Once inside she locks the door and pulls the cling wrapped package from her pocket. She opens the note.

Get the fuck out. TODAY.

"Eloquent." She drops the note and cling wrap into the loo and flushes it. She shoves the phone, key, and cash into her bra thankful for the slouchy jumper, before returning to the kitchen.

She slides into a chair next to Lawrence and grabs two slices of pizza. "How is it?"

"Delicious. Where did you get it? There's no name on the box."

Abbie takes a bite and chews, the saltiness of all the anchovies almost makes her spit it out but she chews slower. "Oh." She swallows. "Some new place in town. I don't remember." She looks down and picks the anchovies off the rest of her slice and the other sitting on her plate.

"Not a fan of the anchovies, then?"

She stops picking and looks up.

"You ordered extra, if you remember?"

"Yes… no. I love them. It's just…" *Shit.*

"It's just… you weren't talking to a pizza place when I walked in?"

"Why would you say that?"

Lawrence pulls a gold chain from his shirt pocket and drops in on the table in front of Abbie. "Didn't I give this to you?"

Did not think that through. Abbie's throat goes dry, despite the water she just swallowed. "Umm…You did. I lost it months ago…"

"Months ago?"

"Yes… where did you find it?"

"In my safe." He frowns.

Abbie puts her glass down, slowly and deliberately, refusing to look at Lawrence's face. "I guess your wife must have found it."

Lawrence grins, but it's more of a grimace. "You think so?"

"Well… how else would it end up in your safe?"

"You're going to blame my dead wife?"

"Not blame… I…"

"Do you think she's to blame for the missing documents from the safe too?"

"Missing documents?" Abbie rubs at her throat.

"You're a liar. Sweetheart." Lawrence moves his chair closer to Abbie and grabs her wrist. He strokes his thumb along where her pulse beats, but his grip hurts. He presses his lips to her ear. "What the hell do you think you're playing at?"

"No. Why would I lie?"

He squeezes her wrist harder. "I'm burying the love of my life tomorrow and here you are accusing her of planting your necklace and stealing my documents?." His eyes flash. "Who do you think you are?" His voice trails to a whisper and he stares at Abbie.

"Love of your life?" She yanks her hand out of Lawrence's and stumbles from her chair. "Love *of your life?*"

Lawrence stands and advances on Abbie. "She was my wife."

Abbie shuffles backwards and stumbles into the worktop and cupboards. "And what am I?"

"You're just the fun little plaything I amused myself with." He stands in front of her and pins her back against the cupboards. "You're nothing," he hisses in her face.

Abbie closes her eyes as the ball of angst and terror floating in her belly swells. She takes a deep breath through her nose before opening her eyes and glaring straight into Lawrence's. "Let. Me. Go."

Lawrence throws his head back and laughs. "You must think I'm stupid. Let you go? And then what? You'll go running to Tom? Tell him all your *unfounded* and *impossible to prove* ideas about me?"

"Nothing is impossible, Matt. Surely you know that?" She pushes him to the chest with both hands and he stumbles back. It's enough room for her to slide out from where he has her pinned and make a run for the front door. He throws a dining chair out of the way and comes after her.

She reaches the front foyer of the house before an arm wraps around her waist and she falls to the floor. Lawrence flips her onto her back. "Where exactly do you think you're going?"

His cologne slides into her senses and his breath blankets her face. She presses her lips together and glares into his eyes.

"Well? My *Sweet*?"

"Away from here. Away from you."

"I'm terribly sorry. But that's not possible." He pins her arms above her head and leans on her wrists. His face moves closer, and he presses his mouth onto hers.

She wriggles beneath him, and he pushes his face harder into hers. *You're stark raving mad.* She manages to turn her head to the side and focus on the hall table.

Abbie heaves her knee upwards and crunches it into Lawrence's groin. He gasps into her neck and rolls off her. She scurries to the table and grabs the letter opener lying next to the keys.

"Abbie. Don't be stupid." Lawrence's voice is wheezy and weak. "Fuck!"

She runs to him and straddles his chest, pinning his arms to the floor with her knees. The letter opener is in her fist, and she holds it up. She stares into his pained face. He glares back a moment before starting to laugh. "What are you going to do, Sweet? Stab me? Like you did *my wife?*" He widens his eyes and tries to thrust her off him. She slaps his face with every ounce of strength in her possession and he stills. "Go on then."

Abbie's vision tunnels and a movie reel plays in her mind. Their intertwined bodies in the upstairs bedroom, them laughing over a bottle of champagne in an expensive hotel room, and the look of utter disregard and hatred he fixed her with in the kitchen only moments ago, play over and over. Her arm shakes and the fist gripping the letter opener tightens.

"I haven't got all day. I do have a funeral to prepare for."

"You killed her."

Lawrence's face stiffens and he takes a long breath through his nose. "What did you say?"

"You killed her. I know you did. Nothing else makes sense."

Lawrence continues to stare at her, and she digs her knees harder into his arms. He grimaces. "You know what? I'm done. I don't need to be scared of you... or anyone else."

"What does that mean?"

"It means you're not leaving this house." He heaves his hips upward and gathers strength to topple Abbie off him.

She scrambles on all fours to the staircase as Lawrence's hand grips her ankle. She kicks him off and runs up the stairs. *Why the hell am I running up?* She runs to the study and gets behind the desk.

Lawrences strides to the door a second later and smiles. "What are you doing?"

"Honestly? No idea. But for the record... I hate you."

He steps into the study and moves towards the desk. Abbie tightens her grip on the letter opener. "I swear to God Matt, I'll stab you."

He stops about three feet from the desk. "No you won't."

They watch each other, both not moving or speaking.

Abbie swallows. "Why Matt?"

"Why what?"

"Why did you kill her?"

He squints at her a moment before giving a slight shrug. "I didn't."

"Neither did I. So I guess it was some kind of divine intervention?"

He runs his tongue along his top lip. "She knew about Amir and the Iranian money. Did I mention? And that you were bribing him."

"I wasn't and you know it."

"That's a strong motive."

Abbie's heart is in her mouth, and she shakes her head at what she's hearing. "You're a monster…"

"Perhaps… but not a killer." He holds a hand out. "C'mon. What say you put the blade down and we move past this misunderstanding?"

A bell goes off in Abbie's head and she jumps over the desk and onto Lawrence. "Fuck you! You selfish piece of shit." She slaps his face and tries to knee him in the crotch again, but he fights back, grabbing both her arms and wrestling her onto her back.

They squirm on the floor, Abbie holding the letter opener and Lawrence struggling to keep her under control.

"Sweet," he pants in her face. "What are you doing? Don't you love me?"

"I hate you Matt… what you've done to me… and for what? Status? Money?"

Lawrence blinks once and grins. "What else is there?"

Abbie uses every ounce of strength in her body and manages to tip Lawrence off her and scurry down the stairs. She reaches the front door and fiddles with the deadlock. *Shit!* She looks at the hall table, but the keys are gone.

A jangle behind her makes her turn and press herself against the door.

"Looking for these?"

"Let me go, Matt. It's over."

"Aren't you going to stab me first?" He chuckles. "Like you did my poor innocent *wife*?"

A single tear rolls down Abbie's cheek. "You aren't worth it."

Lawrence's face hardens and his grin disappears. "Neither were you."

Abbie stops as the poison he shot into her heart stings. She lets out a mangled, gurgling cry of pain before lunging at him and plunging the letter opener into his chest. He stumbles backwards onto the staircase, and sits on the bottom step, the letter opener sticks out just below his shoulder. His face is pale, his mouth agape as he stares at her, all emotion missing from him. Wheezing breaths are all he can manage.

Abbie picks the keys up from the floor and runs to the door, she fumbles with the lock, her sweaty hands getting the better of her. "Shit shit shit…"

The door finally opens, and she runs. Cool air hits her skin and sunlight warms her face. Regardless, a lump of cold ice sits in the pit of her stomach.

What have I done?

21

TOM

Tom's phone pings from the desk and he turns from where he gazes out of the porthole.

Text Message from Melissa Brown

"About fucking time," he grumbles as he flicks open the message.

It's over. Thanks for trying. Don't look for me.

He grits his teeth and throws the phone across the room. It smashes against the wall and explodes into pieces.

He picks up the desk phone and dials Martha. "I need a new phone."

22

TOM

Tom pulls his collar up against the brisk air of the night as he descends the gangway of the ship.

"Wait up!"

Tom stops walking and rolls his eyes. "I didn't invite you, James."

"Don't panic. I have other plans."

"Is that right?"

"That's right."

"What about Sylvie? Iz isn't around to babysit."

"What makes you think my plans are with Mischa?"

Tom turns and tilts his head.

"Okay… I'm going to her flat for dinner."

"Her flat?"

James grins. "Yes. She's cooking me a dish I can't pronounce."

Tom steps closer to James and pokes his index finger into his chest. "Hands to yourself."

"I'm not making any promises." He winks and saunters past Tom. "But I do promise to be a gentleman."

"And I promise to shoot you in the head."

"Noted." He waves and gets into the waiting cab.

Tom purses his lips and glares at the cab as it disappears from view.

"Oh. Good evening, Sir."

Tom turns and smiles at Liam. "Where are you headed?" They walk towards the roadway.

"Just visiting friends." Liam shrugs and pulls his long jacket tighter around himself.

The car Martha sent for Tom arrives and he gives it a wave. "Well… you enjoy yourself."

Liam nods and kicks at the gravel on the road. "Sure."

Tom watches Liam slouch up the road as he slides into the car. "Hey Justin," he says without taking his eyes off Liam.

"Tom." Justin pulls the car away from the kerb. "Who's the kid?"

Tom shakes his head. "No one."

"I believe you wanted a new phone?" Martha's voice fills the car from where she is perched in the backseat.

Tom drops his head against the headrest and closes his eyes. "Did you have to bring her?"

Justin chuckles.

"Cute." She slaps the phone into his arm. "Take it."

He takes the phone without turning. "Did you need an outing?"

"Perhaps. And the prospect of your sparkling company was hard to pass up."

"That's fair. I'm so very effervescent."

Martha snorts. "And... I'm doing your comms this evening."

Tom turns to peer at her. She has a laptop open on her knees and she's tapping away at the keyboard. "You?"

She looks up. "Me. Is that a problem?"

"I'm just following the halfwit. I hardly need comms."

"Do you know where he is right now?"

"Well... no. But I know he's headed somewhere near Charing Cross."

Martha nods once and consults her screen. "Trafalgar Square."

Tom sighs and faces forward again. "I guess you better keep eyes on him then."

"What a splendid idea. And here..."

Tom turns again and she's holding out an earpiece and mic. "I don't need an—"

"Take it."

Tom grunts, takes the earpiece, and shoves it in his ear. "I can't believe I'm saying this, but I should have made James cancel his dinner and work." He clips the tiny, magnetised mic under his collar.

"And miss an opportunity to work with me?"

"Opportunity is such a strong word."

"Hmmm."

"How was the funeral? I'm assuming you went?"

"I did. Lawrence was suitably grief stricken."

"I bet."

"He even had a black sling for his newly acquired shoulder injury."

No one says anything for a second, and Martha taps away on her keyboard.

Tom relents. "I haven't heard from her."

"I assumed not, or you would have told me."

Tom looks out the window and says nothing.

"Right Tom?"

"Sorry what?"

"Don't be an arse."

Tom scoffs. "It's like you don't even know me."

Justin snorts as he turns onto Charing Cross Road.

"Slow down. He's up ahead." Martha keeps tapping her keyboard.

Tom peers down the road. "Maybe he's an avid reader."

"Doubt it."

"I don't see him." Tom unclicks his seatbelt. "Pull over here please, Justin. Time for a stroll."

"You keep me in your ear Thomas Grant."

Tom turns and pokes his head back into the car. "Sorry. Don't know a Thomas." He slams the car door and pulls his hood up.

"Arse." Martha's voice vibrates in his ear, and he grins to himself as he wanders down the street.

The street is scattered with people, browsing closed store-fronts, holding hands, laughing. *Being normal. How lovely.*

Tom squints into the distance and picks Pike. He walks with his shoulders straight and practically marches. *Hard to miss.* "Got him." Tom hastens his stride. "You know, he could balance a book on his head and pass Miss Prissy's deportment class with flying colours."

"What do you know about Miss Prissy?"

"I made it up. Is she real?" Pike turns into Newport Court. "Okay he's going into the pedestrian area towards Chinatown. Park somewhere I'll find you later."

"Keep me in the loop."

"Yeah yeah."

Pike is a few shopfronts ahead when he stops and looks over his shoulder. Tom ducks into a doorway and presses against the glass. He waits a moment before taking a peek. Pike is on the move again. Tom wanders, keeping a safe distance. He stops and pretends to be interested in an antique phone in the window of a store when prickles tingle on the back of his neck. He looks towards Pike; oblivious Tom is there before glancing back the way he came. *Nothing.* "Paranoid," he whispers.

"What's that?"

"Nothing. Shoosh."

Martha huffs and Tom grins to himself as he moves on.

"Go watch Tipping Point or something. I'll let you know if I need you."

His ear falls silent, and he chuckles before a shuffle somewhere behind him makes him stop again. He turns and peers down the road. A few people wandering towards Chinatown pay him no attention. He looks back towards Pike and realises he needs to catch up. He jogs towards the end of the street, but the sensation of being watched continues to distract him and he cracks his neck side to side.

"Keep a track on Pike… I need to check something."

"Check what?"

"Hang on…" Tom backtracks and walks the way he came. Doorways are empty and spaces between buildings undisturbed. He looks up and catches the tail of a jacket disappearing around the corner back onto Charing Cross Road. He runs the fifty metres to the end of the street but by the time he gets there his quarry is gone. "Fuck it."

"Tom?"

"I swear someone was watching me."

"Watching you?"

"Yes." He jogs back towards Chinatown. "Forget it. Where's Pike now?"

"He's gone inside a restaurant called *Duck Soup.*"

"On it."

Tom walks into the restaurant and looks around. Pike isn't there.

"Sir?" The hostess gives him a smile.

"Ah, yeah just me. Thanks."

"Tom! What are you doing?"

"This way." The hostess holds a hand out and Tom follows her, ignoring Martha in his ear.

He sits and smiles as the hostess pours water before walking away. Tom scans the restaurant again. Nothing. "Are you sure he came in here?"

"I'm watching his phone signal flash as we speak. He's somewhere near the back. And I swear if you order a three hundred pound crab I'll throttle you."

"Oh crab. My favourite."

"Tom!"

"Shhhh." He looks to the back of the restaurant. "He's probably in the john."

"Copy."

Tom slaps his napkin on the table and moves to the back of the dining area. He walks into the gents to find it empty. "Or not." A crash from outside sounds through the small open window at the rear of the gents. Tom grabs a rubbish bin and uses it to peer out the barred window at the top of the wall. He can't see straight down, only rooftops and brick. "Dammit."

"I'll get it. Okay?" Pike's voice floats through the window from below.

"Time up." An accented voice answers before what sounds like a punch to the gut.

Pike groans. "He said he'd be here."

"I no see him."

"I can't…" Pike groans again. "I can't explain why."

Tom jumps down from the rubbish bin and runs from the gents. He dodges tables and waitresses and slams out the front door.

"Tom? Why are you breathing like that? What's going on?"

Tom doesn't answer but rounds the corner of the building and sprints down the alleyway. He comes out into the back of the row of restaurants. Pike is on the ground, blood streams from his nose and he is curled in the foetal position, protecting his head. Two men tower over him shouting, but Tom can't make it out. One wears an apron smeared in sauce and grease.

"Hey!"

The two men turn and see Tom. One of them is holding an iron bar. *Well, crap.*

Pike tries to get off the ground but the man without the bar kicks him in the ribs. Tom paces towards the man with the bar. He hoists it above his head, and Tom grabs it as he brings it down and manages to divert it from his head.

"Oh, you want fight?"

Tom smirks at the man in the apron. "Yeah, why not." He raises his leg and kicks the arm holding the bar. The aproned man drops it and before he can pick it up Tom kicks it away and grabs him by the back of the shirt. He slams him into the brick wall, he falls to the ground and Tom stamps a foot into his chest. "More?"

"Sir!" Pike shouts from the ground and Tom turns in time to see the other man running at him. He ducks and swings a leg out, tripping him. He crashes to the ground with his mate. Tom backs away as the pair scramble to their feet.

They glare at Tom, and he grins. "So. Are we done here?"

The man in the apron clenches both fists in front of him. "We are not done with friend." He nods to Pike who is sitting against the wall wiping blood from his nose. "But you can have him tonight."

"How generous. But what do you want with him?"

He smiles. "It's business." He glares at Pike and raises his chin. "Next time maybe your friend will not come to rescue?"

Pike spits blood on the ground. "Maybe."

"Right then. Off you fuck." Tom makes an 'off you go' gesture and the men leave, the one in the apron holds Tom's stare the entire way before walking around the corner.

"What are you doing here?" Pike gets off the ground and leans against the wall, hands on knees and taking deep breaths.

"Who can resist duck pancakes and a side of dumplings?"

"Right."

"Meanwhile… why are you getting beaten to a pulp in a dodgy back alley by a chef and his dishwasher?"

Pike shakes his head and stands up straight. "Gave them a bad review."

"I can only assume you owe them money."

"You know what they say about assuming."

Tom raises a brow. "Did you just call your Commander an ass?"

"*Temporary* Commander." Pike wipes his nose again as the

blood continues to flow. "And no. Anyway... thanks for the help." He goes to walk past Tom.

"That's it?" Tom grabs his elbow. "What the fuck is going on?"

"Nothing. Like I said..." Pike looks Tom in the eye. "Bad review."

Tom pulls Pike closer by the shirt front. "I'm watching you."

"Evidently."

"I also don't like you."

"Noted. But... you're barking up the wrong tree."

"Am I?"

"Yeah. You are." He yanks Tom's hand from his shirt. "Now if you'll excuse me... I'm going to eat somewhere else." He pushes past Tom and slouches to the end of the alleyway.

"My office. Oh eight hundred Monday morning."

Pike gives Tom a wave and keeps walking.

"Well." Martha's voice comes alive in Tom's ear. "That didn't go as planned."

23

TOM

Tom slams another weight onto the end of the bar and stands over it. He bends and grips the bar before deadlifting it. *Fucking heavy.* He straightens before dropping it. He paces the gym and grinds his teeth. *Tonight was a fucking waste of time.* He spins and kicks a punching bag before pummelling it with some one-two-three combinations. He exhausts himself and wraps his arms around the bag, resting his face against it.

He looks up in time to see Liam hovering at the door, looking as though he's about to leave.

"Liam."

"Sir."

"I thought you were out with friends this weekend?"

"Oh. Yeah… I saw one. But the others... cancelled."

"That's a shame." Tom throws himself onto a bench and grabs his water.

"Not really. Anyway... sorry to interrupt." He steps backwards.

"You didn't."

"What?"

"You didn't interrupt. I'm done." Tom screws the lid on his water. "I'm not really feeling it."

Liam shuffles into the gym and sits on a bench opposite Tom. "You looked like you meant it." He nods towards the punching bag.

"Just letting off steam." Tom watches Liam brings his legs up, crossing them under him on the bench and pick at invisible lint on his tracks. "You seem uncomfortable."

Liam chuckles. "I'm always uncomfortable."

"It does seem strange to be coming in here at midnight."

"Well... you're here?" A sly grin creeps across Liam's face.

"You know, I would never come back to the ship when I was granted shore leave."

"No?"

"Nope. Any chance to get away from this place... I took it."

Liam nods and fiddles with his gym towel. "Sir?"

Tom raises both brows and waits.

"Do you ever think about choices you've made and think it was the worst thing you've ever done?"

Tom opens his water and takes another sip. "I've made lots of stupid choices. But…" He shrugs. "They've brought me to some pretty great things."

"All of them?"

"No. Some of them were downright stupid." He grins.

Liam nods again and picks at the embroidered initials on his towel.

"Is there something you want to get off your chest, Liam?"

Liam shakes his head and stands. "I hate it here." He walks out of the gym.

Tom stares at the empty doorway. *Well, fuck.*

TOM PULLED CHRIS'S ARMS FROM WHERE THEY WERE WRAPPED *around his head. "What are you doing? Look at me."*

Chris lifted his head from his knees. "I can't keep doing this. Every day, Tom. I can't."

"Six months to go and you're free."

"It's too long."

"You used to say that about waiting for Christmas too." Tom grinned and slumped against the wall next to Chris.

"Yeah… I was a stupid kid. And anyway, it did take ages. Every year."

"Yeah but it always came around."

Chris pressed his thumbs into his eyes and nodded. "Yeah."

"What happened tonight?"

Chris shook his head. "Nothing. Don't worry about it."

"Are you fucking serious?"

"I said it's nothing." Chris leapt up from the floor. "Stop picking the scab. For Christ's sake."

Tom stood and grabbed Chris by the collar. "You're gonna do this? I'm the only one who looks out for you. The only one who ever has, so what were you saying?"

Chris's lip trembled. "I hate it here." He ripped Tom's hand from his shirt and stormed away.

Tom blinks and drains the last of his water bottle. He throws it in the bin and runs after Liam.

"Hey. Hampshire."

Liam stops at the junction to go to the berths. "Sir?"

Tom stops in front of him. "Are you alright?"

"Never better. Life's a trip." He turns to go, and Tom grabs his shirt.

"What are you doing now?"

Liam frowns and gives Tom a smirk. "Um… going to sleep?"

Tom loosens his grip. "Of course. Yeah." He rubs the sweat gathering above his top lip away and clears his throat.

"Sir?"

"Yes?"

"Are *you* alright?"

Tom takes a slow breath through his nose. "Yeah. Fine. Sleep well." He leaves before Liam can say anything else.

Slamming into his office, Tom throws himself onto his bunk and stares at the ceiling. "Fuck." He takes a moment to steady his breathing and waits for the knot in his stomach to unravel. He scrambles into a sitting position and pushes his hands either side of his head and squeezes. *Make it stop.*

He pulls his phone out and dials.

Isabella picks up on the second ring. "Tom? Are you okay?"

"No."

"Are you hurt?"

"No."

"What's going on?"

"I don't know what's happening to me." His voice is a raw whisper, and he swallows.

"Talk to me."

"You know if I didn't have that job tonight, I could have been with you."

"I know. I'll come home next weekend. Yeah?"

"I don't want to be here for another week. I don't want to be here for another minute." He drops his head against the wall and closes his eyes. *I sound like a bratty five year old.* He fans his shirt away from his sweaty skin.

"Has something happened?"

"No. Yes. Everything keeps happening."

"You aren't making any sense."

"I know. That's why I can't work out what the fuck is wrong with me."

"You're traumatised."

Tom huffs. "Now you sound like Martha."

"Well, sometimes she knows what she's talking about, you know." Her voice is tinged with amusement.

"I'm thirsty, Iz." His throat hurts and he pushes his hand against it. "I... fuck." He squeezes his eyes shut again.

"Tom. Now you're scaring me. I'll come there. I'll come there right now."

He lets his hand slide down to his chest as he imagines her resting against it. "I'm fine. I'm sorry."

"You aren't fine and don't be sorry."

"Next weekend?"

"No Tom. I'm concerned about you. I'll get on a train now."

"No. I shouldn't have called. It wasn't fair of me to worry you."

"Don't be ridiculous. This is the thirst talking. Not you. If it was you, you'd want me there with you. The thirst doesn't because it wants to win."

"It won't win." *Don't make promises you can't keep.*

Isabella says nothing for a moment before sighing. "Are you sure?" she whispers.

"I'm sure. But... please come on the weekend."

"Alright, but... will you call me if you need me? I don't care what time—"

"Okay. I promise." Tom nods. "I need to shower."

"Tom?"

"Yeah?"

"Drink water. Please."

Tom scrunches his face up against the tingle in his nose. "Okay."

———

TOM SNORTS AGAINST SOMETHING HOLDING HIS NOSE CLOSED and opens his eyes. Martha is standing over his bunk, her handbag hangs on her arm.

Tom scrambles into a sitting position. "What are you doing here? Who let you on the ship?"

"I did." James pops his head over Martha's shoulder and waves.

"Isabella called me. She was practically hyperventilating." Martha jerks her head towards the office and walks out.

Jesus, Iz.

Tom stumbles out of his bunk, thankful he slept in tracks and a t-shirt. He flops into one of the chairs and glares at Martha and James. "I'm fine. And tired."

"I brought you coffee." James jumps up and gets it from the desk.

"You're making it increasingly hard for me to hate you, James. And that makes me hate you…"

James grins and sits down.

"We have a situation." Martha picks up her handbag and pulls out some papers. "Matthew Lawrence has filed charges against Abigail Perkins for assault."

Tom swallows half the coffee in one gulp and puts the mug down. "I see."

"And she is currently whereabouts unknown." Martha peers at Tom.

"I don't know where she is."

"I'm glad. Because she is now wanted for assault as well as suspicion of murder. So if you *did* know—"

"I said I didn't know."

Martha closes her mouth and glares at Tom. "Not to mention the incriminating evidence of her involvement in collusion with—"

"Did you come here to tell me things I already know? Or to give me something I can actually work with?"

"I came here because Isabella was convinced you were going to drink yourself into a stupor last night and I… was worried about you." She looks down at her lap and smooths an imaginary wrinkle from her trousers.

Tom massages his temples and slumps back into the chair. "I showered and went to bed. But yes… I wasn't feeling great when I spoke to her."

"And now?"

"I don't know."

"Maybe I should take on some more of the load." James pipes up and reminds Tom he's also in the room.

"How was dinner?"

James frowns. "Dinner?"

"With Mischa."

"Oh… it was nice. I was back on the ship by eleven. Sylvie is teething and wasn't happy and…" He stops and looks between Martha and Tom. "Anyway. It was nice."

Tom nods. "I'm glad."

"James, do you mind giving Tom and I a moment?"

Tom rolls his eyes and stands. He wanders to the porthole and looks out while the door of the office clicks closed.

"Are you alright Tom?"

"I'm ecstatic. Last night was a waste of time. This ship is like some kind of Pandora's box I'd *really* rather not open any further. So yeah… shit's great. Thanks for asking."

"Maybe not a complete waste of time."

He turns to look at Martha. "Excuse me?"

"Last night."

Tom gestures for Martha to keep talking.

"Lawrence was in Trafalgar Square. I saw him as we drove through after you stormed off and refused a ride back." She stops and narrows her eyes at him.

"I needed a walk." He sits back in his chair. "What was he doing?"

"He was on his phone. Looked annoyed. He appeared to be shouting at someone."

"Pike. Too busy getting beaten senseless to make their meeting?"

"Perhaps." Martha picks up her handbag and puts it over her arm. "James needs to get into some phones and computers." She stands and walks to the door. "And you need to calm down and focus."

"Thanks for the hot tip."

"Isabella wouldn't have called me if she didn't think you were in a right state and you know it."

I know it.

24

TOM

Tom walks into the medical office and sits.

Mike flicks his eyes up from the papers he is signing and gives Tom a dry smile. "It's not Tuesday."

"I know."

He leans back and flips the notebook in front of him shut. He looks at Tom and says nothing.

"You're gonna do the interrogation thing?"

"You came to me." He pours two glasses of water from the jug on his desk and slides one to Tom. "A day early no less."

"I'm getting nowhere with this job and it's frustrating. This ship is doing weird things to me. I let it get the better of me on Saturday night."

"Did you drink?"

"Almost."

"But?"

"But… I didn't."

"Because?"

Tom rests his elbows on his knees and massages his temples. "I called Isabella instead."

"Isabella?"

"Yep." Tom stands. "Thanks. Sorry to bother—"

"Sit down. Sir."

Tom stops and stares at the closed door in front of him.

"Tell me about Christopher MacMillan."

Tom closes his eyes and takes a breath. "You aren't going to ease me into it?"

"Do you need to be?"

He throws himself back into the chair. "No."

"So… tell me about him."

"I don't need therapy."

"No? My mistake. You came in here for a physical?" Mike stands. "Behind that screen then. Disrobe… I'll get some gloves on. Be prepared to turn your head and cough."

"Okay… Chris was my little brother."

Mike sits again. "Brother?"

"Foster brother. We lived in the same house for a while. I got moved but we still went to the same school."

"Why were you moved?"

Tom gives a small grin. "Would it surprise you to learn that I didn't like being told what to do?"

"Not at all."

"Apparently I was *hard to handle.*"

Mike snorts. "Go on."

"I don't see what this—"

"*Go on.*"

"I told him I was joining the cadets and he said when he was old enough, he wanted to as well. So… it's my fault he joined up. End of story." Tom stands.

"Sit."

Tom sits with a thud. "Just so you know, I'm regretting this visit."

"I'll keep that in mind. Go on."

"He was targeted by some of the others on day one. He was smaller and… just…" Tom shakes his head. "He wasn't cut out for this life. I should have talked him out of it."

"How were you to know?"

Tom shrugs. "It was obvious."

"He was still capable of making his own decisions."

"Tell me Mike, were you a foster kid?"

"No."

"Then don't tell me what Chris was capable of and what confidence and self-esteem he had squashed out of him by the time he was seven years old." Tom's voice finishes louder than when he started, and he clears his throat. "Sorry."

"No apologies required."

"It was a rough house we lived in. And I moved to a worse one. Before I was... moved to my last home."

"Moved again?"

"Hard to handle…" *And they beat me.*

"And Chris?"

"He stayed in the same home the whole time."

"And it was rough."

"Yeah."

"Have you heard of transference, Tom?"

Tom looks at Mike and says nothing.

"It's when a person transfers feelings or emot—"

"I know what it is. What's your point?"

"You have unresolved issues surrounding Chris's death. And being here is bringing it all back to you. Liam is small, quiet and gets picked on quite a bit…"

Tom stands. "Chris is dead. Liam is not. They're nothing alike. Thanks for the chat." He marches to the door and grabs the handle.

"If you don't talk this through, it's not going to get easier."

Tom drops his forehead against the door and squeezes his eyes closed.

"You're on this ship to do a job. And you can't be objective in this state."

"And what do you suggest I do?"

Mike squeezes Tom's shoulder. "Let's go for a walk."

———

TOM WALKS WITH MIKE AND THEY DESCEND INTO THE LOWER depths of the ship. Towards the berths. Tom stops walking.

"Tom?"

"Where are we going?"

"You don't know?"

"Okay, I'll rephrase. Why are we going to the berths?"

"Because you need to see them."

"I know what they look like. Thanks."

"When was the last time you were in one?"

Tom glares at Mike. "I'm not doing this."

"Why not?"

"Because it's an exercise in futility. What do you expect will happen? Suddenly it will all make sense? That his death had a point?"

"It doesn't?"

"He was twenty-five-years-old. And he died for no good reason. So no. It has no point. And seeing some bunks and family photographs stuck on the wall won't change a thing."

"Maybe that's exactly what your issue is."

"Pardon?"

The sound of a body hitting the floor and a huff of breath interrupts their fireside chat, and Tom pushes past Mike; back the way they came.

Liam is on the floor of the corridor and Pike stands over him. "..so when?"

Liam covers his head with his arms. "I don't know."

"Not good enough."

"I have most of it."

"I need all of it. When are you seeing him again?"

"I don't know. He's... away."

Pike grabs Liam's shirt and lifts him half off the floor.

Tom paces to Pike and pulls him away from Liam, slamming him against the opposite wall. "Pike? Is there a problem?"

Pike's face is bruised, and his nose has dried blood around one nostril. "No. Sir."

"It's fine Sir. We were just talking." Liam gets to his feet, dusts his uniform off and smoothes his hair.

"That's bullshit." Tom glances back to Pike. "You were supposed to be in my office at oh eight hundred."

"My mistake. I must have overlooked it."

Tom steps into Pike so their foreheads are practically touching. "Dismissed."

Pike narrows his eyes at Tom.

"Or would you prefer an infraction? Considering I'm... your *temporary Commander*, I'd prefer to not have to do the paperwork."

"Yes, Sir."

"So let's try again. Dismissed."

He tugs his shirt out of Tom's grasp and lopes up the corridor.

"Can I assist you, Hampshire?" Mike takes a small torch from his top pocket and looks into Liam's eyes.

"No. Thank you."

"What was that about?" Tom leans against the wall and crosses his arms.

"Nothing. "

"It didn't look like nothing."

Liam looks at Tom steadily for a moment before shaking his head. "Nothing."

"Dismissed."

Liam walks away in the opposite direction to Pike.

"Right then. Shall we carry on?" Mike gestures after Liam.

"No."

"Wonderful." Mike strides past Tom and waits at the end of the corridor for him to catch up.

Tom swallows the ache in his throat and clenches his fists as he walks towards Mike. "This isn't necessary."

"Which proves that it is." Mike gestures down the corridor. "After you."

Tom blows a breath out, pushes past Mike and walks towards the berths. "Let's get this over with." As though shot from an arrow a pain so sharp and sudden it causes Tom to stop and slap a hand against the wall, hits him in the chest. "Jesus."

"Tom?"

Tom pulls in another breath only this time its laboured and hurts his lungs.

"Okay, let's have a seat." Mike sits on the floor, patting the spot beside him as Tom slides down the wall and sits next to him.

"What the hell's going on?"

"It's called panic."

Tom shakes his head. "That's ridiculous."

"No. It's normal. In your situation."

"I don't have." Tom gathers himself from the floor. "A situation." He looks up at the numbered berths in front of him. His breathing clears somewhat, and he leans over his knees. "Well? Are we carrying on?"

"You tell me."

"I'm not going near Chris's berth."

"Okay. Let's just see any old berth today."

"I'm also not coming back down here."

Mike grins. "Of course."

25

ABBIE

bbie walks into the Sainsbury's in Penzance. After a little over five hours on a train, she's hungry, thirsty, and irritated. *But now I have space to breathe.* She pulls her hood over her head as she wanders the aisles picking out essentials. *And chocolate.* She grabs a few bars and observes the deserted aisle. Her chest hollows and the blocks of chocolate and crisps on the shelves behind her grow eyes, watching every move she makes. She scuttles down the aisle to the self-service checkouts and scans her haul of comfort food.

The scratchy voice of a two way radio behind her ignites her pulse. She glances out of the side of her eye at the policeman, scanning his morning tea and chatting with the attendant. *Just my luck.* She skims the last pack of sweets through the scanner and keeps her head down. She feeds a ten pound note into the register and shoves her haul into her pockets, not bothering to wait for the few pence change. Looking at the floor she moves past the alarm gates and as the automatic doors open a hand grasps her elbow. Her throat closes and she gasps a breath in.

"Miss?" The scratchy radio is louder now.

She rotates her arm in an effort to keep going but the hand holds firm.

"Miss."

Abbie swallows and turns to face the policeman, keeping her eyes trained on his shiny black boots. "Yes?"

He holds a Mars Bar out. "You dropped this."

She lets out a spontaneous giggle and takes the chocolate. "Thank you."

"Are you alright, Miss?"

He probably thinks I'm high. Abbie nods. "Yes. Thank you." She spins and walks to the doors again. Once outside she jogs to a cab sitting at the rank ahead and slides into the backseat. "Relubbus please."

The cab driver nods and drives. Abbie looks out the back window, half expecting to see the policeman running after the cab. There is only an old woman pushing a trolley and a couple of teenagers smoking next to a skip. "Paranoid," she whispers to herself.

"What's that Miss?"

Abbie shakes her head. "Nothing. Sorry."

"Right you are."

26

TOM

Tom stands in the fresh air on the upper deck and stares at the docks. For the first time since getting on the ship, he wishes it was moving.

"There you are."

"James." Tom doesn't turn around.

"I've been looking for you for ages. Where were you?"

"Sorry Mum."

"There's something you should see."

Tom huffs. "Of course there is."

"Uncle Pete is all over the news."

Tom closes his eyes. "Fuck."

"And he's called me like fifty times, looking for you."

"Excellent."

"Tom! What's wrong with you?"

"It's been a taxing morning."

"How?"

"Nevermind." Tom spins and stalks towards the cabin.

"Have you heard from Abbie?" James scurries alongside Tom, barely keeping up.

"No."

"Ah."

"What else James?"

"Martha called too."

They reach Tom's office, and he slams inside, the door bounces off the wall and almost hits James in the face. Tom picks up his phone and jiggles his jaw back and forth while staring at the screen.

"What is it?"

Tom shrugs. "I'm contemplating which one to call first. Either way I'm going to want to drown myself in a bath full of whisky afterwards so…" He presses Martha's number.

James sits on one of the chairs and watches Tom with a grin on his face.

"Tom."

"You called?"

"Where have you been?"

"Getting a pedicure."

"Moore is headline news."

"Good for him. Some people go their whole career without any acknowledgment of their achievements."

"You know how bad this is. Where are we at?"

Tom lowers the phone from his mouth and looks at James. "Where are we at?"

"Excuse me?" James raises a brow.

Tom turns his attention back to the phone. "He's working on it."

"I want surveillance cameras at the hotel examined and I want Lawrence's inside man."

"Is that all?"

"And Abbie. Where is she?"

"Getting a pedicure."

"Find her."

"No problem, I'll solve the Ripper case while I'm at it."

"You're a pain in the neck." Martha hangs up.

Tom snorts and sits across from James.

"So… what did she say?"

"Not much. She's flexing her little tuck shop arms."

"Huh?"

"Before I talk to Uncle Pete, I need you to get into the surveillance cameras at the hotel and find out what the hell was going on the night Daphne died."

"I have."

"You have?"

"Yeah…"

Tom stares at James and waits.

"They were doctored. Like you said. Some user by the name

of Matthias hacked into the system around four in the morning after the murder."

"And you were going to tell me this…?"

"This morning. But you were M.I.A."

"I was with Mike."

"Mike?"

"The medic."

"Are you sick?"

"No more than usual." Tom stands. "So what was tampered with on the camera?"

"It's been chopped up all over the place." James gestures to the computer on Tom's desk. "Wanna see?"

"Yes. Do we have popcorn?"

"Do you want some?"

Tom rolls his eyes. "Just show me, James."

Tom roams the office while James taps away at the keyboard. Every time he blinks, flashes of Chris's berth and the scene he witnessed there hits him in vivid colour. He rests his head against the wall. "Fucking Mike."

"What's that?"

"Nothing. Are we good to go?" Tom walks around the desk and stands behind James.

"Yep… so… eleven forty five… Moore goes into the room with Daphne."

Tom leans forward as Daphne turns at the door of the hotel room and grabs Moore by the tie. He stumbles off balance and crashes into the doorframe. "Classy."

"Yeah… then there's nothing for around an hour."

"Impressive considering his level of… intoxication."

James grimaces. "That's my Uncle you're talking about."

"I'm just as disturbed as you are. Go on."

"But here's where it gets weird… the time stamp on the footage doesn't change. But when I pulled the layers apart and looked at each frame… it's been cut."

"Cut?"

"Yes... there's around ten minutes of footage missing. It's been spliced together to make it look like a seamless recording."

"But the time stamp doesn't lose time?"

"No. So whoever did it is very, *very* good at sticking everything back together."

"So, something happens in those ten minutes." Tom grabs a pen and writes a scribbly note of the timing. "Next?"

"So here we go… at about ten to one Uncle Pete comes out… looking dishevelled and disappears around the corner."

"Right."

"He's gone until about one fifteen but again… there's another cut and paste on this footage."

"Again?"

"Yes. I want to learn from whoever it is. He's flawless with his work."

"Maybe you can fangirl later?"

"Sorry. So, Uncle Pete goes into the room for five minutes and comes out looking distressed. I've never seen him look like that before."

Tom leans in closer and watches Moore as he leans against the wall for a moment, covers his face with both hands and his shoulders shake. "He's crying."

"Yep. Anyway, he leaves and…more time is cut at this point. And then Abbie turns up."

Tom's phone sounds as he watches Abbie slink into the room and shut the door. He picks it up without checking first.

"Grant."

"Where the fuck have you been?"

"Pete. What a pleasant surprise. How are you this fine morning?"

"How am I? I'm all over the goddamn morning news Grant!"

"I did hear rumours of your television debut."

"You said you'd fix this."

"Correction… I said I'd try."

"Have you?"

"Not yet. My bad. But listen… the footage of you stumbling down the hallway of the hotel with the ice bucket is riveting viewing. You are one suave gentleman at one in the morning after getting your end in."

"I'm not laughing."

"Oh me neither, believe me. My skin is crawling at the thought of it."

"I'm stuck inside my house like some sort of prisoner. There's photographers and journalists outside… TV cameras."

"Give them a wave. That's always a winner on morning TV."

"Fix this." Moore hangs up.

Tom drops his phone on the desk and runs a hand through his hair. "I wonder how much worse today can get?"

27

ABBIE

Abbie pushes the front door of her family holiday cabin with her shoulder. The door flings open, and she stumbles in. "Must have fixed it." She inspects the doorframe and runs her fingers over the recently stained timber.

"Hello?"

Abbie freezes as her mother's voice floats in from the main bedroom. "Shit."

"Who's there?"

She turns to run from the cabin but it's too late.

"Abigail?"

She looks up at her mother standing at the end of the hallway. "Hey Mum."

"Oh Darling." She runs across the lounge and envelopes Abbie in a hug. "How are you, my girl?"

That's all it takes for Abbie's tears to flow. "I'm okay."

Her mother holds her at arm's length. "Why are you crying?"

"I'm happy to see you." Abbie buries her face into her mother's shoulder again, and sobs.

"A few tears I might believe. But not this." She leads Abbie to the sofa, and they sit. "Did you get a key from Mavis?"

Abbie nods and holds the key up.

"Okay, I'll take this back to her while you go and wash your face. Then we can chat."

"Mum?"

"Yes?"

"Why are you here?"

Her mother smiles. "I could ask you the same thing."

"I needed a rest?"

"Funny that. Me too." Her mother winks and walks outside.

Abbie trudges to the bathroom and leans over the wash basin, glaring at herself in the mirror. "Now what?" She turns the water on and splashes her face. The towel she grabs from the rack smells like the washing powder her mother has used forever. She takes in a long nostalgic breath and wishes she could go back to when life was easy and happy. But, when she opens her eyes she is still in the bathroom, wearing the same tracksuit Tom gave her what seems like a lifetime ago.

Cups and saucers chink against each other as Abbie walks into the lounge.

Her mother looks up. "Tea?"

Abbie nods and curls into a ball at the far end of the sofa.

"What's happened Abigail?"

"I messed up." She picks at the edges of a throw cushion as her mother sets a tray with tea and biscuits on the coffee table.

"Messed up how?"

She lifts the corner of her mouth into a half smile. "Fell in love with the wrong man."

"Oh Darling. Join the club."

"No. This isn't like you and dad." *Dad left you. He didn't murder you.*

"Enlighten me."

"He just wasn't what I thought he was."

"Ah. Okay… nothing like your father. He never pretended I was more important than his career. I certainly knew where I stood from day one." She gives a bitter chuckle and stirs her tea.

"You still cried when he died."

"Well. He was your father. And Damien's. I'll always love him for that."

Abbie nods and stares at the opposite wall. "How is Damo?"

"Fine. You should call him. You have another niece you've never met."

Abbie nods and fights back the tears that keep persisting.

"What else?"

"Nothing."

"Are you staying a while?"

"I don't know."

"Well, I can make up your old room."

"I can do it."

"Surely you're sick of making perfect beds and cleaning your quarters by now?" Her mother smiles.

"I've been out almost a month. Time I put my skills to some use."

A hush falls over them. "I'm sorry I wasn't there for your discharge."

"Don't worry about it. It's not like there was a ticker tape parade."

"I know but…"

"It's fine Mum. I know the Navy upsets you since Dad…"

Her mother stands. "Let me make up that room."

Abbie waits until her mother is busy stripping the bed and sorting sheets before she moves from the sofa and picks up the old landline on the side table. She dials and waits.

"Yes?"

"I'm sorry," she whispers.

Tom says nothing.

"Grant?"

"I had a feeling you'd go to Cornwall."

"I just ended up here."

"Did you have to stab him?"

"It happened so fast. I don't even remember doing it."

"Well, he's in a sling so… you did it."

"No but… red mist and all that."

"Abs, you have to come back. I can't help you if you're all the way down there."

"Mum's here."

"How is Marilyn?"

"As put together as always. Asks all the right things but doesn't really care much about the answers. But her makeup and hair are on point."

"Right."

"You don't sound as mad as I expected."

"I'm seething. But…it's been an exhausting morning."

"I'll come back."

"Yes. You'll go to my flat and stay there. Like I told you to, days ago. By the way you've been charged with assault on Lawrence."

Abbie's stomach hits the floor. "That bastard."

"Hmmm."

"Just give me another day here."

Silence falls again and Abbie twists the phone cord around her finger. "Grant?"

"Be on a train tomorrow. I'm not messing with you. If you don't think I'll come down there and drag you back to London…"

Abbie grins. "I know you will."

"Right. So be on a train."

"I really am sorry."

"I know." He hangs up.

Abbie wanders back to the sofa and sits just as the bell outside the door tinkles. *Just my luck she's invited people over for Bridge or something.*

Abbie opens the front door and every muscle in her body contracts.

"Hello, my Sweet."

Abbie's mouth is dry and a truckload of sand sits in her gut.

"Are you going to invite me in?"

"No."

"Come now. Don't be like that. Last time you brought me here we stayed inside for days." He smiles but the chill that comes off his eyes is freezing. "Remember? All wrapped up in... each other."

Abbie goes to close the door and Lawrence slaps his palm against it. "I wouldn't."

"Or?"

"Abigail? Who's there?"

Abbie blinks slowly and clenches her teeth. "No one Mum. Wrong house." She goes to shut the door again and Lawrence pushes harder to keep it open.

Marilyn walks up behind Abbie and upon seeing Lawrence she pats her hair and smiles. "Oh. Hello." She looks at Abbie. "A friend of yours?"

"A dear friend," Lawrence says. "*Very* dear." He stares at Abbie and she blinks again. Everything is in slow motion.

"Oh. Isn't that nice. You didn't tell me you were inviting a friend Abigail."

"It must have slipped my mind." Abbie glares at Lawrence as his smile widens.

"You *have* been quite stressed lately, my Sweet."

"My Sweet?" Marilyn peers at Abbie.

"This is Matthew Lawrence. A… mistake."

Lawrence tips his head back and laughs. "Always one with a sense of humour."

"And are you going to ask your… mistake in?" Marilyn nudges Abbie in the back.

"No."

Lawrence continues to watch Abbie. "That sense of humour could get you into trouble one day." The edge to his voice is sharp, and cuts through Abbie like soft butter.

"Why are you here?"

"Why don't we chit chat about that? My answer may change depending on your attitude." He pushes the door, and it slips from Abbie's grasp, slamming against the wall.

Marilyn looks between the two of them, her hand resting against her throat. "Well… I just made tea. Why don't I add a cup?" She bustles back into the cabin.

"I do love a nice cup of tea." Lawrence pushes past Abigail and moves to the middle of the lounge. "Isn't this quaint?"

"You've been here before. Remember?" Abbie slams her shoulder into Lawrence, right against his slinged arm and he doesn't flinch. She flops onto the sofa and glares at him.

"I didn't think you'd want Mother to know."

"I don't fucking care."

Marilyn reappears with an extra teacup. She puts it on the coffee table and picks up the plate of biscuits. "Matthew?"

"Thank you Marilyn. So kind." He takes a biscuit and smiles

at Abbie. "I can see where Abbie gets her impeccable manners from."

Marilyn sits, picks up her own tea and blows on it. "She's always been a very well-mannered young lady."

"Oh, I certainly believe it." He bites into the biscuit and chews, his eyes never leaving Abbie's face. "I *have* heard her say please quite frequently." He winks.

Rage flames Abbie's face. "Again... why are you here?"

"Abigail! That's no way to speak to company." Marilyn smiles at Lawrence and fiddles with her earring.

"Perhaps not so well mannered these days." Lawrence sips his tea.

Abbie rolls her eyes. "What brings you to Cornwall, Matthew?" Abbie crosses her legs and fixes him with wide, interested eyes.

"Well." He points to his sling. "I'm... recuperating from an accident of sorts." His eyes harden. "And thought the sea air would be just the thing to help."

"Best be careful. You wouldn't want to have another accident." Abbie slurps the last of her tea and slams the cup onto the saucer.

"Thank you my Sweet. Always looking out for me." He leans back in the chair and taps his hand on his knee. "And... we have things to discuss."

"You mean, you have threats to make."

"Yes. That too." He winks.

Marilyn looks between the two of them again, as though

watching a tennis match. "Am I missing something?"

Abbie swallows. "Matt has an… interesting sense of humour."

Lawrence chuckles. "I have missed you, Abbie."

"What do you want, Matt?"

"I want this whole circus to finish. I want my goddamn promotion."

Marilyn looks at Abbie. "Abigail?"

"She's been a very bad girl." He slaps his phone to his ear. "Matthew Lawrence. I found her… yes the location I gave you. She's here. Keep me updated." He drops his phone into his pocket. "We may as well settle in."

Marilyn shifts in her seat. "Why?"

"Didn't I say I needed to recuperate? It's so lovely here this time of year."

Abbie squints at Lawrence. "What are you up to?" She backs towards the wall and side table, as Lawrence turns back to the window.

"Let's shut these curtains. Don't want Looky Lou's"

"Of course." Abbie reaches the table and slips the receiver of the phone off the cradle and presses redial. She moves away and leans on the back of the sofa as Lawrence turns back around.

"Oh my God." Marilyn coughs and pats her chest. "I feel ill."

"Let my mother go."

"Oh. No, this is far more fun. And added insurance for me.

What a delightful bonus. Not to mention a gigantic feather in my cap when I'm the one to turn you in."

Abbie grits her teeth. "What a hero."

"I have set the wheels in motion for your arrest, Abbie."

"Is that right?"

"Yes. That's right. So sit on the sofa and be a good girl."

"Or?"

Lawrence smiles. "Or I'll have to take matters into my own hands."

Marilyn covers her mouth with her hand. Her eyes are dish plates. She shakes her head as tears spill down her cheeks.

Abbie sits on the sofa next to her mother and grabs her hand. "It's alright Mum."

28

ABBIE

The clock on the wall ticks and the sound echoes through Abbie's head, interspersed with the occasional slurping of Lawrence sipping his tea.

"Oh. Don't mind shortbread." Lawrence picks up a biscuit from the plate and takes an exaggerated nibble. "Delicious. Did you make these yourself Marilyn?"

Marilyn startles. "Oh. No. They're from the little bakery in town."

"Ah, well they're still delicious." Lawrence winks and pops the last of the biscuit into his mouth.

"Mum, why don't you go into town and have a walk?"

"Leave?" Lawrence sits upright. "Why, that won't do. It's best she stays here with us."

"So you can use her to threaten me? Intimidate her? Feel powerful?"

Lawrence taps a finger to his chin and rolls his eyes to the ceiling. "All of the above?"

"Why does he need to threaten you Abigail? What's going on?"

"Nothing Mum."

Lawrence leans forward and grins. "Why don't we fill mother in? We have time."

"Abigail?"

Abbie glares at Lawrence, her mouth pinched at the edges and heat rising up her neck. "I don't think Mum needs to know the ins and outs of our... history."

Lawrence stands and wanders the lounge, picking up ornaments and looking at photographs on the wall. "But it's what some might call... an *interesting* history." He spins and looks at Abbie. "Wouldn't you agree?"

"No. You were married, and I knew. That's about as scandalous as it gets."

"Except for the part where I broke it off with you and you were so heartbroken and upset that you killed my wife."

Marilyn gasps. "What?"

"He's lying Mum."

"Lying? I came into the hotel room... you were covered in her blood, knife in hand... I think it's a rather open and shut case."

"Oh my Lord! Abigail?"

Abbie grinds her teeth and glares at Lawrence. "It sure does *appear* that way. Though… she was dead when I got there. And you know it."

Lawrence slaps a hand to his chest. "I do? How could I possibly?"

Abbie's eyes twitch as she watches Lawrence lower himself back into the armchair.

"Abigail? Explain yourself."

Lawrence grins. "Yes Abigail. Tell your mother how in love with me you… still are, and how my wife was an inconvenience to you… a piece of rubbish in your way. You hated her."

Abbie's nostrils flare and she leaps from the sofa. "She hated me more. Because she knew you'd rather be with me."

Lawrence's eyes widen and his grin intensifies. "Interesting."

Abbie swallows and closes her eyes.

"Did I hit a nerve my Sweet?"

"Fuck you."

"Abigail Perkins!"

"Don't upset your mother."

Abbie balls her hands into fists. "Mum. Please stay out of this. Just… please."

"But… did you…"

Abbie whirls around and glares at Marilyn. "Did I what? Mum?"

"Kill his wife?" Marilyn's voice is hushed and her hand plays at her throat.

"Why are you asking me that?"

Lawrence strides across the room and sits next to Marilyn. "Dear woman. Abbie and I were very much in a relationship of… shall we say convenience? Obviously, dear sweet Abbie thought it was more than it was."

"Don't you fucking dare."

"Abigail! Language."

"You told me you wanted me. You told me it was over between you and her. You told me you'd leave her for me."

"Men say a lot of things when women are… servicing them."

"Service…" As though kicked in the back, Abbie lurches forward and jumps onto Lawrence's lap. She slaps him across the face and punches him to the jaw. They topple off the sofa and wrestle on the floor. "I'm not a goddamn prostitute."

The distant cries and shouting from her mother float in and out of Abbie's ears as she fights against Lawrence's free hand around her throat and his legs wrapping her waist. He tips her sideways off him, manages to climb on top and pin her down with his knees on both arms.

"My. Sweet. That was silly and impulsive." He tuts and grabs hold of her jaw, pushing his face into hers. "Stop this nonsense."

"Get off me."

"Do you promise to behave? You're upsetting your mother."

"She's used to it."

A strangled squeal erupts from Marilyn's throat as she pushes Lawrence in the back. It's not enough to push him off

Abbie but it shocks him enough that Abbie is able to thrust her hips and knock him sideways.

Lawrence scrambles to his feet, retreats to the other side of the lounge and stands behind the second sofa. He adjusts his sling and smooths his hair.

"Well? Abigail?" Marilyn fusses with her twin set and runs her manicured fingernails through her hair.

"Nothing Mum. Nothing for you to worry about. Why don't you go for a walk? And then maybe by the time you get back I'll be on my way to jail, and you won't have to deal with me."

"Why would you say that?"

Abbie turns to her mother. "You had to ask."

"Ask what?"

"You had to ask if I killed his wife."

"Well, I…"

"Do you actually think I'm capable of killing a human being out of jealousy or spite?"

"Well Matthew said—"

"I don't give a *fuck* what he said." Abbie ignores the dramatic huff her mother lets out because she swore again. "I'm your daughter. And you shouldn't have to question if I killed another human being because a man you just met said so."

"You can be quite rough around the edges Darling…"

Lawrence snorts and leans on the back of the sofa.

"Shut up Matt." Abbie doesn't take her eyes off her mother. "Look at me Mum."

"I *am* looking at you."

"No. Look at me. And *see* me. For once in your life... see me."

"I do see you Darling."

"You see the parts of me that you're comfortable with. Not the fact I look like Dad... not the fact I wore a Navy uniform for fifteen years... only the parts that sit down and drink tea with you. The parts that don't offend you."

Marilyn looks at the floor and fiddles with her necklace.

"Go for a walk Mum. I'll be gone before you get back. Don't worry, no one in town will know I'm a cold blooded murderer."

"She's not going anywhere."

Abbie turns and folds her arms across her chest. "What? You're going to keep her here against her will? You have no reason to keep her here." She spreads her arms out either side of her. "You got what you came for. She has nothing to do with it."

Lawrence flicks his eyes to Marilyn.

"Holding someone against their will wouldn't look good on a future Admiral I wouldn't think."

"Go on then." Lawrence jerks his head towards the door. "Enjoy your stroll."

Marilyn scurries to the kitchen and comes back with her handbag. "Darling, what is going to happen to you?"

"Not sure Mum. But either way I promise it won't reflect badly on you. God forbid."

Marilyn goes to Abbie and hugs her. "Despite what you think, I do love you Sweetheart."

Abbie ignores the tears pricking at the corners of her eyes. "I know."

Marilyn lets her go and backs towards the door. "It was umm… interesting to meet you."

"You are a delight Marilyn. Hopefully we meet again one day under more amicable circumstances."

Abbie snorts. "Wanker."

"Oh." Marilyn peers at the phone on the side table. "How did that come off the cradle?" She replaces the handset as Abbie's stomach plummets. *Shit.*

Marilyn blows a kiss to Abbie and disappears into the sunlight.

Abbie stares at the closed door. "Well, now what?"

"Who did you call?"

"No-one."

Lawrence walks to the phone and lifts the handset. "No-one?"

Abbie shrugs.

"So if I hit redial…"

Abbie swallows. "Go for it. I'd say Mum called the bakery to check her shortbread was ready before she went to pick it up and didn't hang up properly. So if you wanna chat about pastry and bread, go for your life."

Lawrence narrows his eyes at her and twists the cord around his index finger.

Abbie nods at the phone. "Go on then."

"So you're saying you didn't call... oh I don't know... Tom?"

"Why would I call Tom?"

"Because the pair of you are thick as thieves and if anyone can get you out of this mess... he can."

"You're convinced I killed your wife. How could he get me out of that?"

"Because he's a liar and a con artist. He's your only hope."

"Or... I didn't kill her, and he would help me prove you did it."

"Oh Sweet." Lawrence replaces the handset and sits on the sofa. "When will you let that fantasy go? I could never kill my wife. I loved her so."

"You are such a lying piece of scum."

"I didn't kill my wife."

"I was talking about the fact you said you loved her."

Lawrence slams his mouth shut and glares at Abbie. He checks his watch. "Not long to go." He stands and peers out the curtains. "I hope."

"Whatever."

"I guess bribing a foreign entity wasn't enough for you. You had to add murder to your list of skills."

"Preparing for when you perjure yourself in court are you?"

Lawrence turns from the window. "Perjure myself?"

"I never bribed your Iranian friend, and you know it. I was stupid and naive and did what you asked me to do. I should have realised what it looked like. I'm a fool. That's about all I have committed. The crime of stupidity."

"Handing him envelopes with cheques from your *very own* offshore bank account? Wining and dining him in fancy restaurants?"

"Because you asked me to!" Abbie jumps up again and grabs a vase from the coffee table. "I trusted you. More fool me."

"Are you going to throw that at me?"

"You said it was an invitation. And I believed you." Abbie gives a bitter huff. She puts the vase down. "Maybe I deserve all this. I was so fucking blind."

"Or maybe you and Josh worked together to try and frame me?"

Abbie drags her eyes to Lawrence's face. "You've done an excellent job in making it look the case. Bravo to you."

Lawrence grins and walks to Abbie, stopping in front of her. "My Sweet. You're talking nonsense. I'm so sorry your mental health has deteriorated to this point. I guess murder changes a person."

"You'd know."

Lawrence stops grinning and his jaw tightens.

"But one thing you are right about… Tom will get me out of this. He will expose you. And I will happily sit in a jail cell and wait for it to happen."

"You think he's better than me?"

Abbie pushes her mouth to within a breath of Lawrence's. "He *is* better than you… at everything."

Lawrence's nostrils flare as a loud knock sounds through the room. He steps back and stalks to the door, flinging it open.

Two men in suits stand on the porch.

"Commodore. I'm Benson, this is Fitzsimon."

Lawrence steps back and flings his arm towards Abbie. "Make sure you cuff her. She's feisty."

Abbie rolls her eyes and stays where she is.

Benson approaches her. "Are we going to have a problem?"

"No."

He pulls out a pair of cuffs and Abbie makes no effort to resist him clicking them around her wrists. "Abigail Perkins, you are under arrest on suspicion of murder and treason. You do not have to say anything, but anything you do say may be taken down and used in evidence against you. It may harm your defence if you do not mention something you later rely on in court. Do you understand?"

"Yes."

"Right. Let's go."

Abbie walks to the front door, keeping her eyes ahead and ignoring Lawrence. She slides into the waiting car and says nothing.

Both men get into the car, and Benson slides in next to Abbie. The car is silent as Fitzsimons turns on the ignition and gives Lawrence a nod.

Abbie closes her eyes and drops her head against the head-rest. "Do I get a phone call?"

The car moves away, and Benson pulls his keys out of his pocket. "No need." He jerks Abbie's wrists towards him and unlocks the cuffs. "There's a chopper waiting to take you back to London. Tom expects you to go directly to his flat. Do you understand?"

29

TOM

Tom sucks air through his clenched teeth as he lifts his chin over the bar for the final rep before dropping to the floor. Sweat dribbles down his temples and he grabs a towel, plonking himself onto a weights bench and covering his face.

"She's in the chopper." James' voice cuts through the towel and Tom drops it at his feet.

"Good."

"And Martha has already had a phone call from Lawrence."

Tom grins as he stands. "What a treat."

James huffs out a chuckle and jitters from one foot to the other.

Tom watches him for a moment and raises a brow. "What else?" He gulps from his water bottle.

"I found something."

"Treasure?"

"No." James holds out a piece of paper.

Tom leans forward and squints at the writing. "Matthias."

"Yeah."

"Where did you find it?"

"The berths."

Tom rolls his eyes and glares at James.

"Specifically... Pike's."

Tom's mouth clamps into a thin line. "Find him."

"I told him to go to your office, but—"

Tom pushes past James and out of the gym.

"Tom, wait."

Tom continues to barrel through the ship towards his quarters. "Later, James."

"No but."

Tom stops and turns. "Later."

"Right. But..."

Tom walks faster and waves a hand over his shoulder as he reaches the door of his quarters. The office is empty. He checks the bunk and bathroom before storming back into the corridor where James is leaning against the wall with his arms crossed.

"He's not fucking in here, James."

"I know."

"What?"

"That's what I was trying to tell you when you barged away and wouldn't listen."

Tom curls his lip. "Where is he?"

"No idea. But he was in civvies and didn't seem to give a hoot when I said you wanted to see him."

Tom's left eye twitches. "Is he off the ship?"

"I would assume so."

"Can you track his phone?"

"You know I can."

"Why are you being a smartarse?"

"Because if you bothered to stop and listen to me, you would have had this information and I wouldn't always be copping your attitude when things don't go the way you want them to." James pushes himself off the wall and stands in front of Tom, looking him in the eye.

"Why does this feel like a marital spat?"

"Because you never listen, Tom."

Tom pinches the bridge of his nose. "Did he say anything about where he was going?"

"No. But he was sweating and seemed stressed."

Tom nods. "Can you track his phone please?"

James pushes past Tom into the office and sits at the computer. "Give me a couple of minutes."

"Sorry."

"Pardon?"

"Nothing. Do your geek stuff."

James grins as his eyes stay fixed on the screen in front of him and his fingers hammer the keys.

Tom wanders the office. "He's going to Chinatown."

"He's in Chinatown," James says at the same time.

"Yeah." Tom goes to his bunk and pulls a lockbox from the safe. He grabs his pistol and shoves it into his waistband and puts a jacket on. "Call Justin. Have him meet me up on the street."

"Why do you need a gun? Are your spidey senses going haywire?"

"Something like that."

———

"You want me to wait?"

Tom has one leg out of the car and turns around to Justin. "Hang about. I plan to drag his arse straight to the car when I find him."

"Copy."

Tom slams the door shut and adjusts his pistol. Most restaurants haven't opened yet, but there are people setting up tables and menus on stands outside their respective businesses. He finds himself in front of Duck Soup, which is closed, with no movement inside. *Weird.* Tom walks around the back to the alleyway but overflowing bins and empty crates are all that greets him.

A crash above his head makes Tom push himself against the wall. The gent's toilet window he peered out of a few days earlier is open and another crash sounds into the alley.

"You come with half?" The voice screams in accented English and Tom recognises it.

"I'll get the rest."

Fucking Pike. Tom runs back to the street and shoulder barges the front doors of the restaurant. He crashes inside to an empty room full of half set tables and empty food trolleys. He scrambles through the maze of furniture to the gent's door and presses his ear against it.

"Count it. It's more than half. I promise you." Pike pants before a blood curdling scream fills the air.

"This not our deal."

"Please, George." Pike's voice is strained.

Tom opens the gent's door, slides into the room, and stops in the small vestibule and peeks around the wall. Pike is on the floor against a cubicle, clutching at his crotch. Two men have their back to Tom, one leans into Pike's face and lifts his chin with the blade of a knife.

Tom takes cover behind the wall, poking only his head and shoulder out. He grabs his pistol and raises it. "Drop it."

One of the men spins around and holds a gun out in front of him. He shoots and the round hits the wall, blasting plaster and tiles through the room.

Tom ducks out of sight and holds his breath. *That was a bit close.*

"Come out, come out sneaky snake…"

Tom rolls his eyes and peeks out. His predator shuffles along the tiles towards him. *Amateur.* He squeezes the grip of his pistol, steps out, points and shoots. He catches the man with the gun in the shoulder and his arm flings out, sending his weapon sliding across the floor to George as he crashes onto the tiles.

"Chao!" George shouts. "You fool." He picks up the gun and holds it against Pike's temple. "I will kill friend."

Tom charges at Chao, who is struggling to get off the floor and stamps his foot onto his chest. He points his gun between Chao's eyes and looks over at Pike's captor. "Your move."

"And if I pull trigger?"

"Chao's brains paint the floor."

"Collateral damages?" George chuckles.

"George, please." Pike whimpers. "I'll get you the rest."

"Rest of what?" Tom cups a hand to his ear. "What the fuck are you up to your eyeballs in, Pike?"

George smiles at Pike and pushes the gun harder against his head. "You haven't told friend your… problem?"

"No." Tom lifts his foot and kicks Chao in the face, knocking him out cold. "He has not told me. And we aren't friends." Tom cracks his neck and rotates his shoulder. "So? What the fuck's going on?" Tom points his gun at George keeping his foot in the middle of Chao's chest.

George smirks. "He can't pay debt."

"What debt?"

"He owes me another fourteen thousand."

"What for?" Tom glances at Pike, trembling on the floor with blood dripping from his nose. "Pike?"

"Poker."

Tom leans forward. "Poker?"

"Yes. High stakes Poker."

Tom frowns before shaking his head. "What the actual fuck, Pike?"

"George loaned me the cash to keep playing. I've paid back two thirds."

"Not enough," George says.

"And you *still* owe fourteen?" Movement under Tom's foot makes him kick Chao hard under the chin, without taking his eyes off George and Pike.

"So, now he pays interest." George smiles and his discoloured teeth make Tom grimace.

"Remind me never to eat here."

"You do not leave alive, so…" George shrugs.

Tom grins. "Aren't you adorable."

Pike grabs hold of George's ankle and yanks him off balance. George pulls the trigger and shoots Pike in the lower leg. Pike bellows in pain and thrashes on the floor, blood paints the tiles beneath him.

Tom strides towards George and shoots him three times in the chest. He slams against the wall and slides to the floor, leaving a bright red trail in his wake.

Pike screams and clutches at his leg. Tom shrugs off his jacket, takes his t-shirt off and rips it apart. He ties a rag around Pike's leg, above the wound.

"It's too tight. That fucking hurts." Pike screams and flails on the floor.

"For fuck's sake. Man up, you're in the Navy not playschool." Tom yanks the makeshift tourniquet again and Pike howls. "I need to stem the bleeding."

Pike sobs and bites on his fist. He looks at Tom. "Unbelievable...."

"What's that?"

Pike pants and bites harder on his fist. "Forget it," he mumbles through his fist.

"It's okay. People take a while to warm to me." Tom pulls the tourniquet one more time for good measure.

Pike groans, rolls onto his side and glances up. His eyes widen and he points behind Tom. "Tom... Chao... Tom."

Tom turns and shoots, landing his shot right in the middle of Chao's forehead. Chao crumples to the floor. And Tom admires his marksmanship. "Damn."

"Lucky shot," Pike mumbles into the floor before groaning in pain again.

"Absolutely. But let's pretend I meant it." Tom drops onto his backside and rests his wrists on his bent knees. "Tell me... why are we in the gent's?"

"Priv...acy." Pike huffs and clutches at his leg.

Tom pulls his phone out and calls James.

"Hey, you find him?"

"Yep. We need to go to the hospital."

"Are you alright?" The tone in James' voice is urgent and Tom can't help but feel comforted by it.

"I'm fine. Pike's been shot."

"Bad?"

Tom glances down at Pike, trembling and sniffling. "He'll live." Pike glances at Tom. "For now."

30

ABBIE

Abbie slides the key into the lock on Tom's front door and clicks it open. She's about to step inside when a crackly voice floats across the hallway.

"And who might you be?"

Abbie turns to find an old lady with a pinkish hue to her fluffy hair in the doorway of her flat, holding a cat. In any other circumstance Abbie would giggle and think of villains and cats, but not today. "I'm a friend of Tom's."

"Are you just?" The old woman strokes the cat's head.

"Yes. If you'll excuse me…" Abbie backs into the flat and shuts the door. She rests her forehead against it and blows a long slow breath out. *What I need is for everyone to leave me the fuck alo—*

"I was beginning to wonder where you were. The chopper landed forty five minutes ago."

Abbie jumps and spins around. A tiny woman stands, silhouetted in front of the window with a handbag hanging in the crook of her arm. "Oh my God." Abbie slaps a hand to her chest in an effort to slow her heartbeat.

The woman moves from in front of the window and Abbie realises it's Martha. "Tea my dear?"

"Tea?"

"Yes, I fancy a cup myself." She moves to the kitchen and flicks the kettle on. "Sit down. I expect you're exhausted." Martha places her handbag on the worktop and fetches cups.

"Why would you assume that?"

"You travelled by train all the way to Cornwall this morning, had to deal with Lawrence being... well, Lawrence... and flew back to London. A cat nap wouldn't be out of the question, would it? Sugar?"

Fuck, fuck, fuck. "Oh, ah no thank you. I need the bathroom. Excuse me."

Abbie practically runs to the bathroom and slams the door. She winces before realising she really doesn't care what Martha thinks of her. She sits on the edge of the bath and takes a few deep breaths before going to the sink and splashing her face with cold water. It's invigorating and clears her mind.

"I can't stay here," she whispers while she glares at herself in the mirror.

Abbie steps out of the bathroom, flinching when the door handle gives a mild squeak as she slowly releases it. The kettle clicks off and Martha pours water into two cups. Abbie sidles along the wall towards the front door.

"Running again, Ms Perkins?"

Abbie's stomach plunges and she runs to the door. Grabbing the handle, she pulls it down to find it locked again.

"I always prepare for any eventuality, my dear." Martha returns to the lounge with two cups of tea. She places the cups on the coffee table and points to the sofa. "Sit."

Abbie pushes her back against the front door and stares at Martha.

"Did I not speak clearly?"

"You did."

"And yet you still haven't taken a seat."

"I… I want some answers."

Martha smiles and sits in the armchair. She picks up her cup and sips. She dunks a biscuit and takes a bite before setting her cup back on the table with the biscuit in the saucer. She looks at Abbie again and crosses her ankles. "Why don't you sit down my dear?"

Abbie perches herself on the edge of the sofa, ignoring the tea. "Who were those men that arrested me?"

"Actors."

"Actors?"

"Students at the Cornwall College, actually."

"I don't understand."

"It was the grandson of an old… acquaintance of mine and his classmate. They did me a favour, which now I have to return." Martha rolls her eyes and picks up her tea again.

"Return?"

"I have to endure a night of fine dining and Opera with my… acquaintance."

"Oh."

"As long as he keeps his hands to himself there shouldn't be a problem."

"And if he doesn't?"

"I'll break all ten fingers." Martha locks eyes with Abbie.

I see. "I'm… I'm not afraid of you."

Martha glances at Abbie's fingers, clawed into her knees and nods once. "I can see that."

Abbie folds her hands into her lap. "I appreciate the help in Cornwall. But I think I deserve to know what's going on."

"Do you?" Martha takes another sip of tea and puts the cup down; it clunks against the saucer louder than it did last time. "You think you *deserve* something. Is that correct?"

"Well I—"

"After you come here out of the blue, turn Tom's entire life upside down. Cause him to get into a Naval uniform and go onto a ship that has the potential to destroy him…you keep running away when everyone is working towards *clearing your name...* and you… *deserve* something?"

Abbie bows her head; she knows Martha is right but the fire rising up her body from the embers that had been glowing in her belly take over.

"I don't know you from a bar of soap." Abbie clenches her fists. "How do I know you and Lawrence aren't mates? How do I know you aren't playing Tom? How do I know..." She gestures to her tea. "That isn't poisoned or something?"

"You don't. And there's something I want you to take heed of my dear. I don't get offended by much. Very little, in fact. But if you *ever* insinuate that I would play Tom or put him in danger for my own gain again, poison in your tea will be the least of your worries. Do you understand me?"

Abbie holds Martha's eye contact and says nothing.

"And now you are going to tell me every single dirty, disgusting detail of this mess you've found yourself in the middle of."

"I am?"

"You are." Martha checks her wristwatch. "I have no place to be. Speak."

"Where's Tom?"

"Hospital."

Abbie's throat squeezes. "Hospital?"

"A... colleague got himself wounded."

Relief washes over Abbie. "Oh, thank God. I thought you meant—"

"I didn't."

Abbie slams her mouth shut and swallows. "I didn't kill Daphne Lawrence."

"Go on."

"And I didn't collude with Amir."

"Wonderful. Case closed?"

"Umm…"

"You see my dear." Martha adjusts herself in the armchair to sit taller. "Tom believes you. Therefore, I believe you. But I currently have him on a ship, ready to have a nervous breakdown, a Commodore who thinks he is untouchable and about to become an Admiral, and a First Sea Lord who is currently stood down over very graphic and personal evidence that he was the last to see this dead woman alive. Not to mention a sailor was shot in the leg this morning in the gent's at a Chinese restaurant in Gerrard Street which believe it or not is also connected." Martha takes a sip of her tea. "Quite the sticky situation wouldn't you agree?"

"He's ready to have a nervous breakdown?" Abbie's voice comes out softer and squeakier than she wanted, and she puts both hands over her mouth, resting her elbows on her knees.

"More or less." Martha leans on the armrest. "And he's there to help *you*."

"God." Abbie drops her head and runs her hands through her hair.

"And he won't leave until he clears you from all of this."

Abbie claws her fingernails into her scalp.

"But you know this. That's why you came to him. You knew he would go above and beyond for you."

Abbie looks up. Martha's face is hard, and her eyes bore into Abbie's. "But I didn't think…"

"Selfish people rarely do."

"You don't like me."

"I don't know you. But as I said, if Tom believes you, I trust him therefore... I believe you."

"There's nothing to tell. Daphne is dead and I was covered in her blood." Abbie shrugs and slumps back into the sofa.

Martha purses her lips in a very tight little circle and squints at Abbie. "You aren't helping yourself."

A phone rings and Martha goes to her handbag to pick it up. Abbie's shoulders relax a little now Martha's eyes aren't examining every inch of her.

"Tom."

Abbie's heart wakes up and she stands. Martha gestures for Abbie to sit back down. She lowers herself onto the sofa, her eyes never leaving Martha's face.

"Yes, she's here. We're having tea and a chat... Yes. A chat... I'm being the perfect hostess." Martha glances at Abbie. "No she hasn't... rather difficult actually." Martha returns to Tom's armchair and holds the phone out to Abbie.

She takes it and bites her lip. "Hello?"

"Are you alright?"

His voice washes over her like a whiff of calming lavender and she sits back. "Yes. Are you?"

"I'm wonderful. Hospital coffee and limp lettuce sandwiches have come a long way."

"They have?"

"No. Listen to me Abs... Martha will *not* mess around. And she doesn't want to hear bullshit. Shoot straight with her and tell her fucking everything. Even things you may not have told me yet, things that make you uncomfortable. All of it. She just saved your arse."

"I know but—"

"And frankly I don't want to hear her moaning about going on a date with crusty Harold. So make it worthwhile."

"What do I need to tell her?" She flicks her eyes to Martha who is sipping tea and apparently ignoring her.

"Everything. Every single detail of that night. Every single detail about Lawrence's house. *Everything*. I'll be there as soon as I can."

"Okay."

"Abs?"

"Yeah?"

"It'll be alright. But you have to stop running from it. And listen to me… I trust Martha with my life. If I was flying into a shitstorm, I'd want her piloting the plane. Do you understand what I'm saying to you?"

"Yes." Abbie's nose tingles. "I'm sorry," she whispers.

"I know."

The phone goes dead, and Abbie puts it on the coffee table. She wipes her nose on the back of her hand. "He's complaining about the hospital food."

"Of course he is. He's always complaining about something."

Abbie nods and gives Martha a small smile. "I'll tell you anything you want to know."

"How long were you having an affair with him?"

"Too long."

"Did he ever give you any indication that he was capable of hurting his wife?"

Lawrence wrapped a hand around Abbie's throat and pushed her against the wall in the women's locker room.

"What did I tell you about staying quiet?"

"I didn't tell anyone."

"I'm about to be promoted to Commodore. If you fuck this up I'll throw you overboard. Do you hear me?"

"I hear you." Abbie held her breath and met Lawrence's eyes. "I didn't tell anyone. You're being paranoid."

He stared at her for what felt like days, gradually loosening his grip around her throat, but keeping his hand there. Abbie's heart didn't stop slamming itself against her ribs.

"Good girl," he whispered against her lips, kissing her, and making her forget he still held her throat.

"He panics when he thinks his authority is threatened or he is going to be duped out of something he sees as rightfully his."

"Like a big promotion for example?"

"Yes."

"What would offing Daphne have to do with that? Surely the woman would have supported his promotion. Unless of course she found something she shouldn't have."

"She was a trophy to him. Someone who wore expensive dresses and sipped champagne at all the events." Prickles crawl up Abbie's spine. "A wet dishcloth has more personality than she did."

Martha lifts her chin and her eyebrows dip slightly.

Abbie springs off the sofa and paces in front of the coffee table. "He never shared anything with her. Would keep important information locked away from her. Hell... she didn't even have the pin numbers to their accounts. He controlled every..." Abbie's hand flies to her mouth. "Holy shit."

"What is it?"

"She knew."

"She knew what?"

"About Amir." Abbie stops pacing. "How did I not see this before? He set this up from the beginning. He used me to pass money to Amir and set me up so that it looked like I had a motive to kill her."

"How does that give you a motive to kill her?"

"Because he made it look as though I was the one bribing him. The only way she knew about anything is because *he* told her."

"That's quite the long game on his behalf."

"You don't know him like I do. He finishes his Christmas shopping in March and sets reminders for every birthday and anniversary in his diary on the first of January every year. He's meticulous. He colour codes his socks for crying out loud." Abbie tugs at her hair and walks to the window. She peers through the crack in the closed curtains to the street below. "He used Josh as a backup so the Iranian stuff could never be pinned on him." She turns to Martha. "How do we prove this? We need to get Josh out. He's innocent too. Lawrence has played everyone."

"And what will he do if he realises you figured this out?"

"Kill me. He killed his own wife. I am a threat. He will do the same to me." This thought strangely, doesn't upset Abbie. Determination blossoms in her belly and a sense of justice hits her right between the eyes. "So what do we do? What do you need from me?"

"An assurance you won't disappear again would be a good start."

"I won't."

"Wonderful." Martha fetches her handbag and slides it over her arm. "I'll be in touch."

That's it? "But... what next?"

"Don't open the door to anyone. The only people who need to be here have a key."

"Okay."

"Go and have a snooze. You look like you need it."

"I can't *snooze*. I want to find Lawrence and end this."

"And we will. In good time." Martha opens the front door and turns to Abbie. "From now on you do exactly what you are told. Do you understand me?"

31

TOM

Tom moves his eyes to the clock on the wall, not sure it has moved since he checked last time. Two minutes ago. *Three seventeen.* He plonks his head against the wall and closes his eyes.

"Sir?"

Tom jumps. "Yes. Sorry… long day."

The man in scrubs pulls his mask down and smiles. "That chair is slept in more than any other chair in this place." He holds his hand out. "Dr Andrew Simmons."

"Tom."

"Well, your mate is lucky you were there. We managed to stop the bleeding and remove the bullet from his shattered bone. Although without that tourniquet…"

"Yeah right. Is he awake?"

"He's being wheeled to his room from recovery now. But I wouldn't expect too much sense out of him until morning."

Tom purses his lips. "I see."

"Talk to him, by all means but don't expect much is all. I'm sure he will appreciate a friendly face."

Tom swallows a snort at the suggestion of being a friendly face to Pike and nods instead. "Thanks so much."

"He'll be in room four-oh-six." Dr Simmons juts his hand left then right to show Tom the way.

Tom shakes hands again with the doctor before walking the hospital corridors. He wrinkles his nose at the sterile, antiseptic smells and gives the nurses a smile as he walks past their station. A particularly round faced nurse giggles and tucks her hair behind her ear while another drops a file she is carrying to a metal drawer.

He arrives at a door with a white plate reading *406*. The door is open a few inches and Tom pushes it open all the way. Pike's eyes are closed. His leg is resting above his hipline on a platform with straps.

Tom drags a chair across and sits next to the bed. "Well… shit."

Pike drops his head to the side and his eyelids slowly peel apart. "You're not my mum." His voice is scratchy and weak.

"Not last time I checked." Tom picks up the lidded cup of water with a straw and offers it to Pike.

He takes a mouthful and licks his lips. "Thanks."

"Don't mention it."

"I assume you aren't here to bring me chocolates?"

"Sharp."

Pike winces as he tries to adjust his position and flops back on the pillow. "I feel like I'm off my face."

"Anaesthetic and morphine will do that to you."

"So… what do you want?"

"You have a gambling problem?"

Pike closes his eyes and Tom grabs his earlobe and pinches.

"Ow! What the fuck?"

"I'm asking you questions. I'd appreciate it if you stayed awake to answer them. How long has this been going on?"

"Years. It started small but…" Pike yawns. "Anyway, it got me shot so maybe I'll stop."

"Just like that?"

Pike nods.

"Have you ever tried to *just stop* an addiction before?"

"No. But it's not like... I'm on heroin or some... thing." Pike does a heavy blink, his eyes glassy.

Tom snorts. "Okay."

Pike blinks again, his eyes staying closed a tad longer than before.

Strike while the iron's hot… "So, Matthias."

Pike lifts his chin. "Huh?"

"Matthias."

"What's a ma... thigh... us?" Pike's eyes droop and a sliver of dribble runs from the side of his mouth.

Tom's phone pings in his pocket and he checks the screen.

I'm in the cafeteria. You need to come down here. Now.

Tom huffs and types a reply.

Two minutes

32

TOM

"Luckily for you I'm hungry. Have a snooze. I'll be back."

Pike doesn't answer apart from a snore and snuffle.

"Fuck's sake." Tom stalks to the lift and punches the button.

"Having a bad day?" A woman holding a toddler stands next to him at the lift.

Tom gives a tight smile. "I've had better."

"Haven't we all?" The woman smiles as her daughter grabs her ponytail and yanks on it. The woman winces. "Kids. Such treasures."

Tom laughs. "Better you than me."

The lift opens and they walk inside. The woman puts her daughter down and she proceeds to go to all the buttons and pushes the ones she can reach. "Oh shit. No Maddie." She grabs the girl's hand and pulls her away from the buttons. The girl squeals and tries to wriggle out of her mother's grasp.

"Sorry," the woman grunts. "Looks like we're taking the scenic route." She picks up her daughter again and the little girl peers at Tom over her mother's shoulder.

Tom slumps against the back of the lift.

The doors close and the lift jerks and rattles downwards. It stops one floor below and Tom contemplates getting out. The doors slide shut without anyone else getting in. *Too late.*

The girl giggles and points a chubby finger at Tom. "Daddy."

"Daddy's at work sweetheart."

Tom laughs and makes a face at the girl who giggles again. The girl's curls remind him of Sylvie and for the first time in days, warmth fills his chest.

The woman turns to Tom. "I'm sorry. She calls every man she sees daddy. Let's hope she grows out of it." The woman rolls her eyes as the lift stops again and no one gets in.

Tom huffs out a chuckle and nods.

"So, you're visiting a friend?" The woman seems intent on chit chat, and Tom looks up to see how much longer this lift needs to travel. *Two floors. Thank Christ.*

"No. I actually despise him."

"Oh… I see."

Tom grins as the lift stops on the first floor. "I don't think you do."

"Right well… you have a good day."

"You too." Tom gives the little girl a wave and she bites her mother's shoulder in response.

The doors shut and Tom blows a breath out. "Wow."

A moment later, the lift rattles to a stop and the doors wobble open.

"Death box," Tom mumbles as he follows the signs to the cafeteria. He reaches the entrance and sweeps his eyes around the room before they rest on James'. *At least he sat in the back corner.*

Tom thwacks James on the back of the head. "Up."

James frowns and rubs his head. "What?"

"I'm not sitting with my back to the room." Tom swirls his finger in the air. "Swap seats."

James sighs and slides into the chair across from him. "How's Pike?"

"Shattered tibia. But he'll live. Sick leave though so let's sort this shit out while I still have unfettered access to him."

"Yeah so... I've been digging."

"And..."

"I managed to recover the original surveillance." James slides his phone across the table and presses play.

Tom leans over the phone as the scene plays out.

Daphne and Peter Moore go into the hotel room. Daphne is pulling Moore by the tie. He is running his hands down her dress. Tom grimaces. "I could have gone my whole life without seeing that."

"Think yourself lucky he isn't your uncle who looks exactly

like your dad." James spins the phone back to him. "Anyway, they go at it for almost an hour. And no one else walks down the hall in that time."

"An hour? I hadn't given him that much credit. Maybe they watched a video for fifty eight minutes."

James snorts and taps the video forward. "The video we saw first of all was cut from here until Abbie turns up. But now…" He pushes the phone back to Tom.

As the time stamp reaches 12:50 Moore walks out of the room, his shirt is open and his trousers appear to be hastily pulled on, his belt flops unbuckled, and his fly isn't done up all the way. He stumbles down the hall towards the lifts. Seconds later Lawrence appears from the other end of the hall and goes into the room, shutting the door behind him.

"You bastard," Tom mumbles.

"Wait for it…" James skips the video forward a little more.

Ten minutes after he went in, Lawrence leaves the room. Tom picks up the phone and peers closer. "He hasn't got a drop of blood on him."

"Nope. Keep watching."

Moore comes back into view five minutes later with a bottle of whiskey and opens the door. He drops the bottle and disappears into the room. Within moments he runs from the room with his jacket and tie balled up in his hands. He leans against the wall for a moment and covers his face with his hands before wiping his nose and leaving.

"Reputation first." Tom shakes his head. "He could have called an ambulance at the very least."

"That's when he stabbed her."

James shrugs. "Check out this next bit."

"Right. So this is where the video picked up again after it had been cut." James taps the screen to move it along.

Abbie arrives at the room and pushes open the not quite closed door. She steps back and slaps her hand over her mouth before running into the room. She leaves the door open.

Seconds later, Lawrence is back and stands at the door, digging his fingers into his hair and appears to shout before running into the room.

Abbie runs from the room almost immediately; her hands and the front of her hoodie are smeared in blood.

Tom leans back in his chair and interlaces his fingers behind his head. "Well. Fuck."

"Ambiguous. Though it does prove Lawrence was there."

"It does. But it also shows Abbie with blood all over her and Lawrence without a drop, at least until *after* he goes to her again, once Abbie arrives."

"Right."

Tom scrubs his hands through his hair and leans on the table. "Matthias?"

"Still digging… but some things aren't adding up."

"Such as?"

"Well… during the Iranian debacle the electronic signatures on the photographs say Matthias."

"Yeah… not a newsflash."

"But Pike was in the middle of the Atlantic Sea at that time doing an exercise for three months."

Tom frowns.

"And again…Even on the night of the murder, he was in Scotland visiting a cousin or something. He had authorised leave until the day you and I arrived on the ship."

"He couldn't access a computer from Scotland?"

"Of course, but the I.P. address wasn't in Scotland. And I even checked to see if he had been issued a VPN or used his phone. But nope."

"Maybe he wasn't in Scotland."

"I checked. He was there. I hacked his texts. Found some very willing ladies while he was there too, might I add."

"Again… I could have gone my whole life…"

James laughs. "Sorry."

Tom taps the table with his index finger and runs his teeth along his bottom lip. "So where was the IP address coming from?"

"Brighton."

"Excuse me?"

"Brighton."

Tom leaps from his chair. "Fuck."

33

TOM

Tom marches into the mess and glares around the room. "Hampshire."

A sailor looks up from his tray. "He's in the berths, Sir."

"Why?"

"He has late watch again. He's sleeping."

Sleeping. Tom holds his breath and nods. "Right." He leans over an empty chair in front of him and ignores the tightness gripping his lungs.

"Sir? Are you alright?"

Tom looks up. "Yes." He turns and stalks out of the mess towards his quarters. He slams the door shut behind him and stands in the middle of the office. Images of Pike throwing his meal tray at Liam, wrestling Liam to the ground and Liam

promising to 'get the rest' play on repeat in Tom's mind. *Fuck.*
He goes to the bathroom and turns the shower on. While it heats
up he grabs his phone and dials Isabella's number before
deciding at the last minute to hang up. He drops the phone on
the bunk and peels his clothes off.

Under the running water he waits for his chest to relax and
the tension in his shoulders to melt away. *Nope.* He slams a
palm against the wall and dips his head into the water. "Fuck!"
Ten minutes later he emerges into the office space wearing utili-
ties to find James sitting at the desk typing away at the
computer. Tom sits in the chair opposite.

"Have you spoken to him yet?" James looks up from the
monitor.

"Not yet. How many other crews come from—"

"Two."

"And?"

"No dice."

"Shit." Tom rubs a towel over his wet hair before throwing it
on one of the leather chairs. "Let's get this over with." Tom
paces down the corridor, knowing James is trailing along behind
him. He keeps his eyes fixed ahead of him and people in his
way move before he steamrolls straight over the top of them.

His pulse pounds in his ears and sweat stings his spine as it
beads down his back. The closer he gets to the berths the harder
it is to breathe freely, and a weight descends on his chest,
pushing against his lungs. He stops and leans forward over his
knees.

As though experiencing signal interruptions, scenes keep flashing in Tom's mind. *Chris laughing while eating in the mess, Chris smoking a cigarette while leaning on a railing looking out to sea, Chris sitting in a bar on shore leave flicking his lighter on and off. Chris deteriorating the more the others bully him, Chris hating his life, Chris crying when he thinks no-one is watching.*

Chris. Dead in his bunk.

Tom squeezes his eyes shut and pushes his thumbs into his eye sockets.

"Tom?" James puts a hand on his shoulder. "Why don't we send for him?"

"No." He stands and cracks his neck, which usually prepares him for a task but this time it sends pain into the base of his skull. He continues down the corridor, massaging his temples. But as he gets closer to the berths, the pain gets worse.

He stops at the end of the corridor leading to where he doesn't want to go and pushes himself against the wall.

"You want me to get him?"

Tom shakes his head. "No."

He swallows the obstruction blocking his throat and takes a step forward. His knee buckles and he slaps a hand against the wall. James grabs his elbow, and he yanks it away.

"I'm fine." His own voice reverberates around the corridor walls as they close in on him.

"Okay." James holds both hands up and steps back.

Tom clears his throat and continues slower, as though the

floor may open up and swallow him whole. He slaps his hand back onto the wall and uses it to counterbalance as his vision tunnels and the inside of his head fills with cotton wool. *One foot in front of the other.*

A couple of people walk towards him. Their faces have no features and their voices are muffled to Tom's ears.

"Is he alright?" A distant voice asks James.

"I'm *fucking* fine."

The pair of sailors scurry away and James sighs. "This is a bad idea, Tom."

"Yep." He keeps going.

"Okay... it's the next one on the right." James' voice sounds a million miles away, but Tom hears him and nods. "You want me to—"

"No!" Tom sucks in a breath and turns to James. "No, James. Shut up. Please." Tom pushes the heels of his palms into his eyes. *Fuck.*

"Where are you going, Chris?"

"Tired."

"Bullshit. What happened?"

"Nothing." Chris put his hand on Tom's shoulder and squeezed before pulling him into a hug. *"See you soon."* He turned and loped along the corridor towards his bunk, leaving Tom standing alone.

"Chris?"

Chris stopped but didn't turn around.

"What are you doing?" Tom's gut writhed.

"Going to sleep." He continued walking away.

Tom blinks and looks at James. "I should have stopped him."

"Who?"

"I knew he was going to hurt himself."

"Tom... what are you on about?"

Tom shakes his head and squares his shoulders. He marches to Liam's berth and yanks back the curtain to his bunk.

His own voice from years before, echoes through his head.

"Wake up. This isn't funny."

The outline of a body under the blanket on Liam's bunk induces the same panic and acidic burn in his throat from years before. The edges of his vision morph and he shakes his head. A tremble hits his knees, and he lurches forward, grabbing at the shoulders of the body in the bed.

"Wake up." He shakes the body as the pillow falls off the bunk and the blanket falls away from his face. "Wake up!" A hand on Tom's shoulder irritates him and he shrugs it off. "Leave me alone." He shakes Liam again.

He knows it's Liam... he can see the confusion on Liam's face and his startled eyes, but it doesn't register.

It's Chris. Dead in his bunk. And no pointless shaking and yelling will bring him back. Tom grips the front of Liam's shirt tighter and drops his head against the mattress. He lets out a sound almost like a scream and moan mixed together.

Liam grabs Tom's hands and pries them off him. "Sir?

What's going on?" Liam shuffles up the bunk and hugs his knees to his chest.

"How could you do this?" Tom lifts his face and peers at Liam, seeing Chris's mottled grey skin and lifeless, half open eyes. He scrambles back against the wall and drops to his backside.

James appears in front of Tom's face. "Tom? Take a breath."

Tom balls his shirt into his fist over his heart. The pain is unbearable. "I don't know what's happening."

"I've sent for Mike. Just breathe."

Tom shakes his head. "I... I need to get out of here." He leans over his bent knees and claws at his hair. "I can't breathe."

"Tom?"

Tom looks up. Mike is in front of him.

"I can't breathe. Why can't I..." He gulps and drags in a breath.

"Panic. Slow down and breathe, Tom."

"What the fuck is happening to me?" He balls both hands into fists and pushes them against his temples. "Stop..." He takes another breath against the burn in his chest.

Somewhere around him he can hear voices, muffled at times but some words hit his ears.

"... to the warehouse... Tom?"

Tom looks up, through blurred, tired eyes at Liam, being held by the upper arm. Liam's head is bowed, and he doesn't resist.

Tom hauls himself off the floor and leans against the wall on shaky legs.

"Tom?" James asks. "I'll take him to the warehouse?"

"Wait." He takes a breath and looks at Liam. "Are you Matthias?"

Liam drags his eyes from the floor to meet Tom's face and nods.

Tom drops his head again. "Take him."

Tom doesn't watch as James leads Liam out of the berth. He stares at the unmade bunk. The empty, unmade bunk. He bends forward, resting his hands on his knees. Tears prick at the edges of his eyes. *Fuck.*

"C'mon Tom. Let's go have a cuppa." Mike slides an arm around Tom's shoulders.

———

"I want you to take some long deep breaths in and out."

Tom clenches his jaw. "I'm fine. Whatever it was is over now."

Mike sits across from Tom on the leather chair. "Whatever that was?"

"Yeah." Tom stands. "I've got places to be."

"Sit down Tom. Please."

Tom walks a full circle around his office before sitting down again.

"That was brave of you."

"What was?"

"Going down to the berths like that."

Tom rolls his eyes to the ceiling. "You and I have a very different definition of what *bravery* is."

"You think so?"

Tom shrugs and picks at a piece of thread on his shirt. His heartbeat isn't as noticeable anymore and the pain in his lungs is dull.

"I'm going to assume you won't be coming back on board after today?"

"I'm never getting on this or any other ship again."

"No?"

"No. And this time I mean it."

"How do you feel, Tom?"

Tom looks up and jerks a brow. "How do I feel?"

"Yes. What's your anxiety level out of ten?"

Tom snorts and storms into his bunk. He grabs a bag and shoves his clothes into it, leaving anything uniform related in the locker.

Mike leans against the doorframe.

Tom goes into the bathroom and grabs his razor and toothbrush before stalking out, past Mike and into the office. He picks up his phone and looks at the screen. Five missed calls light up from Isabella. *Shit.* He shoves it into his pocket and does one more sweep of the quarters.

"You don't think this will follow you?" Mike moves from the bunk door to the middle of the office.

"No. It stays here."

"Are you sure?"

"Positive." He goes to walk from the quarters and stops at the door. "I appreciate that you tried, Mike."

"You know how to reach me."

34

TOM

Tom puts a hand on the glass door of *The Whisky Exchange* and pauses. Martha's pinched, disappointed expression floats past his mind's eye, as does Isabella's. His mouth waters and sweat dots his top lip.

He pushes open the door and walks in.

Anxiety level, Balvenie.

A bell tinkles above his head. A man in an apron stacking shelves looks and smiles. Tom gives him a tight, reserved for strangers, smile and wanders to the shelf he has visited many times before. The rows and rows of bottles with smooth amber contents call to him and for the first time since losing his mind, his shoulders relax. He pulls his old favourite off the shelf and trudges to the register. He puts the bottle on the counter and places both hands, palm down on either side of it.

"Ah, nice choice," a voice behind him says, as the man in the apron moves to the register.

Tom continues to stare at the bottle. *The self-loathing starts about now usually*. He taps his card on the reader and picks up the bottle, now in a paper bag. *Classy*. "Thanks."

"Enjoy."

Tom snorts and walks out.

Fifteen minutes later he walks into the warehouse and for the first time in a long time, it feels like home.

"Tom! Hey. Wow… you look tired. Can I get you a coffee or something? Here let me take your bag." Penny waddles out from behind her desk.

Tom grips his bag and hugs it against himself. "No. It's fine. Thanks."

Penny raises a heavily coloured in eyebrow and her cheeks glow pink. "Sure. Um… are you okay?"

"Peachy." He walks onto the main floor.

He ignores James, sitting at his computer and walks straight into Martha's office. She is behind her desk on the phone. She points to the chair in front of her and Tom sits.

"Thank you. That's good news. Please keep me abreast of progress." She nods once and hangs up. "You look terrible."

"You need your roots done yourself."

Martha smooths a hand down her hair and huffs. "What's in your bag?"

Tom glances at the bag on the floor next to his chair. "My clothes."

"Why?"

"Because I'm not going back to the tub." He peers at Martha. "Ever again."

Her eyes soften. "Are you alright?"

"I'm wonderful."

"The medic called me."

Tom nods. "Where's Liam?"

"I have him in a holding room."

"Okay. Let me get this over with."

Martha studies Tom's face for a moment. "Be careful. You've lost your objectivity with him."

Tom frowns. "What exactly did the medic tell you?"

"Just that you visited the berths. Not enough to breach your privacy."

Tom snorts. "Like I have privacy around here." He stands.

"Before you go."

Tom grunts and sits again.

Martha nods at her phone. "That was the Secretary."

"And?"

"Lawrence has been taken off the promotions list."

"Because?"

"I told him we had Liam. Along with Abbie's statements and the surveillance. Also... were you aware Liam is Commander Andrew Hampshire's son?"

Tom's gut wrenches and he drops his head. "Well... shit."

"Liam won't speak. Maybe you can... encourage him?"

"If he doesn't think I'm completely insane."

"You really didn't have Liam in the frame?"

"No." Tom stands again. "I guess I let personal stuff get in the way. Like some sort of amateur." He grits his teeth.

"Like a human."

"Whatever." He grabs his bag and walks out.

He goes to James' desk and picks up a sticky note. He pulls the cap off a pen with his teeth and writes a name. "Bring me his service records."

"Um. Now?"

"No James, maybe in a month or two?" Tom throws the pen on the table and stalks towards the holding rooms.

———

TOM LOOKS THROUGH THE RECTANGULAR GLASS WINDOW IN THE holding room door. Liam sits at the desk with his head buried in his arms. Tom flicks his head at the agent sitting on the fold-up chair outside the room.

"You'll be alright?" he asks, standing.

"I think I can take him."

The agent chuckles and walks away.

Tom opens the door and Liam looks up, squinting against the bright artificial light. His eyes widen and he sits straighter as Tom sits across from him. "Sir."

"Rule number one. If you call me Sir, again, I'm going to box your ears."

Liam bites his lip. "Right."

"Rule number two. Don't lie to me."

"Okay."

Tom nods. "So. What the fuck?"

Liam presses his mouth into a thin line and stares at Tom.

Tom shrugs and leans back in the chair. "I have all day."

"You hate the Navy. Don't you?"

"I'm the one asking questions, Liam."

"Why?"

"Because I'm on the good guy side of the table."

"No… why do you hate the Navy?"

"Because I believed in it."

"That doesn't make sense."

"Welcome to adulthood."

"I love the Navy." Liam sniffles and pulls a tissue from the box on the table. "My father was a Commander. I wanted to be just like him."

"Your father is Andrew Hampshire."

Liam nods. "He was ashamed of me."

"Because?"

"I wasn't the son he wanted me to be I guess."

"You told me he took you to watch the Seagulls."

"Yeah… he did, but when I turned fifteen…" Liam stops and shakes his head. "Our relationship changed."

"But you still joined the Navy?"

Liam nods. "He retired four years ago."

"I know."

Liam slides his hands along the table, perspiration streaks along in their wake. "Why are you doing this?"

"It's my job."

"You want to know why I worked for Lawrence."

"It had crossed my mind."

"Let's just say he gave me no choice and leave it at that."

"Let's not." A knock at the door makes Tom roll himself backwards in the chair and open it. James holds a folder out. "Thanks."

"No worri—"

Tom pushes the door closed and wheels himself back to the desk. "Okay…" He opens the folder. "Let's see."

Liam's fingers dig into the tabletop as Tom flips through the photocopied pages.

Tom lets out a low whistle. "Impressive. He's got more commendations than he's had hot breakfasts."

"Yeah."

"That's quite the family reputation to live up to."

Liam folds his arms on the table and drops his face into them.

Tom studies the top of Liam's head for a moment. "Wouldn't you say?"

Liam emerges from his arms. "He told me not to join."

"Why?"

"Because… and I quote… *it would embarrass me*."

Tom flips the folder shut and rests his hands on top of it. "Embarrass him?"

"Don't pretend you didn't notice how much I didn't belong on that ship. I know you noticed."

"So why would you embarrass him?"

Liam gives a bitter laugh. "I'm sure he thinks I joined up just to get the uniform."

"Excuse me?"

Liam meets Tom's eyes. "I quite like a man in uniform."

Tom blinks. "A man in…" The cheeky voice of a certain Australia popstar from a year or so earlier sounds in his head, *I quite like a man in a suit.* "I see."

Liam shrugs. "Dad can't handle who I am. But my whole life I wanted to be just like him. A respectable Naval Officer. I wanted to impress him and make him proud of me. But… I don't belong in the Navy. I know that now."

"It never pays to try and live a life to please someone else."

"Maybe some of us don't see another way to live."

Tom swallows against his dry throat and slides his hand into his pocket, squeezing the silver lighter inside. He shakes his head and stands. He walks to the door and rests his forehead against the cool glass of the window. Demons claw at his throat and he takes a raspy breath in.

"S… Tom?"

Tom turns. "Yes?"

"You said you believed in the Navy and that's why you hate it now?"

"I believed in what it stood for."

"Until?"

"Until... I didn't anymore."

Liam clears his throat. "What happened today, in the berth?"

Tom pushes himself against the door and looks at Liam. "You deserve an explanation."

"No. I don't I just... I was concerned..."

"You do. Because it was more than what happened today." He sits again and cracks his neck. "You remind me of someone... of my best..." Tom scratches the back of his head. "My brother."

"Your brother?" Liam's eyes widen and he sits up straighter.

"My... foster brother. I don't have any siblings of my own."

"Okay."

"He followed me into the Navy when he was old enough. But... he shouldn't have."

"Why not?"

"He wasn't cut out for it. He was timid and smaller than me and just..." Tom shrugs. "He should have been an accountant."

Liam smiles.

"Anyway. He used to get bullied quite a lot. Picked on because of his size, his nature, his refusal to fight back. But he... he just wasn't like that. He was a prankster. Loved a laugh, loved being outside, loved..." Tom's nose tingles and he sniffs to make it stop. "He just wanted to be free."

"Did he leave the Navy?"

"He took an overdose of pills in his bunk. I... went to wake him." Tom closes his eyes, squeezing tight. "I knew he was going to hurt himself." He shakes his head and opens his eyes again. "I mean... I didn't *know* but I had a feeling something wasn't right."

"That's heavy."

"So when I saw you today... sleeping... I don't know what happened, but I couldn't stop seeing Chris. Dead. It was like it was happening all over again."

"And I already reminded you of him?"

Tom nods.

"I'm sorry."

"What for, Liam?"

Liam shrugs. "Everything I guess. All of it."

"You can't help reminding me of him."

"No. But it's because of me that you came aboard the ship. Isn't it?"

"Indirectly, I suppose."

"So... I'm sorry." Liam sits back in his chair and fiddles with his hands in his lap.

"Well... how about you tell me everything and we call it square?"

Liam stands and paces behind the desk. "Short story. Commodore Lawrence blackmailed me into helping him. He figured out I'm gay and threatened to out me to the whole ship. I was terrified. I already got picked on."

"How did he figure it out?"

Liam scratched the table with his index finger. "He's evil. Manipulative and just... *evil.*"

No shit. "What happened?"

Liam's adams apple bobbles as he swallows and he lifts his eyes to the ceiling, tears glisten at the edges. "When I was assigned to his ship… he knew I was Andrew's son. He took me aside and said he thought a great deal of my father." Liam gulps in a breath. "He said if I ever needed anything I could go to him. He would help me. And I…" Liam drops his head. "God this is humiliating. I started to like him. A lot."

"Okay…"

"Anyway, time went on and whenever anyone picked on me or I was hassled in front of him, he would step in and look out for me. I thought of him like a protector almost."

"But?"

"One day he calls me to his office. The office you were in."

Tom nods.

"We sat in those leather chairs, and he said it upset him to see how much being on the ship was destroying my confidence…" Liam pulls his collar away from his neck. "He said he had developed feelings for me."

"He what?"

"And he couldn't deny them anymore. He asked me to kiss him. Anyway… I went to oblige because… well I kind of had feelings for him too. Anyway, just before I touched his mouth he pushed me away and called me…" Liam shakes his head, and a tear rolls down his cheek. "Some pretty awful names."

"Then?"

"After that he said he had the whole thing on video and

pointed to his bookshelves. I saw a go pro sitting on the shelf. He said he needed my tech expertise, and I had no choice."

"Jesus *Christ.*"

"He said if I didn't do as he asked he'd have a movie night and show the entire crew the video."

"I knew he was a bastard but that takes the cake."

Liam takes a tissue and blows his nose. "Anyway… I was so frightened he would follow through with it I did whatever he told me to. I was being extorted for months."

"But... did he not pay you?"

"Yes. He insisted on paying me. I guess it was so it would implicate me if we got caught… unexplained money in my possession and all that. And no trail back to him because it was all cash." He sits again and taps his fingers on the table.

"So how did Pike end up with your money?"

"He found out what I was doing. He's pretty good with tech as well. He hacked into my laptop and found things."

Tom rolls his eyes. "And then?"

"He needed money because he has an outrageous gambling problem. So he said if I gave him cash, he would keep his mouth shut to everyone. Including Lawrence."

"I see."

"But then it was like he thought he could just treat me badly all the time and I'd take it."

"You *did* take it."

"I was terrified." Liam closes his eyes and shame veils his face.

Tom slams his fist onto the table and Liam jumps. "Why didn't you go to someone? Why didn't you turn Lawrence in?"

"Who would listen to me over a Commander?"

"You still should have gone to someone."

"He would have outed me."

"So instead you help him frame people for bribery, murder, collusion…"

Liam nods. "Yeah. I did. All of it." He drops his head.

"Do you have any idea of the innocent people caught up in this shitshow?"

Liam brings his eyes to meet Tom's.

"*Do you*?"

"I knew I was doing the wrong thing."

"That wasn't my question."

"Yes. I knew I was potentially ruining lives."

Tom stands and wanders the room, interlacing his fingers behind his head. "So now you're looking at serious jail time. Do you know that?"

"Yeah."

"Dishonourable discharge. The whole nine yards." Tom sighs and kicks over the chair he had been sitting in. "I don't even know how to help you out of this mess."

"Why should you?"

"Excuse me?"

"Why should you help me? I deserve whatever happens next."

"No well…" *He isn't Chris.* "I just mean… you were forced into it. Right?"

"Only because I'm weak."

"You aren't weak." Tom swallows. "Me on the other hand?"

"*You*? Yeah right."

Tom pictures the bottle of Balvenie in his bag and his mouth waters. "Yeah. Me."

———

TOM RETRIEVES HIS BAG AND SLAMS HIS LOCKER SHUT. HE leans his head against the locker. "Did *not* see that coming."

The door to the locker room opens. Tom straightens and slings his bag over his shoulder.

"Hey." James walks over and sits on the wooden bench between the rows of lockers.

"Hey."

"How did that go?"

Tom slumps back against the lockers behind him. "I didn't want it to be him."

"Yeah. I was surprised to be honest."

"He's not a bad person."

"I know. But…" James shrugs.

"I had this… this need to help him. And I know where it came from but… fuck." Tom sits next to James on the bench. "It got all confused and messed up in my head."

"I've never seen you so helpless before."

Tom thinks again, of the bottle in his bag and holds back a snort. "Not pretty, right?"

"I was scared."

"Of what?"

"Nothing. I was scared *for* you."

The same warmth that crept into his chest seeing the little girl in the lift, threatened to come back. *Won't be having any of that!* "Well shit, James. Don't go soft on me."

"But I could see the pain and… fear in your face. And it wasn't because your chest hurt or whatever. It was because of what you could see in that moment, that Liam or I couldn't."

Discomfort forces Tom to his feet. "It's over."

"But shouldn't you—"

"It's over."

"Well, if you need to talk…"

"I'm fine."

"Sure. But… I'll talk back. Unlike Jack Daniels or Johnnie Walker."

Tom blinks and peers at James, he looks different but there's nothing different about him. *Now who's going soft?* "Thanks James."

35

TOM

Tom trudges down the hall towards his flat. He remembers at the last second that he should have been quieter as Lorna's door opens. A silent groan sits in his throat. *Not tonight, Lorna.*

"Tom! What a coincidence, I was checking to see if Pebbles was wandering the hall."

Tom watches the cat jump onto her sofa inside the flat behind her, but smiles. "Such a happy coincidence."

"Oh my, you look tired."

"Yes. I'm exhausted so… see you next time." He slides his key in the lock, not waiting for an answer. His mouth waters as he closes the door behind him and rests his head against it. *I'll make it up to her. Poor old duck.* He turns to face the room and his eyes land on Abbie. She's standing next to the coffee table. The TV is silent behind her.

"Hey Grant."

Relief washes over him and he walks to her and pulls her in for a hug. "You're a pain in the neck. You know that?"

"I'm sorry."

"I know."

She pulls away. "Are you alright?"

"No." He drops his bag on the floor and sits in the armchair. "But it's over."

"It is?" She sits on the edge of the sofa and fiddles with her hands in her lap.

Tom rubs his eyes. "Almost. You'll be off the hook. But we need to find Lawrence."

"Find him?"

"Yes. He's been taken off the promotions list and suspended. And gone AWOL."

"Oh wow. He's going to be beside himself."

Tom snaps his eyes to hers. "Don't you dare feel sorry for him."

"No... I don't. But... everything going tits up for him is going to send him loopy."

"Yeah well he should have thought about that before."

Abbie leans over her thighs and rests her chin on her knees. She fiddles with the cuffs of her tracks. "He would have."

"What?"

"He would have." She drags her eyes from where she is staring at the floor and meets Tom's. "He thinks of everything."

"So what's he about to do, Abs? Storm Parliament? Graffiti

Big Ben? C'mon. It's over. He knows it. He will run until he's caught. Like any other piece of shit criminal."

"Maybe…"

Exhaustion hits Tom in the face like a shovel and he stands. "I need to sleep. But Abs… I'm glad you're okay and we'll talk more in the morning, yeah?"

Abbie nods and, as though remembering something, she jumps from the sofa. "Oh… Ummm…" She looks at Tom's bedroom door.

"What?" Saliva whooshes onto his tongue, knowing in one minute he can quench the thirst. *Sitting in bed, in the dark like a crack addict.*

Abbie smiles and shakes her head. "Sweet dreams." She sits again before stretching out and pulling the throw over her legs. "Just keep it down, yeah? Some of us want to sleep." She winks.

Tom quirks a brow. "Right." He picks the bag with his contraband inside and walks to his bedroom. It's dark, but the slice of moonlight cutting across the bed illuminates her. His heart expands five times its size and slams into his ribcage. He drops his bag and watches her; the gentle rise and fall of her chest; her ethics textbook open and lying on the bed next to her. His throat aches but not because of thirst and he swallows the lump away.

He crawls onto the bed and nuzzles his face against hers. A moment later, he breathes in her flowery shampoo and presses his lips against hers.

She stirs, opening her eyes, she blinks and smiles against his mouth. "Surprise," she whispers, kissing him back.

Her warmth spreads across his face and down his body as her presence numbs the trauma and pain invading his thoughts.

Isabella pulls her face away. "Talk to me."

"About?"

"What's going on in your eyes?"

Tom drops his gaze from her face and rolls onto his back, pulling her with him onto his chest. "I'm just tired, Iz. Lots going on today."

Isabella sits up and tilts her head. "I *know* you aren't going to brush me off like that."

Tom reaches up and cups her cheek in his hand. "Martha called you. Didn't she?"

Isabella nods. "She pulled strings so I could get away early for the weekend."

Tom sighs and closes his eyes. "Do something for me?"

"Of course."

"Tip the whisky down the sink?"

"What whisky?"

"The bottle in my bag. Because if I try to… it won't make it down the sink."

Isabella leans into him and runs a thumb over his bottom lip. "What happened to you?"

Tom shakes his head. "Bottle first. Please?" His bottom lip wants to curl and tremble as tears prick in his eyes. "Fuck." He squeezes his eyes shut and drops onto the pillow.

"God." Isabella rests her mouth against his forehead and kisses him. "I'll be right back." She scrambles off the bed and takes the whole bag out of the room with her.

Tom stares at the light flitting as the sobs waiting to come out fade away. *I need to dust that.* He pushes himself into a sitting position and leans against the headboard. The silence of the room envelops him and the sounds from inside the berth haunt him.

Isabella comes into the room and closes the door softly. "It's gone."

Tom nods as she sits against him, nestled against his heart. "Some demons are easier to fight than others."

"Tell me about the others?" She runs her hand to the middle of his chest and keeps it there.

"I don't know how to."

"Something happened on the ship. Didn't it?"

"Yes. But that's not where it began. I've been carrying it for years."

"It?"

"You'd think with everything else that's happened… Claire, drinking, you, Russia… blood, death… you'd think it would fade away. But… it doesn't."

"Well…" Isabella adjusts herself so she's sitting across from Tom, their legs tangled together. "What does *it* mean to you?" She looks into his eyes and waits.

"My first foster family… all their kids were foster kids. And Chris and I were the oldest."

"Chris?"

Tom nods. "He was a brother to me in every sense of the word. I was only in that house for a few months, but we remained brothers after I left. I'd see him at school." Tom shrugs. "He was a couple of years younger than me, but we always played together. Never lost contact."

"He was your family."

"Closest thing I had… until Martha."

"Right."

"I should have stopped him from joining up. He'd still be here."

"What happened?"

Tom drops his head against the headboard and after a few minutes of regulating his breath he swallows his emotions and speaks. He tells Isabella the story that he had kept locked away and unacknowledged for too long. When he gets to the part about Chris being bullied and picked on, Isabella rests her head on his chest. When he gets to the part about Chris breaking down because it was too much, Isabella bunches his shirt in her fist over his heart. When he gets to the part about Chris going to sleep for the final time, Isabella kisses away the lone tear rolling down his cheek. And when he tells her about finding Chris's lifeless body in the bunk, she pulls his head under her chin and wraps her arms around him.

"It's not your fault," she soothes.

"I knew, Iz." The vision of Chris walking away down the corridor is as fresh in his mind as the moment it happened. His footsteps echo in Tom's ears. "He told me what he was going to do. I didn't listen."

"He said he was going to sleep."

Tom looks into her eyes. "Exactly."

She bumps her forehead against his and slides her hands into his hair. They sit together for a while, neither saying anything. The silence in the room comforts him because for the first time today, the noise in his head settles into a distant hum.

"Iz?"

"Yes?"

"When you came face to face with Damir again... after all that time and what he had done... how did it feel?"

"Like the last time I ever saw him. All the hatred, pain, and sadness inside me bubbled to the surface. I heard voices from that time in my head, and tasted blood in my mouth." She sits up and holds his gaze.

"Like your chest was being wrapped up in a thousand rubber bands?"

Isabella nods.

"I walked into that berth today and I saw a body under the blanket. That one moment took me back there. I grabbed Liam, but to me it was Chris. I pulled him towards me. He was so heavy. Heavier than he had ever been before. He slumped against me, and I shook him and shouted in his face." Tom's voice rasps and he stops. "I shouted and shook him until someone pulled me away. And today made me feel all of it. The sounds of the room, the noise and commotion of people trying to prise my hands off his shirt. The rushing of white noise in my ears." He stops and covers his face with his hands. "I could smell his aftershave today."

"Liam's?"

"No. Chris's. He always wore cheap shit from Boots. Awful stuff."

Isabella lies against Tom's chest. He drops his hands from his face and wraps them around her, holding her securely against him.

"And I heard the same voices telling me to stop and move away from him. It was so…" Tom swallows and huffs a harsh breath. "Confusing."

"What happened then?"

"I don't know. I was stuck in this… moment in time that kept circling me… shouting and invading every part of me. And I couldn't make it stop." Tom's heart doubles in speed and his breaths become shallow. "No…" He buries his face in Isabella's hair. "No more today." He hears Mike's voice. *Deep breaths, Tom.* "No more ever again." He steadies his breathing as Isabella gives him her warmth and strength to calm down.

He lies down and pulls Isabella against him. She covers his arms with her own as he buries his face into her back and closes his eyes.

———

Tom's eyes spring open and he scrambles to sit up.

"Tom?"

Tom blinks in the dusky light and remembers he isn't on the ship. He's at home with Isabella. "Did you hear something?"

Isabella sits up and yawns. "When?"

"A thud."

"A thud? No... you were probably dreaming." She lays back down and pulls him on top of her. "But now you're awake..."

Tom swipes his thumbs across her cheeks and pecks her lips. "But... something feels off."

"No Tom. Everything's fine. You had a really stressful time and you're still processing it."

"I'll just go and check—"

"Tom. Relax. Abbie is out there. Don't you think she would have come and got us if something was wrong?"

"I heard a thud..."

"She probably stumbled into a wall going to the loo."

Tom looks at her and the desire to go running into the lounge fades. He runs a hand down her neck and under her cami.

"Now, this is a more worthwhile activity." She pulls his face to hers and wraps her legs around his waist.

Forty five minutes later Tom strokes Isabella's sweaty hair from her face and rolls onto the mattress next to her. "God I missed you."

She props herself up on one elbow and leans down to kiss him, her hair falls around his face and tickles his neck.

Tom chuckles against her lips. "Stop. Or I'll never get out of bed."

"You don't need to. We could stay here all day."

"Tempting."

"I'll go make some coffee." She swings her legs to the floor and pulls her robe around her. "Stay." She points a finger at Tom and frowns.

"Okay." He holds both hands up in surrender. He kneels up, pulls open the curtains and stares out the window.

"Tom!"

His muscles tense and he scrambles off the bed and pulls on his tracks.

He runs into the lounge and finds the coffee table on its side, the seat cushions from the lounge on the floor and… no Abbie. "Fuck." He runs to the bathroom, knowing it will be empty before bolting out the front door to the stairs, taking them two at a time.

"Jesus. What happened?" Isabella is right behind him.

"Abbie."

"She ran again?"

"No. No way." He scans the street and finds nothing out of the ordinary. It's too early for office workers or anyone else to be up and about who isn't walking a dog or running in too short shorts. Tom huffs out a steamy breath in the cold morning air and puts his hands on his head. "C'mon." He grabs Isabella's hand, and they go inside. He pulls her up the stairs behind him and as they pass Lorna's door it opens. *Fuck's sake.*

"Ah… early start?"

"Yeah. Sorry Lorna, can't talk we—"

"You saw your friend?"

Tom turns from his door back to Lorna. "Excuse me?"

"I heard a noise when I was pottering about with Pebbles and assumed you were leaving for the day, so I opened the door to say hello but… it was someone else."

"Someone…" He turns to Isabella. "Get Martha on the phone."

She runs into the flat and Tom turns his attention back to Lorna. "What did my… friend look like?"

"Rather suave I must admit. Quite the silver fox." Lorna chuckles and winks at Tom.

"What was he wearing?"

"A long black coat and a flat cap. To be honest if it was eighteen eighty I'd have thought he was Jack the Ripper. Gave me chills when he looked at me. Ice cold eyes, that one."

Tom inspects the lock on his door to find it broken off. *Jemmied.* He looks up at Lorna. "Did he speak to you?"

"He said he was here to pick up his friend for work and I should pop back inside before I caught my death." She huffs. "Honestly, treated me like I was some sort of old loon. But I saw him breaking your lock."

"And then?"

"Well, naturally I closed the door and kept watching through the peephole."

Isabella appears in the hall with the phone and taps Tom on

the shoulder with it. He takes it and slaps it to his ear. "Hey. Give me a sec…" He holds the phone against his chest. "Lorna. What happened when you watched through the peephole?"

"Well a few minutes passed, and he came back out with your blonde friend… you know the sassy one?" Lorna raises a brow and gives Isabella a sidelong glance.

"Yes. She's an old friend. Was she struggling?"

"No. But he did seem to be whispering some rather strong words in her ear. His teeth were all clenched and she was crying."

Tom nods. "Okay. Thanks Lorna. I'll pop in again in a while."

"Oh wonderful! I'll put the kettle on." She disappears into her flat.

Tom walks into the lounge and sits next to Isabella. He puts the phone to his ear again. "Lawrence took Abbie almost an hour ago." He pulls Isabella against him and kisses the top of her head.

"This isn't good." Martha crunches on something that sounds like toast. Tom imagines her in her hair net and dressing gown.

"Yes. Thank you Nostradamus. I'd predicted that on my own."

"I'll be right in. I expect you will too?"

He looks down at the top of Isabella's head, knowing she will insist on helping. "We're on our way."

36

ABBIE

A bbie sits, leaning against a freezing cold concrete wall, her hands are bound and tied to a water pipe. A rag is shoved in her mouth; held there with tape. The room smells like motor oil and the floor is sticky with years' worth of dirt and grease.

Sunlight pushes its way through a grimy window above a well-used workbench. She watches Lawrence as he sits on an ancient vinyl covered stool with stuffing poking through the olive green trim. He taps on a laptop and grumbles to himself.

Given the daylight and the numbness in her backside, she calculates they have been here now for a few hours. Her back aches and trying to move makes it worse. He hasn't said a word or acknowledged her since he threw her into the corner and tied her up.

Not a single word.

He stands and crosses the floor towards her. He leans over her and doesn't look down or say anything, he reaches into an open shelf above her head.

"There was some copper wire here…" He fumbles around and dust rains onto Abbie, but he takes no notice. An old pickaxe handle with no axe attached falls and hits her on the ankle. She squeals into the rag in her mouth and squirms. He pays no attention. "Damn. The old coot probably sold it…"

He walks back to his laptop, leaving Abbie squirming and breathing loud heavy breaths through her nose. Her skin crawls with imaginary bugs while her stomach bubbles red hot. She clenches her fists and tries to stretch out the nylon ropes tying her hands together. She tries to sit up a little straighter, but as soon as she moves her feet, pain shoots from the left ankle where the axe handle fell. She slumps against the wall again and blinks against the tears pooling in her eyes. *If my nose blocks, I'm screwed.*

"Ah ha!" Lawrence jerks his head and peers at the edge of the grimy window where an old coiled up strimmer cord hangs. He jumps and flicks it off the window frame, catching it on the way down. He walks back to Abbie, still not looking at her face and kneels in front of her. He inspects her neck and unravels the cord. He pulls it taut between both hands as though about to floss his teeth and pushes it against Abbie's neck. She gasps through the dirty rag and coughs as dirt coats the back of her throat. She tries to shuffle away but he grabs her shoulder and slams her against the wall, still not making any acknowledgement of her. He presses the cord against her skin again and lengthens it. "Perfect. It's not copper but..." He shrugs and stands.

A tin bucket sits on top of a stool just out of reach of where Abbie is tied to the water pipe. She slides her backside forward, keeping her eyes on Lawrence as he concentrates on his laptop screen. She pulls hard against her restraints and stretches out, shuffling her backside further forward. She draws a long, deep breath through her nose and uses every ounce of strength within her and kicks the stool. The bucket tumbles to the floor with a reverberating crash.

She kicks at anything she can reach with her feet and thrashes against the water pipe. Lawrence continues typing for a few seconds, before pressing one last button with a flourish and turning to Abbie. She stops kicking and making noise, so he turns back to his laptop. She starts again. This time as she pulls against the water pipes they move imperceptibly but for a tiny sprinkle of dirt flakes hitting her in the face and a quiet grind of metal on metal. Her heart flutters and hope springs into her head.

Lawrence stands and his stool tips over. He paces across the room to her.

She stops moving so he doesn't notice the pipe giving.

He rips the tape from her mouth.

"God *damn* it!" Abbie's eyes squint shut of their own accord as the sting from her mouth prickles her entire face.

"You shout, scream or make one sound higher than a whisper and I'll break your neck. Don't… provoke… me."

"Like you did your wife?"

Lawrence whips his hand back and slaps her across the face.

Tears cloud Abbie's eyes and she gasps in a hard breath. "What are you…"

"This is all your fault Sweetheart. You know that don't you?"

Abbie blinks and glares at him. "How do you figure?"

"You ran off and wouldn't stick to the plan."

"Plan?"

"Plan." He stands and looks out the grimy window. "This was meant to be over, and I was meant to be promoted and free of all the shackles. But you fucked it up, Sweetheart."

Abbie peers at Lawrence in the dingy light of the old garage. "What fantasy world do you live in?"

"It's no fantasy. I deserve what's coming to me. I just need to tie up some loose ends."

"You definitely deserve it."

"What's that Sweetheart?" Lawrence turns from the window and leans against the workbench as though waiting for a bus.

Abbie bites on her bottom lip. "You certainly worked hard." She turns her mouth up at one corner.

Lawrence squints at her. "You know I did."

Abbie holds her breath a second. "I can understand why you killed her."

"Pardon?"

"I understand why you killed your wife."

He pulls the stool across that had been holding the tin bucket and sits. "It wasn't her fault, you know. She knew too much and then tried to blackmail me. Can you imagine? *She* tried to blackmail *me*." Lawrence shakes his head. "Poor stupid woman."

"She knew about Amir."

"No Sweetheart. She knew *everything*." Lawrence crosses his legs and flicks a hand out as though telling the most obvious of stories. "She knew about Amir, yes. But that was on purpose. However, it appears in the days leading up to the banquet she had found out about you and I."

Abbie averts her eyes from Lawrence and closes them. The last time she saw Daphne breathing flashes behind her eyelids.

"Must be my fault for being attracted to powerful men." Daphne winked and sipped her white wine spritzer. "Or maybe I told him something he didn't like?" She shrugged.

"I'd love to stay but just heading to the Ladies. Lovely to see you again."

"And you Darling, good luck in your... future endeavours." Daphne's eyes flashed for a second before her face softened into a smile.

"What did she threaten you with?" Abbie shimmies into a

sitting position against the pipe, it jiggles against her back. She holds her breath. Lawrence is too busy inspecting his fingernails to notice anything and Abbie exhales.

"She did herself no favours. She wanted a divorce and half of *my* money. And if I didn't give her what she wanted she would expose our affair. *Right* before my promotion. I told her I was deeply sorry of course and grovelled. She thought I was so terribly remorseful."

"Why not just give her what she wanted? You'd be rid of her and get your promotion."

"My dear girl… she wanted *my* money. She was a gold digging old witch who had aged out of her younger charms and… assets. And she wanted to take half of my wealth and go live it up in Spain or France? No, no, no. That would never do."

"Your ego is your worst enemy."

Lawrence curls his lip and leans into her. "Behave yourself, my *Sweet.*" The snarl in his voice is nasty.

Abbie drops her head. "Sorry." *Not.*

"So, we left in a car after the dinner," Lawrence continues as though Abbie never spoke. "And I picked a fight with her so she would go rushing back into the hotel. So I followed her back in and gave her the key to our room… peace offering. Let her have some time alone. I'm such an adoring and thoughtful husband after all."

"What for?"

"Admiral Moore."

"You knew about him. You were going to frame him for her murder."

"Oh Sweetheart, there's no *gunna* about it. I wanted him in the frame all along. But I used you as a backup. Really quite ingenious. I had intended to blackmail Moore, but things didn't go exactly as I would have liked…" He glares at Abbie. "Did they?"

"Guess not."

"Now tell me, what's Tom going to do when he finds you're gone?"

Abbie stops herself from snorting and shakes her head. "Assume I ran again, I guess."

"You and I both know that's not true."

"I ran before. There's no reason to think I wouldn't run again. Right?"

"And the old bag across the hall?"

"Please. She can't even remember what day it is, let alone who she spoke to three hours ago."

"She seemed rather spritely to me."

"She's a lonely old woman who lives across the hall from Tom Grant. I'd be spritely too." As soon as the words leave her mouth she knows they are a mistake.

Within microseconds Lawrence is in front of her with his hand around her throat. "You *still* think he's better than me?"

Abbie swallows against his thumb and says nothing.

"Answer me."

She pushes down the words she wants to say and grits her teeth. "Of course not."

"Then at the house, why did you say—"

"I was upset."

Lawrence's fingers loosen but his hand remains. "Why?"

"I was *so* in love with you." The words cause Abbie nausea. "I didn't want you to see how heartbroken I was…" Abbie holds his glare, softening her gaze, and waits.

Lawrence's eyes are blocks of ice and they freeze her blood. "You're a liar."

"No. It's true. I was devastated."

Lawrence's hand slips a little down her neck.

"I'm sorry this has been so difficult for you, Matthew."

"I got complacent. I won't make that mistake again."

"Complacent?"

"But not again. Never again. New day. New plan."

"What's your obsession with Tom?"

"Obsession?"

"Obsession."

"He irks me."

"Because he's younger, better looking and better in the sack? Or is it something else?"

Lawrence grabs a handful of her hair and yanks her head to one side. She winces and a squeak sticks in her throat. "You listen to me. He won't rest until he has me cornered like some helpless rat in a maze. Because you *had* to get him involved. I won't let that upstart who never made it in the Royal Navy, win. Do you understand?"

Abbie nods but doesn't look at him.

"He won't find us here. No one will."

"Where are we?"

Lawrence throws his head back and laughs. "I always did love your sense of humour." He stands and goes back to the desk and snarls at the screen. "Where the fuck are you?"

Abbie pulls against the pipe, watching the back of Lawrence's head as he leans into the keyboard and pounds on the keys. The bracket holding the bottom third of the pipe against the wall has one screw in it and it's rusted away. The filthy old sink the pipe runs into is rickety and appears as though it could fall over with a gentle nudge. *Pull, slide and kick. Easy.* Abbie snorts softly but Lawrence is too busy taking his frustration out on the keyboard to notice.

She looks at the door to outside. It's made of wood and rotting at the bottom. Sunlight streams in through the gaps in the moisture eaten wood. One hard kick and it should open.

Lawrence growls at the laptop and slams the screen shut before tapping his fingers on it and opening it again.

"Are you okay?" Abbie tests the waters.

"I'm wonderful. Thank you."

"Yeah. I can tell."

"Just shut your mouth, Abigail."

Abbie presses her mouth together and flares her nostrils at Lawrence as he starts typing again. *Go time.* She clasps her hands and musters every ounce of fortitude she possesses. With a hard and sharp yank she pulls the pipe away from the wall and slides her ropes along it towards the sink. Once close enough, she kicks the tiny old sink. It comes away from the wall and the pipe falls out of its fitting. She pulls her tethered hands away from the pipe and turns to run.

She sees the back-side of the shovel coming for her face too late and then... nothing.

37

TOM

Tom traces circles on the top of Isabella's hand as he stares straight ahead. The sofa in Martha's office is as lumpy as always but today he doesn't care. The door opens and Isabella lifts her head off Tom's shoulder.

Martha nods at the pair of them. She continues to her desk where she places her handbag and reads some slips of paper left for her.

Tom tightens his grip on Isabella's hand. "No, no. Please take your time we have all day."

"I had to drive in from Islington, Tom. I'm terribly sorry you made it here before I did. Quite astounding how you possibly made the ten minute journey on your bike and beat me here." She drops the paper she had been reviewing and looks up. "Good morning Isabella, dear. You look well."

Isabella leaps from the sofa and bounds across the room, enveloping Martha in a hug. "Nice to see you, Martha."

Tom bites his cheek as Martha pats Isabella on the back with all the awkwardness of just being told her fly was undone. Isabella points to the door. "I'll go make some coffee."

Tom stays on the sofa and waits until Martha finishes fussing and joins him. "How did he get in?"

"Broke the lock."

"You didn't hear him?"

Tom tilts his head and frowns. "Of course I did. I wandered out in my birthday suit and had a quick yarn about the weather before he asked *very* politely if he may take Abbie with him, and I said yes, obviously."

Martha purses her lips. "Drop the attitude."

"I was exhausted and slept until some sort of thud woke me."

Martha nods once and picks some lint off her cardigan. "That's better."

"Lorna spoke to him, but he didn't give her much."

"We need more information." Martha taps her chin with her index finger.

"Wow yes—"

"If you call me Einstein I'll throttle you."

Tom slams his mouth shut and folds his arms.

"I've had James trying to track his phone and ISP since you called me. Nothing yet. He's now on his way to pick up Liam from the holding cells in town."

"So we have nothing?"

"I'm warning you, Tom. Don't lose your temper."

Tom stands and walks the perimeter of the office, his arms firmly folded against his chest. Dregs of the anxiety and panic from the ship creep into his thoughts but he stomps on them. *Don't you fucking dare.* He digs his fingers into his biceps and stops at the window, glaring at the carpark out the back. "What about his car?"

"His car?"

"Yeah. He has one of those schmick cars with a computer doesn't he? Have we tracked that?"

The door opens and Isabella walks in, balancing three mugs on a plastic 'in-tray' that has *James* written on it.

"See? He *does* come in useful." Tom joins Isabella at the desk and grabs his mug. "Ta."

"James just got here with someone." Isabella sips her coffee.

"Which begs the question of why they are not sitting in this room already?" Tom raises both palms and peers at Martha.

Isabella rolls her eyes. "Relax, Tom. They're—"

"Morning." James saunters in pushing Liam along in front of him like a kid on his first day of kindergarten. Liam has a bruise on his left cheekbone and his eyes are red with bags under them. He keeps his eyes down and sits in the chair offered to him by James.

Tom grips his coffee mug tighter as Liam sits, without acknowledging him.

"Good morning Liam." Martha pours some water from the jug that always sits on her desk. "Water?"

"Thank you Ma'am."

"Martha is fine."

Liam nods and picks up the water with a shaky hand. He puts it down again without taking a sip.

"What happened to your face?" Tom nods towards Liam's cheek.

Liam's eyes stay trained on the floor. "Fell over."

"No, Liam. You didn't."

Liam squirms against the backrest of the chair. "What am I here for?" He addresses Martha.

"Are you fucking kidding me?" Tom's neck heats and he slams the coffee mug on the desk.

"Tom," Isabella whispers and grabs his elbow.

Liam's shoulders rise and fall with a sigh as he looks at Tom, towering over him.

"What happened to your face?"

Liam swallows. "Fell."

"Because?"

Liam shrugs. "Clumsy."

Tom squints and clenches his fists by his side.

"We think you might be able to help. Matthew Lawrence has gone to ground and taken Abigail Perkins with him." Martha's voice is loud, and she glares at Tom and motions to his seat with her eyes. He sits and glares past Martha at the wall behind her.

Liam clears his throat. "He took her?"

"Yes. Early this morning."

The dull thud Tom now knows was the coffee table falling over sounds in his ears. Tom shakes his head and runs both hands through his hair before standing. He paces behind them all.

"I'm not sure how I can help."

Something in Tom clicks and he stops pacing. "For fuck's sake, Liam."

Isabella and James turn to look at Tom. Liam remains sitting with his head bowed.

Tom darts across the room and grabs Liam out of his chair by the front of his shirt. "He will kill her. So use your damn smarts and think. You helped him. Now you help us."

"Tom. Stop right now." Martha stands and leans forward on her desk with both palms down.

Liam blinks and stares at Tom.

"It's time to make it right, Liam." Tom drops Liam into his chair.

"Does he know you found out about me?"

"No. So here's what's going to happen. You're going to contact him asking if there is anything he needs you to do."

Liam's posture stiffens. "Okay."

"And I want to know where he is."

"He won't tell me if he's on the run. He's not stupid."

"We're going to trace his location, Liam." Tom picks up the phone on Martha's desk and holds it out to Liam. "Start dialling."

Liam takes the phone and taps the screen. He put it to his ear, his hand trembling. "Yeah Um. Hey. Hi. It's me."

James starts tapping the keyboard to trace the call.

Tom pinches the bridge of his nose and cringes at Liam's timid, shaky voice. "Wow." He sits on a chair next to Liam and rests his elbows on his knees, hands under chin and glares at him.

"No, Sir. Sorry I... I've been distracted." Liam shifts his eyes to Tom and gives a half shrug.

"Fucking firewall," James mumbles to no one in particular.

"Well, I'm calling because... do you have any work for me? Or someth—" Liam squeezes his eyes shut. "I could do with the money is all..." Liam jerks his head up and looks at Tom, his eyes like saucers. "What? No... why would you—"

Fuck. Tom shakes his head and crosses his forearms. "Don't you fucking dare," he hisses at Liam.

"Ahhh... I don't know why you would think *he* was here with me."

Tom bites the inside of his mouth so hard an ulcer emerges before he lets go. He grabs a post-it and scribbles a note. *Tell him to meet you somewhere.* He slides the paper to Liam and taps it with his index finger.

"Why don't we meet? You'll see I'm not with him and we can get some jobs on...hello?" Liam holds the phone out to Martha. "He's gone."

James pushes the keyboard away and grunts. "I didn't have enough time. He's blocked himself good and proper."

"How much more time do you need?" Tom nods at the computer.

James shrugs. "How long's a piece of string?"

Tom's pulse spikes. He spins and stalks from the room before the expletives he is swallowing find their way out.

He kicks the first chair he comes across and swipes a daily planner and telephone off the accompanying desk. "Fuck!" He glares at the ceiling with both hands on his head.

Arms slide around his waist and Isabella rests her head in the middle of his back. "Calm down."

"I am calm."

Isabella laughs and the vibration shudders down his spine. It's oddly comforting, and he turns to face her. "If anything happens to—"

"It won't. You'll find her. But not if you're out here rearranging desks and cursing at the ceiling fans."

Tom drops his cheek onto Isabella's head. "I need five minutes, or I'll snap Liam's neck."

"Why?"

"I don't know. Yesterday I felt sorry for him but, today, I want to shake sense into him."

"There are stakes today."

"There were stakes yesterday."

"Yes. But Abbie was safe in your flat yesterday."

Tom pulls Isabella's hair into a ponytail at the nape of her neck and kisses her forehead. "Go in. I'll be five."

"Tom—"

"Five." He steps back and shoves his hands in his pockets. "I need a minute. Unless you want me to give him a shiner on the other cheek."

Isabella narrows her eyes at him for a second. "Okay. Five minutes. No more."

"So bossy."

Isabella snorts and closes the office door.

Tom stares at the closed door for a minute before blinking and heading to the back of the office space. *Fresh air.* He pushes the heavy back door open and takes a breath. The nausea and waves of anxiety rising in his gut settle a little. He walks the perimeter of the car park; past the shooting range at the rear of the block where he pauses a moment. *I could unload fifty clips right about now.* "And achieve what?" he whispers to himself.

"Tom?"

He closes his eyes and takes a long breath in. "Not now, Pen." He doesn't bother turning around.

"No but... it's important." Her heavy, clumsy footsteps sound across the deserted car park and Tom drops his head. *Fucks sake.* He turns and she holds a phone out to him.

"You should take this. It sounds... important."

Tom looks at the phone, his hands firmly shoved in his pockets. "You can't take a message? I mean... isn't that seventy percent of your job?"

Penny's already rosy cheeks deepen. She huffs, "Well, he said if I don't find you, he'll kill some girl called Abbie. But if you prefer I take a mess—"

Tom snatches the phone from Penny and slams it against his ear. "Grant." His heart staccatos and his throat dries up.

"It was so easy to manipulate, you know." Lawrence's voice is freezing cold.

Tom lowers the phone from his mouth. "Tell James." He mimes to Penny. He flicks his head to send her inside.

She waddles away and Tom watches her disappear into the warehouse before he speaks.

"Is that right?"

"Yes. Such a cowardly, scared little runt of a kid."

"Makes sense. It's not like you could intimidate anyone of note."

Lawrence chuckles. "Like you?"

"I'm no one, but no… you don't intimidate me. You never did, to be honest."

"Well you did have Jack looking out for you in the end."

"He hated me. He only did that because Claire begged him to get me out. But you didn't call to chat about old times."

"No. I didn't. Tell me are you tracking me?"

"Is there a point?"

"No."

"Put Abbie on the phone."

"She's… a little tied up." Lawrence laughs at his own joke as Tom's jaw tightens.

"Put her on the phone."

"She's sleeping."

Tom kicks the tyre of the car next to him and slumps against the roof with his face in his arms. "Did you call for a reason? Or just to gloat?"

"You'd like Abbie back in one piece I assume?"

Tom grits his teeth. "Ideally."

"Wonderful. I want a chopper."

"Are you insane? You've kidnapped a woman, killed your wife, bribed foreign entities... And you want a chopper?"

"Killed my wife?"

"Killed your wife."

"That's rather presumptuous of you."

"I've seen the footage from that night."

"As have I."

"The unedited footage."

A rough, whirring noise accompanied by random squeaking travels down the phone line.

"Are you going to speak?" Tom wanders back to the door and inside the warehouse.

"I'm thinking." The whirring sound rises and falls as though it slows and speeds up again. It claws at the back of Tom's skull with familiarity.

"First time for everything I suppose."

Tom's curiosity gets the better of him. "What the hell are you doing?"

"I fidget when I'm bored."

"I see."

"And you're boring me."

"I tell you I know you killed your wife and you're... bored?"

"I want a chopper. Tonight. I'll send coordinates." His voice has taken on a sharp, cold edge. "I get a chopper, you get Abbie. Quite simple. Oh and another thing... charge Moore for my *darling* Daphne's death and have this over with. It's carried on for far too long."

"Moore?"

"Yes. He was sleeping with her was he not? All the... *evidence* is there."

"Charming."

He walks into Martha's office where James and Liam are sitting behind her desk, eyes glued to the screen of her computer. Martha and Isabella stand behind them and look up as Tom sits in his chair. "So let me get this straight... you want a chopper, Moore charged, and you'll give Abbie over... that's what you're saying?"

Martha shakes her head and frowns. "Is he insane?"

Tom nods as Lawrence laughs down the phone. "That's what I'm saying... but if Abbie doesn't cooperate... I can't be held responsible for my actions."

The last line grates on Tom and he leans forward slamming his fist on the desk. "Held responsible for your actions? No... of course not... Why should you face any justice whatsoever? I mean... you're far too important right?"

"Now you see it from my side of things. Well done. I'll be in touch." The line goes dead.

Tom throws the phone onto the desk, and it slides onto the floor.

"Didn't I warn you about losing your temper?" Martha picks the phone up and puts it on the desk.

"I think we both know it was inevitable."

Isabella sits next to Tom. "Is Abbie alright?"

"No idea. She was *sleeping*."

"Oh, crap."

"Hmmm." Tom scratches his hands through his hair as the squeaky, grinding noise rings in his ears. "What *is* that sound?" He leaps from his chair and paces.

"What sound?" Martha drops her glasses onto the desk as James whoops and grins at Tom.

Tom glares at James. "Why so cheerful?"

"I broke through his firewall."

Tom holds both palms up. "And?" Just as he speaks, a vision of an old grinding wheel in Martha's work shed floats through his mind.

Tom cranked the handle faster and faster and watched the stone wheel spin. It squeaked a bit.

"There you are." Martha's voice was at the shed door. "You'll get dirty in here."

"But it's fun." He cranks the handle again.

"Ah, Dad's old grinding wheel. He used it to keep his wood chisels sharp."

"What's it made of?"

"Stone."

"Why does it make that squeaky sound?"

"It needs oil." Martha reached into an old biscuit tin and found a bottle of Singer oil. *"Here… let me show you…"*

"Tom?"

Tom looks up and Isabella's face is in front of him. "Are you okay?"

"It's a grinding wheel."

"What?"

"Lawrence. He was winding a grinding wheel."

James leaps across the floor. "He's in Oxford."

"Oxford?"

"Rose Hill to be exact." James puffs his chest out as though he's just cracked the enigma code.

"So… he's winding a grinding wheel in… Rose Hill…"

"Tom? What's with the grinding wheel?" Martha peers at her computer screen.

"I could hear it. He started winding it while he was talking to me…"

"He grew up in Rose Hill," Liam says quietly.

Tom snaps his head towards Liam. "Pardon?"

"He grew up in Rose Hill."

38

ABBIE

"How stupid do they think I am?" Lawrence's irritated voice creeps into Abbie's ears as she blinks her eyes open.

Her head aches. Her nose is blocked. She moans as she shifts from lying on the floor to half sitting. Lawrence doesn't turn around and she glances down at her shirt, covered in dried blood. She presses her nose with her tightly bound wrists and the pain shoots through her entire face. "God," she rasps.

"Ah, my Sweet. You're awake." Lawrence spins on his stool and stands. "And not going anywhere this time."

She tries to move her feet, but her ankles are tied together so tight, they mash against each other sending sharp pain up her leg akin to blades cutting skin.

Lawrence crouches in front of her. "Don't be too sad. I haven't tied you *to* anything this time. And I haven't gagged you. So don't make me regret it." He winks and returns to the workbench. "Oh and Tom says hi."

Abbie's gut convulses. "What?"

"Tom. We had a lovely chit chat about half an hour ago… he sends his regards."

Abbie looks around the tiny garage, expecting to see him tied up in an opposing corner, but there's no one else there. "Where is he?"

Lawrence bends forward and reads his laptop screen. "I don't know, having tea and scones with that old bag across the hall?"

"He doesn't like scones."

Lawrence laughs and spins around on his stool again. "No I don't suppose it would fit with his workout regime. He's got some muscles hasn't he?"

Abbie glares at Lawrence and says nothing.

"Big strong arms… must have been nice for you… while it lasted."

"Are you jealous?"

Lawrence's nostrils flare but he grins. "Of that no hoper? Please."

Abbie stares at him but says nothing more.

Lawrence flinches and his skin deepens in colour. A sense of dread creeps up Abbie's spine as the energy in the room shifts.

"You think you're so clever. Don't you?" He walks around the garage, with his hands on his hips. "You think Tom's going to come crashing through the door and rescue you like some kind of damsel in distress from a Disney movie." He turns and glares at her. "Don't you?"

"I'm no damsel." Abbie struggles into a sitting position against the wall. "And I'm not in distress."

Lawrence raises his eyebrows. "Oh no?"

"No. You don't scare me."

"I smacked you in the face with the backside of a shovel, my Sweet."

"You did. But only because you know in a real fight... I'd win."

Lawrence screws his face into a distorted caricature of himself and laughs. "I hit you with that shovel harder than I thought."

"Not hard enough, actually." Abbie bites the inside of her lip as she imagines Tom hissing at her to shut up.

"Is that so?"

"I woke up. Didn't I?"

Lawrence crouches in front of her and strokes hair off her forehead gently, pity paints his face. "Oh Sweet. You are so full of hope and positivity."

Abbie pushes her head harder against the wall, though it makes no difference.

Lawrence leans in and kisses her softly on the temple. "It's going to be a shame to snuff your shining light when you've served your purpose."

Abbie closes her eyes and holds her breath. When she opens them again Lawrence is back at his laptop, typing. The only sound in the garage is of Lawrence tapping on the keyboard. He refers to a laid out map on the workbench and plots some points with a pen.

"Going somewhere?"

"We both are my Sweet. You'll love it."

"I'm not going anywhere with you."

Lawrence laughs as he picks up his phone. "You're sexy when you're angry. Ah… Martha. How lovely." He spins back to the workbench. "I've sent coordinates to you. I expect everything will be as I instructed?"

Abbie's skin prickles and sweat breaks out on her face, running down her temples. *I'm screwed.*

"You are a delightful woman." Lawrence ends the call and drops the phone onto the bench. "Old hag."

Abbie sweeps her eyes around noting the door she assumes leads to the side garden and small square window. The only two escape routes, apart from the up and over garage door. *All impossible.* She lifts her wrists and inspects the bindings. Rope and gaffer tape. *He's gone all out this time.* A quick check of her ankles reveals the same.

Maybe… "I need to use the toilet."

"That's unfortunate."

"I'm hungry."

"Cupboards are bare."

"I hate you."

Lawrence picks up the roll of gaffer tape and turns to face Abbie. "Do I need to shut you up?"

"Why are you doing this?" Abbie's voice is huskier than she would have liked, and she hates the fact Lawrence grins at her obvious emotion.

"My Sweet. Because you get nowhere in this world without fighting for what you rightly deserve."

"Deserve?"

Lawrence gets off the stool and wanders the garage. "My father taught me everything about being a man. Being in control and getting what you want. Most of his lessons in this very garage might I add."

"We're at your father's house?"

"Don't interrupt."

"I thought you hated your father?"

"I said… *don't* interrupt." Lawrence stops walking and glares at Abbie. "I do hate him. When he would push me to get top grades, whip me behind the knees when I failed to score a goal in football… when he would berate my mother for making the eggs too runny." Lawrence stops and swallows. "But now I know he was asserting his authority. Preparing me for the real world. He used to make sure my bedroom was meticulously tidy. Everything has a place." He stops and looks at Abbie. "Much like people. We all have our rightful place. And if something isn't in its rightful place, that's when everything falls apart." He sweeps a hand out as though showing his point.

"Are you mad?" Abbie can't help but jerk her lip and stare at him.

"This garage… always tidy, everything labelled, everything

clean and put in the right spot. He wasn't to be messed with. And I… My Sweet, am also not to be messed with."

"Is your father dead?"

"Dead? No. Though he may as well be. He's a dribbling shell of the man he used to be."

"He's frail?"

"Yes. And can't remember what he had for breakfast. It's pathetic." He spits out the word pathetic like it was poison on his tongue.

"Where is he?"

Lawrence points at the back wall of the garage. "About fifty feet in that direction. Sitting in the living room, staring out the front window with a blanket over his knees. Dribbling." The disgust screwing up Lawrence's face jabs Abbie through the heart. "I hired a full time nurse to look after him. Hopefully he doesn't last much longer." Lawrence shakes his head. "*Pathetic.*"

Abbie's heart aches as she tries to remember what she ever saw in Lawrence. "You're a monster." A tear rolls down Abbie's cheek.

"*I'm* the monster? I'm putting everyone in their rightful place, including myself. How is it that I'm the villain?"

Abbie shakes her head, slowly, gaping at him. "Insane."

Lawrence's eyes squint and he creeps across the garage towards her. "Insane?" His voice is quiet. He reaches Abbie and crouches in front of her. "Did you think I was insane when I would undress you?"

Abbie's throat closes up. "No."

"When I would trail my finger down your spine?"

Abbie blinks again and sends tears toppling down her face. "No."

Lawrence leans in and rests his lips against her ear. "When I made you scream my name?"

"Stop."

"But you remember." His lips drop from her ear, and he pushes them against the pulse in her neck. "Don't you?"

"Yes," she whispers. "I was blind. And stupid." She pushes her nose into Lawrence's as she grits out the words.

Lawrence chuckles and wraps his hand around the back of her neck and grabs a handful of her hair. A squeak escapes Abbie's throat and she locks eyes with Lawrence.

"Get used to pain my Sweet. This is *just* the beginning."

"You can't hurt me anymore. It's done. I feel nothing."

"I bet I can make you feel something." He puts his other hand against her throat before sliding it to her chest. "Well, this won't do." He releases her hair and grabs the front of her shirt with both hands and rips it open.

Every muscle in Abbie's body tenses as though paralysed. "What are you doing?"

"We have some time to spare."

"Get off me." The pleading in her voice belies the strength she is trying to give off.

"Maybe I can make you scream my name… one more time."

Abbie's paralysis disintegrates as her heart hums and her pulse thumps in her ears. "No!" She squirms beneath his weight.

He slaps a hand over her mouth and leans into her face. "You will do as you're told My Sweet.

Flight kicks in and Abbie bites Lawrence's fingers while thrashing her body beneath him. He grabs her around the soft part of her waist and squeezes. Air huffs from her lungs and Lawrence leers at her. "You know how much I love your warm breath on my skin, My Sweet." He grabs the waistband of the tracks she is wearing and pulls them down to her knees. He pushes his face against her stomach and his tongue trails down to the top of her underwear.

Abbie throws her head back, screams and thrusts her hips upward.

Lawrence sits up on his knees and glares at her. "Why won't you lie the fuck still?"

"Please, Matt. Stop. Why are you—" He swings his arm and slaps her across the face. The sting travels through her face, her neck, and into her heart. "How could you…"

He holds a hand over her mouth and with the other he twists the elastic of her underwear and yanks, snapping it loose. Abbie sobs into his hand as her body tires and she can't fight anymore. Pain throbs through her broken nose and the sting of his slap lingers.

He slides his hand off her mouth and unbuttons his own belt and trousers.

Abbie openly wails, not caring about staying quiet, not caring about following orders. *It's over.*

She sniffles as her nose blocks and razor blades dig into her throat; her voice spent. She squeezes her eyes shut and waits for it to be over. He pulls at her now loose underwear, and she opens her eyes in time to see cracks of light appear from beneath the large up and over garage door behind Lawrence. The old wooden door cracks as someone with a crowbar yanks at it from the outside, and the sound rockets through the small garage like thunder.

"God damn it. "Lawrence pushes himself off Abbie and bunches his trousers at the open fly.

Abbie rolls onto her side and draws breaths in against the grimy floor, tears mixing with dirt coat her cheeks as she cries against the hard concrete.

The side door leading to the garden slams shut as the garage door swings open.

Tom runs into the garage followed by Isabella. "Where is he?"

"He ran out there." Abbie nods at the side door and Tom crashes through it. Purple wisteria flowers rain down from the trellis above the doorway as Tom disappears, leaving it open.

"Abbie!" Isabella's face is in front of her. She pulls Abbie's tracks back up over her hips and clasps her bound hands in her own. "It's over now." She pulls Abbie against her and holds her while she trembles.

Isabella grabs a knife from her waist and Abbie gasps.

Isabella smiles. "I'm going to cut your wrists and ankles free."

Abbie lets her breath out and a giggle starts in her throat, and she lets it bubble to the surface. "I'm so sorry. I don't know why I'm laughing."

"You're in shock." Tom's voice is next to her. He dusts dirt from his shirt and elbows, a graze colours his left temple.

Isabella peels the tape off Abbie's hands, and she grimaces as it rips at her raw skin. "What happened to your head?" She rotates her wrists as they become free.

"He was closing the door to his car when I caught up. I grabbed hold of it. He slammed his foot down and tore up the driveway, leaving me in the gravel."

"He got away?"

"Yes. But you're safe. He won't find you again. I promise." He kneels beside her, wraps an arm around her shoulders and pecks her on the head. "Abs?"

"Yes?"

"Why were your tracks around your knees?"

Abbie looks at Tom's jaw, knowing it will be rigid and tense. "Why are you asking a question you know the answer to?"

"Hoping I'm wrong."

"Well there's a first time for everything… thankfully."

"We have to get out of here." He drops his arm from her shoulder.

Isabella frees Abbie's ankles and holds a hand out. "Can you stand?"

"Yes." She gets to her feet and puts a hand against the wall for support. "I'm fine."

Isabella holds Abbie's elbow as she hobbles to the door.

Tom stops at the workbench and scoops up the laptop. "At least we have something useful to take back to Martha."

"Will she be angry he got away?" Abbie steadies herself by holding the doorframe and waits for Tom.

"Livid. I can't wait."

Abbie grabs him in a hug. "You're a pain in the arse."

39

TOM

Martha paces back and forth in front of Tom while he sits on the lumpy sofa.

"This is typical of you Tom. It's like the time you left Kat alive in the old boarding house. You let your emotions and concern for people you care about cloud your judgement."

"It's actually not."

Martha stops and glares at him. "We have no idea where Lawrence is now."

"Thanks for the newsflash."

"Why didn't you grab him?"

"Excuse me? I'm terribly sorry I couldn't crowbar open a garage door in silence. I'm terribly sorry he was out the garden door before I could get inside. And I'm even *more* sorry I got hold of his open car door and got a hand on his shirt, might I add, before he stamped his foot on the accelerator and I fell off a speeding car. I'm a failure. Obviously."

"Didn't think to go around and find the possibility of another exit point *before* using a crowbar on the up and over?"

"Yes. We were working that out when I heard Abbie screaming blue murder... so y'know..."

"As I said... emotions and concern."

"I'll try and be a cardboard cut-out in future."

Martha huffs and sits. "You're impossible."

"There's also that little matter of me giving his laptop to James. But... let's not mention what I was actually *able* to achieve. It's far more fun to talk about what I *couldn't* do."

Martha narrows her eyes at Tom but says nothing.

James bursts through the door, breaking the seething silence between Tom and Martha.

Tom leaps from the sofa. "So?"

James looks around. "Where's Isabella?"

"At the hospital with Abbie." Martha ushers everyone to her desk.

"Where I'd like to be. So if we could hurry this up?"

James frowns at Tom. "Why aren't you there now?"

Tom tilts his head at Martha and purses his lips. "I had to come here and be berated." He looks back at James. "But also... girly examinations and whatever. I'll pass."

"Oh." James grimaces. "Alright. Seems Lawrence is a little more tech savvy than we gave him credit for."

Tom's phone rings as James brings information up on the laptop. "Grant."

"Where are you?"

"Pete. How lovely to hear from you." *Could today get any better?*

James looks up and gestures at the phone. "Give it."

Tom glares at James and turns his back on him. "Why are *you* calling me?"

James reaches over Tom's shoulder and tries to grab the phone. Tom turns, covers James' face with his hand and pushes him back down on the chair. "Do you *fucking* mind?"

"No, but—"

Tom turns his back on James. "C'mon Pete. Out with it. Kinda busy here."

"Where are you?"

"Getting my nails done."

"Don't fuck me around Grant. I'm here. Where are you?"

"Here where?"

"Your office. And if you think that doesn't make me cringe having to call it that…"

"My off—"

James rips the phone from Tom. "Get out. Tom's not there. Get out. I'll explain when you're safe."

Tom's heart ignites. "Fuck."

"Uncle Peter, listen to me. For once in your miserable life. Tom didn't send the text. It was—hello?" James' face pales and he holds the phone out to Tom.

Tom snatches the phone, glaring at James. "Pete."

"Tom. How are you after your heroics earlier today? I must admit I almost thought you'd got me in the car."

"You really have lost your mind. Though, it was never complete to begin with."

Lawrence laughs. "So... I shall expect you soon?"

Tom's gut writhes as he pictures the ship, the berths, all of it. Sweat prickles all over his skin and he opens his mouth, but no words come out.

"Tom? I assume you'll be coming to save the day again?"

"You've taken the First Sea Lord hostage on a navy ship." Tom flicks his eyes to Martha, and she picks up her phone and wanders off with it against her ear. "Do you honestly think the sailors aren't going to get in your way?"

"Ahhh... They haven't noticed anything amiss. I'm the perfectly sane Commodore, coming on board with the First Sea Lord for a visit. Unlike some people... who shall remain nameless. Tom Grant. I think about the long game and plan things meticulously."

"How fortuitous you have that luxury."

"Indeed."

Tom grips the phone tighter as the realisation he's getting back on the ship. It can't be avoided sinks in. "What's next?"

"Come have tea with me. Or scotch. Whichever you prefer." The phone goes dead.

Tom lowers himself into the chair and places the phone on

Martha's desk. He drops his head into his hands and digs his fingers into his hair.

"Tom?" James' voice is soft.

"What?" He doesn't look up.

"Is Uncle Peter okay?"

"I don't know."

"Shit."

"I thought you hated him?"

"I do. But… he doesn't deserve to die."

"Agreed. Tell me what we know."

"Lawrence sent a text via his laptop making it look as though it came from you. He asked Uncle Peter to come to *Arrochar* and assist with some enquiries."

"He's dumb enough to fall for that?" *Of course he is.*

"You also apparently told him the killer was in custody, so it was simply some loose ends."

Tom sighs and shakes his head. "Then?"

"Then—"

"Alright." Martha's voice is behind him. "The crew are under the impression Moore and Lawrence are wanting to *observe* the ship. I just spoke with the medic."

"Mike?"

Martha nods. "The secretary is aware of the situation, at least what we know at this point."

"Which isn't much."

"No. Not until you get onboard and end this circus."

At the mention of going on board, Tom's throat dries. "C'mon then." His gestures to James.

"One moment. Tom?"

Tom blows a long breath out. "Meet me in the car, James."

Martha waits until James shuts the office door and turns to Tom. "Can you go back there?"

"Piece of cake."

"Don't lie to me. I'll mobilise another team if you can't do this."

"Are you joking? I'm fine. We're wasting time with this non discussion."

Martha gives him a hard stare.

Tom draws a circle in the air with his finger in front of her face. "Don't do that."

"Do what?"

"That stern business. You know it doesn't work."

"I'm concerned."

"Don't be. Are we done? I've got to go onto a ship I hate to rescue a man I hate and stop another man I hate. It's been a lovely day, frankly."

"Keep me in the loop."

Tom's phone rings again and he slaps it to his ear as he jogs from the office. "Grant."

"Very formal." Isabella's voice is soft and comforting in comparison to Lawrence's bark.

"Hey. How's Abs?"

"She's fine. A bit bruised and sore but fine."

"Bruised and sore?"

"Face and back. Relax."

"Right."

"You sound like you're running."

"We found Lawrence."

"Where?"

"Just stay with Abs okay?"

"Don't you dare. Where are you going?"

Tom gets to the car and finds James in the driver's seat. He opens the driver's side door and yanks James out by the sleeve. He dips the phone under his chin. "Nice try though."

"You're talking on the phone." James scowls as he trudges to the other side of the car.

"Tom!"

"James is with me. Don't panic."

"With you where?"

"Iz, I have to go. I'll be fine. Everything's fine. Don't leave Abbie okay?"

"Tom Gra—"

Tom throws the phone into the cup holders and starts driving.

"Did you just hang up on Isabella?"

"Yep."

James winces.

"I like to live on the edge." Tom takes a sharp turn and James slams against his door. "Sorry."

"No you aren't."

40

TOM

"Are we going aboard?" James hops from one foot to the other.

Tom stares at the imposing ship, gently pulling against its restraints. "You know, some people think ships look majestic."

"They do?"

"Yeah. I don't."

"What does it look like to you?"

"A floating torture chamber."

"Where my uncle is currently on board with a psychopath…"

"Yes. And the crew."

"So…?"

Tom squints at James. "Lawrence won't do anything to him if we aren't on the ship."

"Why won't he?"

"Because he likes to be the star of the show. And if no-one is there to watch and applaud… it's a wasted effort." Tom's phone rings and he grimaces. He puts the phone to his ear but says nothing.

"Are you going to stand there staring at the ship all day?"

"Maybe. It's very majestic."

James snorts.

"Your tea's getting cold."

"I thought you said we could have scotch?"

"Your ice-cubes are melting."

"I drink it neat."

"Of course you do. Straight from the bottle."

Tom's nostrils flare and he grits his teeth. "Put Moore on the phone."

"I'd love to oblige but… no."

"Put Moore on the phone."

"Tell me Tom, Why haven't you run onboard, guns blazing to save the old coot? Isn't that more your style?"

"I adjust to the circumstances."

"Hmmm. What makes you think I haven't done away with him yet?"

"Where's the fun in that?"

A scuffle sounds down the phone line and Tom flicks his eyes to James. "He's alive. Stop stressing."

"I'm not stressing. Much."

"You're way too nice to him after what he did to you—"

"Tom." Peter Moore's voice is urgent.

"Pete. Not having a good day are you?"

"He's insane. Come and get me out of here. I swear I'll send Isabella back to Russia if you—"

"First of all. You'd be dead. So… no you won't. Second, we made a deal. Third, I'm coming to get you, so stop getting your petticoat in a twist."

"I bet you love speaking to the First Sea Lord like that, don't you?"

"It's rather liberating."

"Tom. Please. I've tried to reason with—"

"And he was unsuccessful." Lawrence's voice is back, louder, and far more jovial than Moore's. "I'm beyond reasoning. No-one listens to reason it seems."

"Including you. What say… you get off the ship and we have that cup of tea." Tom pauses, knowing his attempt is futile.

"Ten minutes or he's dead. I love a good game of hide and seek." Lawrence ends the call and Tom keeps the phone held against his ear.

"Well?" James chews on his bottom lip and looks at Tom.

Tom continues to hold the phone against his ear and says nothing.

"Tom? What's he saying?" James hisses.

Tom swallows the dread building in his throat and fills his lungs before letting out the breath slowly. He lowers the phone and slides it into his pocket. "We have to find him."

"Huh? We know where he is. He's on the ship. So why aren't we?"

"No, I mean… he wants us to find him on the ship like we are playing some children's game in the back garden." Tom cracks his neck and keeps trying to keep his breath even.

"Then, shall we?" James flips his wrist as though showing Tom to a table in a fancy restaurant.

"Yep." Tom's feet are cemented to the spot. *This isn't ideal.*

James walks a few steps before stopping and looking over his shoulder at Tom. "Whoa. Are you alright?"

"I'm fine."

"You're all pale and…" James walks back to him, peering at his hands. "Are you trembling?"

Tom gives himself a shake and clears his throat. "Adrenaline. Let's go." He walks towards the gangway. "Are you coming?"

James jogs up beside him. "You still look like you've seen a ghost."

Tom reaches the gangway, and his feet stop again. His gut writhes like a pile of garden worms and he clutches the railing to stay upright.

"Jesus, Tom. Did you eat a bad curry or something?"

Tom swallows and squeezes his eyes shut. "No."

"Are you scared?"

"No I'm not fucking scared."

"Then?"

"I don't *know*." Tom pinches the bridge of his nose. "Just

give me a sec and shut up." Tom winces inwardly, knowing he's being unfair to James. He sighs and turns to him. "I can't explain it. I'm… it's making me..." Tom leans over the railing. "Fuck."

"Making you what?"

"Anxious. It's making me anxious." He blows another breath out as his vision sways. He grips the railing tighter and slowly stands upright.

"The situation makes you anxious?"

"No. The ship."

James nods. "Of course it would."

"What?"

"You've had bad experiences here. Really bad ones. So… it makes sense."

Tom blinks. "Since when did you turn into Dr Phil?"

"I'm just saying…" James looks around and scratches his head. "I know it's not Lawrence or Moore or the gun shoved in your belt freaking you out. But... I'm coming with you. I won't let anything happen to either of us."

Tom looks at the ship and back to James.

"I've got your back, Tom."

He does. "You do."

"I do."

"Well, fuck. This is inconvenient."

"What is?"

"Realising you aren't a completely useless git."

James grins. "It's going to be fine. And we have to save

Uncle Peter, or I'll never hear the end of it from my father." He rolls his eyes.

Tom nods. "Right. Let's get this over with." He turns and walks up the gangway, knowing James is right behind him.

Tom sets a foot inside and looks around. The corridor is deserted in both directions. *Weird. Where is everyone?* He moves aside to let James in and holds a hand out to stop him walking any further. Tom takes out his gun and flicks his head to make James follow.

"Shhh." Tom listens to the sounds of the ship and takes a deep breath, the familiar metallic, chemical smells fill his nostrils and the sweat trickling down his back intensifies. "Office," Tom whispers, nodding in the direction.

"He won't be there," James mumbles behind Tom.

"I know."

"Huh?"

"Follow me and shut up."

They reach the office, and the door hangs open. After clearing the room Tom sees amber liquid in a glass in the middle of the desk. A note is propped up against it reading **I dare you.** The back of his tongue floods and he swallows three times. The urge to lift that glass and down the nip is almost overwhelming. He squeezes the grip of the gun and walks around the room, stopping at the porthole.

"Hey, do you think old lady Maxine's dog ate her finger like she said?"

Tom rolled his eyes and kept tinkering with the antenna on his remote control car. "No Chris. Don't be daft. She's scaring you so you don't short cut through her garden again."

"How do you know?"

"Cause she has a fluffy little yappy dog. It didn't eat her finger."

"Dare you to go through her garden."

Tom looked up. "Why?"

"To prove you aren't scared of her dog."

"I never said I was."

"Yeah but you also don't shortcut through her garden."

"Cause I'm not a disrespectful git like you."

"Chicken."

"I'm ten. I'm not a chicken."

"I'm eight and I cut through her garden." Chris started clucking like a chicken.

Tom shook his head. "Fine." He stood and threw the remote control for the car to Chris. "Hold this."

"You can never say no to a dare." Chris laughed as Tom jogged away towards the fluffy white dog he could already hear barking.

"What's with the whisky?"

Tom huffs a chuckle. "To remind me of my place." Tom walks to the desk and picks up the glass. He hurls it across the room, and it smashes against the wall, whisky splashing all over the floor.

James stares at the broken glass a moment before turning back to Tom as though nothing had happened. "Your place?"

"My weakness. My…" Tom shakes his head. "He's mind-fucking me."

He takes another look at the desk and notices empty pill bottles. Nausea swells in his gut and he bends forward over the desk, glaring at the empty bottles. "You bastard," he mumbles.

"C'mon Tom, you need to get it together."

Tom squints at James. "Did you just tell me to… get it together?" He stands upright. *He's right though.*

"Yes."

"Who do you—"

A gunshot sounds from deep within the ship. Tom's head snaps to the door and he's running before he realises what he's doing.

"Where are we going?" James keeps up.

"He's in the berths."

"How do you know?"

Tom stops and James runs into him. "Because he wants me in the one place he knows I don't want to be." Adrenaline peaks through Tom's blood and the tremble starts again. He pushes both hands against the wall and leans forward to catch his breath. "And I should have realised it before now."

"Can you go there?"

"Yep." Chris's laugh fills his ears, and he closes his eyes. *Not now.*

"Dare me."

"What?"

"Nothing. C'mon. Let's retrieve your useless uncle."

"You good?"

"Fucking fantastic." Tom pushes himself off the wall as another gunshot echoes through the ship.

Finally sailors emerge from different corridors and rooms.

Tom's pulse ignites. "Marshall on deck," he shouts as he runs. "Now!" He turns corners, ducks under bulkheads not stopping to think or make sure the sailors did as he ordered. He skids to a halt as he and James reach the berths and slaps both hands against the bulkhead above him, his gun makes a clanging sound of metal on metal.

"He could pop out of any of them." James pants behind Tom.

"No. I know where he is." Tom drops his hands and racks the slide of his gun.

"Where?"

"Chris's berth." Tom steps forward and his gut plunges. "Where Chris died," he whispers.

"I'm right here." James' voice is soft behind him, and it makes Tom drop his head and pause.

"Thank you, James."

They hasten their pace towards the berth and Tom halts just before it. He pricks his ears and waits. He swallows against his arid throat and taps the barrel of his gun against the wall.

"Take your time." Lawrence's voice sounds from behind Tom. "We can wait for you to have your meltdown." A gun is pressed to the back of Tom's head.

"Of course you were hiding… like some kind of rodent."

"I left a drink for you to calm the nerves. Did it help?"

"Pete?" Tom ignores Lawrence's baiting. "You alright?"

A mumble and humphing answers him.

"There's your dulcet tones… very nice."

"He's alive," James whispers behind him.

"Weapons, if you please?" Lawrence grabs hold of Tom's gun while pushing his own harder behind Tom's ear. "Yours as well hero sidekick…"

Movement next to Tom tells him James hands over his weapon. *Well, shit.*

"There's good lads." The gun slides around Tom's head as Lawrence moves in front of them. He lifts the gun away and grins at Tom. "So obedient. I'm impressed." He gestures towards Chris's berth as he walks backwards. "Why don't you come in?"

James turns and nods at him. "Let's go."

Tom swallows. "Yeah. Right." *One foot in front of the other.* He follows James into the crowded space and looks into the eyes of Admiral Peter Moore.

Moore has his hands tied behind him, tape over his mouth and he appears to be tethered to the bunk by a rope around his neck.

Tethered to Chris's bunk. *The bunk where he took his last breath.*

"You certainly spared no effort." Tom looks at Moore as he speaks to Lawrence and concentrates on keeping his voice even. His insides may as well be on fire.

Lawrence sits casually on the opposite bunk to Moore and smiles. "Well, now we're all here, let's have that chat?" He gestures for Tom and James to sit on the bunk alongside Moore.

James sits next to his uncle and Moore fixes him with watery, uneasy eyes.

Tom lowers himself onto the bunk, ignoring the wrenching of his gut. He glares at Lawrence. "Now what?"

"We fix this mess."

"This oughta be good." Tom folds his arms.

"Moore killed Daphne. Moore is charged with such. Abigail is charged as an accessory. I am cleared of any wrongdoing or involvement. I get my promotion. Life goes on."

Tom huffs a laugh and claps his hands. "You're more insane than I gave you credit for."

Lawrence raises both brows and tilts his head. "Hmmm? I don't see any insanity in this plan."

Tom leans forward and squints. "You're holding the First Sea Lord hostage… and now James and me by default. You tried to rape Abigail Perkins after beating her with a shovel. You killed your wife, bribed an Iranian oil tycoon, and have black-mailed all and sundry. You also have crew on this vessel that you are putting in danger, who by the way, are going to know something isn't quite right by now. I don't understand how you think this can be… salvaged."

"Don't you have quite the imagination. And how pray tell… do you intend to prove any of this?"

"We have Liam Hampshire. Remember?"

Lawrence throws his head back and laughs. "That insipid little germ? Good luck getting him to hold up under pressure. He's pathetic."

"We also have Abbie. And after today we will have Pete. We also have the unedited CCTV footage. I'd say you're well and truly fucked. Excuse my French."

"You know all this could have been avoided if everyone just stayed in their own lane and left me to my job." Lawrence's face deepens in colour, and he stretches his arm out, pointing the gun at Moore's face.

Moore grunts and pushes himself back against the wall while James grasps his leg and squeezes. "It's okay Uncle Peter. Stay calm."

"Yes Admiral." Lawrence stands. "Stay calm… I can help you with that if you desire."

Bile rises in Tom's throat as Lawrence pulls a handful of pills out of his trouser pocket. "These should do the trick. Tom? Would you agree? And this bunk is the perfect place for such a demise. No?"

"What the hell is wrong with you?" Tom grips the mattress either side of his thighs. He wants to stand and wrestle Lawrence to the floor, but his body is rigid and won't move. The sounds of voices echoing through the berth trigger everything from years ago and his brain can't connect with his limbs. Sweat dots his brow and breathing is an effort. *Fuck this.* He glares at Lawrence as the walls close in and his vision fogs.

"Problem Tom?"

Tom draws in a breath and curls his lip at Lawrence. "No."

"Nice try. I'm not buying it."

"I don't give a fuck what you're buying. You know as well as I do you aren't getting out of here a free man. So… let's finish this charade?"

Lawrence pushes the muzzle of the gun against Moore's temple.

Moore closes his eyes as Lawrence rips the tape from his mouth. He takes in a gasp of air and clamps his mouth shut.

James jumps up and grabs Lawrence by the arm.

Before Tom can react Lawrence has jabbed James in the jaw, and he falls to the floor.

Lawrence leans over him and jams the gun into his ribs. "What the hell do you think you're doing?"

James dabs a finger against his fat lip and glares at Lawrence.

"I want my demands met. Then we all walk out of here happy as pigs in shit."

Tom grabs James by the collar and pulls him up onto the bunk. "That's not going to happen. And you know it."

"Okay fair. One or two of you may die." He grins at Moore. "*You* are a definite." He pushes his face to within an inch of Moore's. "You sleep with my wife and think you can get away with that?"

"She hated you Matthew." Moore's voice is raw, but anger sits in his words. "You were nothing to her." He juts his face forward so their noses touch. "Fucking nothing."

Lawrence grins, points the gun at the mattress between Moore's legs and pretends to shoot.

Moore startles and shouts indecipherable garble.

"It's alright Peter. Your manhood's intact. For now."

Moore pants as sweat streams down his face and his body trembles.

Lawrence grabs the back of Moore's hair and jerks his head back.

Tom moves to get up and Lawrence turns the gun on him. "Try me."

James scrubs his hands over his face and into his hair. "Fuck," he squeaks.

Tom nudges him with his elbow as he stays seated. "Trust me," he mumbles.

Lawrence turns his attention and the gun back to Moore. "Open your mouth. "

Moore stares into Lawrence's face and keeps his mouth pursed shut. The tremble in his body increases.

"Open your goddamn mouth, Admiral." Lawrence jams the gun harder into Moore's ribs causing him to release air. Lawrence takes this moment to shove a handful of pills into his mouth. Moore can't move his head away given the way he's tied by the neck, but his body squirms and moans escape his throat. Lawrence slaps his hand over Moore's mouth. "Swallow."

Tom's pulse may as well be thunder in his ears. His eyes are glued to Moore, whose jaw isn't moving.

Lawrence swats him in the back of the head with the butt of

the gun. "I said swallow."

"What are you giving him?" Tom's voice comes out forced and higher than usual. He clears his throat and glares at Lawrence. "Well?"

Lawrence winks at Tom. "Opioids. Got myself a little mixture here from the shoulder injury dear Abigail caused me. She stabbed me. Remember?"

"Yes. You seem to have recovered quite well."

"I may have embellished my injury... for dramatic purposes." Lawrence grins.

"There's at least eight pills in your hand."

"Correct."

Tom narrows his eyes. "You were always going to kill him."

"Correct again! You win."

James twitches next to Tom. "We have to do something," he hisses.

Thanks for the hot tip. Tom glances around the berth looking for something, anything he can use as a weapon.

Moore gasps and coughs. "Water," he whispers.

"I'll allow it." Lawrence grabs a water bottle from the top bunk and throws it to Tom. "You want to help so much... give the man water."

Tom catches the bottle and crouches in front of Moore. Lawrences pushes the gun into Tom's back. Tom squashes a sigh of irritation and holds his breath instead. He tips the water into Moore's mouth. "I'm not going to let you die. You understand?" he whispers.

Moore nods as Lawrence laughs. "How many times have you made promises you can't keep, Tom?"

Before Tom can answer James jumps from the bunk and pushes Lawrence to the chest with both hands. Lawrence stumbles backwards and his gun goes off, hitting the ceiling. James jumps on top of Lawrence and punches his face. He makes a grab for the gun, but Lawrence has hold of it with both hands.

Tom drops the water bottle and stamps his foot into Lawrence's crotch. He howls and rolls onto his side but somehow the gun goes off.

Tom blinks and everything slows to a crawl as James topples off Lawrence to the floor. Bright red blood colours the front of James' shirt. Tom forgets about Moore and Lawrence, dropping to his knees next to James. He pushes his hands onto the wound in James' abdomen.

"Breathe James. It's alright." Tom straightens and takes his shirt off. He balls it up and pushes it against the wound.

Lawrence huffs and puffs behind Tom and he turns back to land a cross to Lawrence's jaw.

He squawks and lies on the floor, blinking at the ceiling.

Tom looks back into James' pale face. "I need you to hold this." Tom pushes the t -shirt harder against James' body. "Can you do that?" James nods before his eyes widen at something behind Tom.

Tom ducks to the left as Lawrence's hand holding the gun narrowly misses the side of his head. He twists and kicks his legs out, hitting Lawrence in the back of the knees. He slams onto his back and his gun slides out of his hand.

Tom climbs over Lawrence to get to the gun but an elbow to the gut stops him short. He doubles over as Lawrence wriggles out from under him.

Tom gasps in air as Lawrence pulls himself off the floor using Moore's bunk for support. Tom grabs at Lawrence's shirt but Lawrence kicks him in the chest. Tom stumbles backwards and falls on the floor. Lawrence stamps his foot down on Tom's arm.

Tom tries to catch his breath as everything slows again. He looks around the berth from where he is splayed on his back. James holds Tom's shirt against his wound, bright red blood colouring the once grey material. Moore's eyes are closed and vomit dribbles down his chin, more of it paints his front.

"This… this is your last chance to do what's right," Tom manages between breaths. "Call nine nine nine for them."

Lawrence throws his head back as he points his gun square into Tom's face. "An absolute riot you are, Tom. It's been a real pleasure outplaying you. Any last words?"

Tom stares at the ceiling above him, Chris's laugh echoes in his ears before Isabella's citrus shampoo fills his nostrils. *This is it?*

"What on earth…?" Lawrence's voice is full of irritation.

Tom squints as he tries to make out the object flying through the air above him towards Lawrence.

A soft, wet thud sounds and Lawrence drops the gun.

41

TOM

Tom scrambles off the floor and picks up Lawrence's gun. He stands over Lawrence and points it at him as he writhes on the floor, gasping for breath. A knife sticks out of his chest, half a blade deep.

Tom looks at Isabella and Abbie standing at the entrance to the berth. "Not all the way in, Iz?"

"I wasn't sure if you wanted him dead or not." She runs to James and presses her hands against Tom's balled up shirt seeped in fresh blood.

Abbie drops to her knees, her eyes fixed on Lawrence.

"Abs? I need you to call nine nine nine."

Abbie nods and grabs the phone Isabella holds out to her. She sits next to Moore and feels for a pulse. "Yes… I need an ambulance, three of them…Um sixty something, male." Abbie holds the phone against her shoulder with her chin and takes the rope away from Moore's neck. "Yes he's breathing but… barely. His lips are blue. He has sick down his shirt…" She looks at Tom. "What's he had?"

"Fentanyl."

Lawrence wheezes and half chuckles from the floor. "Nice… guess."

"Chris used Fentanyl." Tom glares at Lawrence. "Tell them he has ingested about eight pills around ten minutes ago."

Abbie nods and keeps talking into the phone. "We also have a gunshot victim…"

"Tick… tick, tick." Lawrence gasps another breath in. "There may have been some codeine in there as well." Lawrence huffs and sucks in a breath. "Who can say?"

Tom grabs the rope Abbie discarded from Moore and yanks Lawrence's hands behind his back.

Lawrence groans. "I've got… a damn knife sticking… out of my… chest."

"Well spotted."

"So… do you mind?"

"Not really."

Isabella squeals and pats James' cheeks. "James. Open your eyes. C'mon."

Tom's heart squeezes. "Fuck." He loops the rope around one of the bunks and secures Lawrence before jumping over to James and Isabella.

"Tom… he closed his eyes and hasn't opened them for about a minute now…"

"Calm down Iz… you know how this works. He's lost a lot of blood." Tom turns back to Abbie who has started CPR on Moore. "How long?"

"I don't know... she said she's sending three to us, priority one... three, two…"

"Fuck." Tom moves the balled up shirt and inspects James' wound. "It looks like it's gone all the way through."

"Tom we need to keep him alive," Isabella's voice wavers and tears slide down her cheeks.

"Let's hope it hasn't hit his spleen." Tom grabs a sheet from the top bunk and rips it in half. He balls it up and replaces the sopped shirt, pushing the sheet against the bloody wound. "Pressure on this. Don't let go."

Isabella nods as sobs escape her mouth and she pushes both hands against the sheet. She rests her forehead against James' and whispers to him.

Tom goes to Abbie as Lawrence moans and whines from the floor.

"I'm... here too." Lawrence gripes. "My blood... will be on... your... hands."

"I'll be sure to paint a picture."

"Someone... else… dead in this very… spot… because of... you." Lawrence drops his head back and gasps air. "*Three* someone's... is that a ... record for you?"

Tom's jaw tightens and he kneels on the floor beside Lawrence. "You need to shut your fucking mouth."

Lawrence leers at Tom. "Or?"

As though moving independently of his body, Tom's arm swings and he uppercuts Lawrence, snapping his head back against the wall.

"Tom!" A voice from the berth entrance barks.

He turns to find Mike moving towards him through the cramped space. He pushes Tom out of the way and opens his medical bag. He pulls out a thick bandage and hands it to Tom.

"Wrap the knife."

Tom grabs the bandage as Mike turns his attention to James.

Lawrence laughs as his face glistens and his breaths wheeze.

"Save James. Please." Tom wraps the bandage and Lawrence yelps.

Tom fixes eyes with Isabella, her face is blotchy, and tears stain her cheeks. Tom tries to soften his eyes for her, but it starts the flip flopping in his gut and the tightness in his chest.

Mike grabs Isabella's hand pushes it against James' side and her attention is back on James.

Tom pushes his free hand against his lungs, willing them to relax and let him breathe freely. If anything, it tightens his chest more and his glares at Lawrence as the walls around them inch closer and closer together.

"You thought you'd win down here." Tom grabs Lawrence's jaw and jerks his face towards him.

"I *was*... winning... until your... angel of... death turned... up." Lawrence pulls in a ragged, raw breath.

"You aren't dead."

"No. I... refuse... to let you... kill me."

"James needs a transfusion." Mike turns to Tom. "The ambulance has been called?"

"They said first available." Abbie pants as she continues CPR on Moore.

"We need them now. Can you continue CPR?"

Abbie nods, counting in huffs.

"Are you sure? That's the First Sea—"

"She's sure!" Tom glares at Mike. "Keep James alive."

Mike grunts, turning back to James. He pulls another sheet from a bunk and tears it into strips. He winds the strips around James' waist and pulls them tight.

"Breathe!" Abbie sniffles and coughs as she keeps compressions up on Moore.

"Iz." Tom waves Isabella over now that she has been relieved of pushing against James' wound. "Can you hold this? I need to help Abbie."

Isabella nods and wipes the back of her hand across her eyes.

Tom waits until her hands cover his before letting go. "If he gives you any shit, punch him in the throat."

Mike huffs but doesn't turn around.

"You'll go... inside if I... die." Lawrence glares at Isabella.

"And if you don't die, you go inside." Isabella shrugs.

"I'm the... victim in all—" Lawrence howls in pain.

Isabella lets go of the handle of the knife. "You need to shut up. Or I twist it harder."

"Good luck." Tom grins at Lawrence before turning his attention to Abbie.

Tom puts his hand on Abbie's shoulder, and she looks up at him. He flicks his head, and she moves out of the way so Tom can take over compressions. "Go outside, I can hear sirens… get them in here fast. Yeah?" Tom pushes on Moore's chest and sweat streams down his back. "C'mon Pete… keep breathing."

Abbie runs from the berth.

Tom keeps up compressions as Lawrence hollers and moans behind him. Tom grits his teeth. "If you could shut the fuck up… that'd be helpful."

"I… need aid… Mike... "

"You need to wait your turn." Tom pants as he pushes into Moore's unresponsive chest.

"I'm a fucking… Commodore…" He wheezes.

"Were…" Tom pushes again.

"What?"

"*Were*. You certainly won't be after today…" Tom puts his ear against Moore's mouth as six paramedics rush into the already cramped berth. Tom jumps up to make room. "Fentanyl and codeine pills and who knows what else…" He shoots a glare at Lawrence.

A paramedic nods and pulls a needle and vial out of his kit. "How long ago?" He fills the needle.

"Around twenty minutes by now."

The paramedic nods again and slams an injection into Moore's thigh. Within a few seconds Moore gasps and his eyes pop open. He tries to move and sit up and flails his arm, hitting the paramedic in the face. Tom grabs Moore's shoulders and pushes him back down.

"Pete. Stop. Look at me." Tom rolls him onto his side. "Can you hear me?"

Moore blinks and nods. "What…?"

"You overdosed." Tom checks the paramedic who has resumed his position on the bunk next to Moore. "Pete… this medic is going to help you. Do you understand?"

Moore heaves in a breath and frowns. "Corpsman?"

"Paramedic." Tom looks at the paramedic's name badge. "This is Mitchell. And he's going to look after you." Tom nods at Mitchell and moves out of the way. He falls onto his backside and drops his head between his knees.

Mike is talking to two paramedics who are busy pulling things out of their bags.

Another pair are with Lawrence as Isabella stands next to them, watching James. Her face is pinched, and she pulls a rag of discarded sheet from the floor to blow her nose.

The frantic noise and sounds of paramedics working hastens Tom's breathing, and he tries to ward off the panic rising in his chest. He squeezes his eyes shut as the noise and frantic commotion fade into a foggy blur of white noise. He gasps for air as though drowning.

"Tom?" Isabella's arms slide around his shoulders and her warmth surrounds him. He drops his head against her chest. "They're taking James to the hospital."

Tom nods but can't bear to look up and see a stretcher being carried from the berth. *Never again.* "How is he?" Tom keeps his eyes closed.

"Critical."

Tom's chest implodes and he concentrates on breathing. He slaps both palms to the floor to ground himself as the tiny space contorts and sways around him.

"We need to take the stab victim with us." A muffled female voice says over Tom's shoulder.

Rage fires Tom's gut and he grits his teeth. "He's not a victim."

"I'm sorry?"

Tom looks into the face of a female paramedic. "He's not a victim." Her face is blurry at first but slowly clears as Tom pushes his palms harder against the floor.

"Ah… right well. He needs treatment we can't give him here, so…"

"I'll go with him." Abbie's voice is cold, and it helps snap Tom out of the cocoon of white noise.

He notices MP's in the corridor and nods. "I'll organise a relief for you." He swallows as he hears his own voice come out shaky and weak. *Stop.*

"Take your time." Abbie glares at Lawrence as he's being helped onto a stretcher. He moans and winces as they strap him in.

Tom clenches his fist and glares at him.

Get it together.

Tom gets off the floor and ignores Lawrence as they take him from the berth. "You'll be okay?" He pulls Abbie into a hug, and it helps his bearings come back, but the tremble in his knees threatens to stick around.

"Yep. I have things I need to say. And he can't get away from me in the hospital. Under guard."

"Or attack you with a shovel."

"That too." Abbie smiles. "I owe you."

"No you don't." Tom steps aside and gestures Abbie through. "I'll be at the hospital soon."

Abbie nods and smiles at Isabella before disappearing.

Tom holds Isabella against him and kisses the top of her head.

"Right." Mitchell is next to Tom. "His vitals are back up. He's refusing to come to the hospital, so I advise he sees his GP sooner rather than later."

Moore moves to the edge of the bunk and sits forward over his knees, gripping the edge of the mattress with white knuckles. "Where's James?"

Tom drops his arm from Isabella's shoulder. He sits next to Moore. "They've taken him to hospital. Where you should be going too."

Moore massages his temples. "Is he okay?"

"He's critical."

Moore looks up at Tom. "He's alive though. Right?"

"So far." A knot tightens in Tom's gut. "You need to go too."

"I don't need a hospital."

"Well, my mental health doesn't need me on this ship... but here I am."

Moore stares into Tom's face, his own softening at the edges. "Yes. You are."

"So maybe you do me a solid and go to hospital, so I don't feel like it wasn't worth it."

Moore stares at the opposite bunk. "You said you wouldn't let me die."

"That's right. So go and make sure you stay breathing through the night?"

Moore inhales and winces. "I feel like I've been hit by a truck."

Tom raises his eyebrows and says nothing.

Moore sighs. "Okay fine. I'll go." He stands. "But I'll walk off this ship with my own two legs."

Mitchell nods and holds a hand out, gesturing Moore past him. "Fair enough, I'll walk with you."

Moore turns back to Tom as Isabella stands next to him. "Thank you. Both."

Tom tips his head and Moore nods once before shuffling away.

Tom spins slowly, looking over the empty berth. Isabella takes his hand, and he stops in front of Chris's bunk. Tom blinks and squeezes Isabella's hand tighter.

"Tom?"

He blinks again as the familiar wave of panic and heart thumping hits him in the throat. He releases a heavy breath before letting go of Isabella's hand. He grabs hold of the rumpled blanket and sheet with both hands and rips them from the bunk.

"What have you done?" He grips the blanket against himself and drops onto his knees beside the bunk. He opens his eyes, and the pillow is dipped in the middle, as though someone has their head on it. He drops the blanket and sheet and grabs the pillow. He hugs it against his chest and drops his face into it. He lets out a shout, or scream he can't be sure, into the down and holds his breath to stop the unshed sobs in his throat.

A hand touches him on the bicep, and he tenses.

"Tom? It's alright. It's a pillow. And an empty bunk."

Tom buries his face further into the pillow and shakes his head. "He... he was here."

The pillow slides away from his face as Isabella's pulls it from him and puts it on the top bunk. "It was just bundled up bedsheets. There's no one there." Her voice is gentle and calm, and it sets a wave of grief flooding over him.

"But... he was right there. I could... I could see him. His face was pale, and his lips were blue... I..." Tom falls onto his backside and drops his forehead against the mattress. "I should have come earlier." He looks at Isabella. "He'd still be here. I could have stopped it."

Isabella runs her hand through his hair and rests it at the back of his neck. "It's not your fault."

"This place..." Tom looks around. "It's always noisy. For

me." He rests his eyes back on Isabella's serene face. "You can't hear it. But I can."

"I know."

Tom studies the blue of her irises and he swallows the pain down. "You do know." He reaches to her face and cups her jaw in his hand. "I'm sorry."

"For what? Being human? Having emotions?" She smiles and rubs her face into his hand. "You're allowed to feel things Tom."

He gazes at her, and he can breathe again.

"I'm going to give you a minute." She stands and his hand slides down to her shoulder before he drops it to the mattress. "I'll be right outside. Okay?"

He nods and pushes his face against the mattress as she leaves. When he looks up again he is alone. *I'm never alone in this berth.*

He sits on Chris's bunk and grips the mattress either side of his legs.

"Will you still visit?" Chris dropped his scooter on the grass as Tom followed the woman from Children's Services out the front gate.

"Yeah." Tom turned around. "And I'll see you at school."

"Why won't they let you stay here?"

Tom shrugged. "It's just how it is, I s'pose."

Chris jumped over his scooter and ran to Tom. He hugged him and cried. "I don't want to stay here by myself. Can I come too?"

Tom wrapped the arm not loaded with a suitcase around Chris's shoulder. "It'll be okay Chris. I'll see you on Monday. At school."

"Thomas?" The social worker woman stood at her open car door. "Come along. Your new family is waiting for you."

"New family?" Chris looked up at Tom, tears filled his eyes.

"You're my family. Doesn't matter where they take me. Okay?"

Chris nodded as Tom dawdled to the car.

"C'mon lad... in you get." The woman ushered him into the car.

Tom pushed his suitcase onto the backseat and got in. He sat up on his knees and rested his chin on his arm, watching as Chris disappeared into the horizon.

Tom sweeps his eyes around the deserted berth. He hears the noise, but it's duller somehow. He pulls the silver lighter out of his pocket and flicks the flame alight.

It's time to go now.

Tom looks at the empty space next to him on the bunk as Chris's voice rings in his head. "You're not the boss of me." Tom smiles to himself and watches the flame flicker.

Tom closes his eyes.

I dare you.

He opens his eyes and blows out the flame.

42

ABBIE

Abbie stands in the sterile hospital room while Lawrence is wheeled in from recovery. She grits her teeth and turns to look out the window while the nurses fuss. *Don't bother. He's a waste of space.* She takes a sip from a water bottle she bought and waits.

"You press this buzzer if you need me, okay Mr Lawrence?"

"Thank you... my dear." His voice is so weak it makes Abbie smile.

Abbie keeps her back turned and waits. *He can't help himself.*

"You... came to... apologise?"

Abbie snorts and keeps her back to him. "For what?"

"Causing all of this?"

She finally turns and has to swallow back the immediate shock at how frail and old he looks. He has an oxygen tube clipped to his nose and a drainage tube trailing out under his right arm. She strolls across to his bed and stands at the foot of it. "You look about eighty five."

Lawrence's eyes narrow. "A knife to the chest ages a person. But... I'll bounce back." He huffs a breath before sucking one in, wincing as his chest expands. "And that Isabella girl will be in prison."

"She should have thrown it harder."

"You know you don't... mean that." He pats the bed beside him. "Come... sit so I can touch you. You like that... remember?"

Bile threatens to climb up her throat, but she forces it down and leans forward on the end of the bed. "I'm good at faking it."

Bright pink spots appear on Lawrence's cheeks. "Does Tom know you're good at faking it?"

"Doubt it. I never had to."

Lawrence takes a breath in and coughs. Pain screws his face up and he reaches for the water cup and straw on the table next to him. He misses and it falls to the floor. "God damn it."

Abbie watches the water spread across the linoleum but doesn't move.

"Think you could assist... me?"

"I did once. Assisted you. It didn't work out so well."

Lawrence huffs and drops back onto the pillow. "I need water."

Abbie pulls her water bottle from a plastic bag and takes a

gulp. She pulls the wheelie hospital table towards her and puts the bottle on top, out of Lawrence's reach.

"You really are a… bitch of a ... thing."

"I'll take that as a compliment."

"Get out."

"Gladly. But first... I want you to know something. When you are convicted of your multitude of crimes, I am going to be front row centre in that courtroom." She leans forward again. "When you are sentenced to the best part of the life you have left in prison I'll stand and applaud. And when anyone asks me why I bothered with you, I'll tell them I was bored and you were easy, if not a little clumsy."

Lawrence curls his lip, and his eyes turn colder. "Anything else?"

Abbie picks up her water and takes another slow, nourishing gulp. She replaces the lid and leaves it on the table, still out of reach. "Yes. Don't drop the soap." She walks out the door, past the uniformed guard, without looking back. A garbled, frustrated shout follows her down the corridor, but she smiles and keeps walking.

She rounds the corner before leaning against the wall and letting out a long breath that had filled her lungs for too long.

"Abbie!"

She looks up and Isabella jogs over and hugs her. "Are you okay?"

Abbie hugs her back as she trembles and sobs sputter from her mouth. "Yep."

"Oh sweetheart." Isabella pats her back.

"I'm fine. I'm good." She pulls away from Isabella and dabs at her eyes. "I'm such a fool."

Isabella smiles. "We all fall for the wrong man at some point in our lives. Don't we?"

Abbie laughs and they walk to the waiting lounge and sit. "Have you?"

"Have I?"

"Ever fallen for the wrong man?"

"I'd never *fallen* for a man before... well... before now."

"No?"

"There have been men but... I was in hiding for many years so..." She shrugs. "I could never really pursue anything meaningful."

"One day you are going to have to tell me your story."

Before Isabella answers, an arm snakes around Abbie's shoulders and Tom hugs her against him. "You okay?" His voice and warmth bring back the tears. He releases her and sits next to Isabella. *Where he belongs.*

"Yeah. Lawrence will be fine. In case you were wondering."

"Not really. But the thought of him languishing in a jail cell kind of warms the cockles."

Isabella leans into Tom's side. "You know... he could be quite handsome. For an evil piece of trash anyway."

Abbie nods and stares out the window. "He is. Was." She shakes her head. "Whatever."

"Any news on James?" Isabella sits up and looks at Tom.

Tom shakes his head. "Still in surgery. He lost a shit-ton of blood."

A fresh wave of tears tumbles down Isabella's face and she nods, snuggling back against Tom.

"I'm so sorry," Abbie whispers.

"What for?"

"This is all my fault, Tom. If I hadn't come to you, none of this would have happened. I should have taken my medicine."

"Abs, you're innocent."

"But now your friend is… fighting to survive and you went through hell on the ship. I just…" She leans over her knees and claws her fingers through her hair. "Because of me."

"Someone thinks a lot of herself." Tom taunts and moves to sit next to Abbie. "Hey…"

She looks up through a blur of tears and sniffles.

"We would have become involved at some point anyway. It's our charter." Tom shrugs.

"It's not your fault Abbie." Isabella smiles and reaches across to grab her hand.

"And listen, I can't tell you how uncomfortable it is to be surrounded by weeping women. I'm kind of nervous."

Abbie coughs out a laugh while Isabella slaps him on the back of the head and stands. "Coffee? We'll be here a while."

Tom and Abbie both nod and she wanders away down the hall.

"I like her." Abbie wipes her nose and pulls away from Tom.

Tom opens his mouth but clamps it shut again and stands up.

Abbie looks back over her shoulder and a surgeon in scrubs, pulling his mask off stops in front of them.

"Doctor Renshaw." He shakes Tom's hand and nods to Abbie. "He lost a huge amount of blood."

Abbie holds her breath and closes her eyes.

"Fortunately the bullet missed any major arteries, but we had to remove his spleen. He's in recovery now but the next twenty four hours will be critical."

"So… not in the clear yet?"

"I'm afraid not."

Tom nods. "Ah, his mother was waiting downstairs."

"Yes, I saw her first. She was with a rather short stern woman."

"Don't mind her, that's just Satan."

Doctor Renshaw quirks a brow and squashes a grin. "I see. Well in any case, you can stay or come back in the morning."

"Thanks. We might stick around if you don't mind?"

"Not at all." He sweeps his hand towards the seats behind them. "Make yourselves comfortable."

Abbie sits. "Where's his father?"

Tom paces in front of her. "They don't get on."

"But… he could die."

"Yep."

"Wow."

Abbie looks up and sees a familiar face walking towards them.

Mike nods at Abbie and turns his attention to Tom. "Tom. I thought you'd like an update on James."

"His surgeon just saw us."

"I see. So you understand he isn't out of the woods yet."

"Yes."

Isabella reappears holding three paper cups with lids. She looks between them all and her face drops. "Oh my God. What happened?"

Tom takes the cups and hands one to Abbie. "Relax. He's alive."

"Oh thank God."

"For now," Abbie whispers.

"What?"

Mike clears his throat, and they all look at him. "Tom? If I might have a quick word?" He flicks his head down the corridor.

Tom rolls his eyes and walks past Mike down the corridor.

Mike chuckles. "He's softer than he makes out."

"I know." Both girls answer at the same time.

Mike winks at them and follows Tom away.

Abbie sips her coffee. "Thanks Isabella."

"Of course. I wasn't sure if you took sugar but—"

"I'm not talking about the coffee."

Isabella raises her brows.

"I turn up, covered in blood on your doorstep and you have no issue with helping me… knowing that Tom and I have… history."

"Why would I?" She sips her own coffee, keeping her eyes on Abbie.

Abbie shrugs. "I know I'd probably feel uneasy if it were the other way around."

"I trust him with my life. And you're his friend. He would do anything for the people that mean the most to him. I couldn't stop him even if I wanted to."

Abbie looks at the ceiling to stem the tingle in her nose. "I can't thank you enough." Her voice is husky, and she takes another sip of coffee to try and push the pain away.

"Then don't." She holds her coffee cup out to cheers it with Abbie's.

Abbie obliges before leaning in and hugging Isabella.

"Anyway," Isabella whispers. "Wait til he decides to get angry at us for risking our safety and coming on the ship."

Abbie laughs. "I have found over the years that the trick is to just ignore him 'til he finds something else to complain about."

43

TOM

Tom stops halfway down the corridor and waits for Mike to catch up. He gulps his coffee so he doesn't have to say anything as Mike stops in front of him.

"Ah, perfect." Mike gestures towards the lift. "Shall we?"

"You can't say whatever it is here?"

"There's a very comfortable lounge area up on Orthopaedics. I thought we could make use of it."

"Isn't this a quick chat?"

The lift dings and opens. Mike waves Tom in before following and pressing the button. "Did I say quick?"

"Yes."

Mike raises his brows and shrugs. "Well, maybe not quick per se…"

Tom huffs and slumps against the back of the lift. "I'm not in the mood for a fireside chit chat."

"No, I don't suppose you are." The lift opens and Mike stands back to let Tom out.

"You don't have to open doors for me."

"I know. But if I had got out of the lift first… what would you have done?"

"Pushed the door close button and gone back downstairs."

"Exactly." Mike taps his right temple and grins.

Tom follows him to the comfy lounge area that looks suspiciously like the comfy lounge area they just left. He sits and stretches his legs in front of him. "The floor's yours." He sips and waits.

Mike sits across from him and steeples his fingers under his nose. "How are you?"

Tom squints. "I'm not doing this now."

"You weren't in control in that berth today."

"Are you kidding? I was jumping between three victims —*two* victims and a piece of trash, all of which could have died at any moment."

"Yes."

"And I wasn't in control?"

"On a surface level you did what needed to be done."

"Exactly." Tom nods. "Wait. Surface level?"

"Underneath you were rocking back and forth in the corner, unable to breathe. Correct?"

"No." *Yes.*

Mike stares at Tom and waits.

"That doesn't work on me."

"What?"

"The whole *waiting for me to speak first* thing."

"You did speak first."

Tom rolls his eyes and presses his mouth shut.

"We have a good rapport, you and I."

Tom nods but keeps his mouth closed.

"Today would have been horrific for you."

"Would have?" Tom can't help himself and it annoys him. "It *was* horrific. I have a colleague who is in a critical condition and still may die, The First fucking Sea Lord needing Narcan injected into him… and well... Lawrence doesn't count. But… I'd say that was pretty *horrific* for a day at the office wouldn't you?"

"I would. But you forgot something."

"What?"

"What happened to *you* in there."

Tom holds both arms out and wiggles both his legs. "I seem to be rather intact."

"Physically. I agree."

Tom stops and sits still in the chair. "Can we not do this now?"

"You need to process—"

"No. I need to be downstairs with Isabella and Abbie. I need to be there for when James wakes up. I need to do… things."

"Of course you do. Because it distracts you."

"Look… I don't know what you *think* happened to me today but—"

"I saw you."

Tom's gut plunges. "Pardon?"

"I was coming back in after they took James to let you know his condition… but I stopped as you dropped onto the floor and ripped the bunk apart."

Tom's nostrils flare and he breaks eye contact to look anywhere but at Mike.

"I heard you and watched you, until Isabella came out. I ducked out of sight and waited until you both left together."

Tom's heart thumps and he picks at imaginary lint on his trousers. "Isn't that a bit creepy?"

"In my opinion you required my help. So… no. I don't believe it was creepy."

Tom nods but doesn't look up.

"You thought he was in the bunk?"

"I… I saw him. I blinked and he was there. And I blinked again, and he was gone. I needed to… find him again."

"But he was gone."

"He was never there."

"But he was once."

"He was never there today."

"No. But your brain didn't know it was today. It was back on the day Chris died."

Tom stands and walks around the waiting lounge. "Can we stop now?"

"Only if you come and see me—"

"Sorry. No go. I'm never getting on a ship again. In my life. Not even a P and O. Nothing. I'm done." Tom's voice slowly climbs, and two nurses look up from their station. "Never again," Tom finishes in a whisper.

"No trouble. I'm out in a month and a half. You can see me in private practice. Until then... we can video call."

Tom snorts and stares out the window. "Talk about ambulance chasing..."

"I have a responsibility to all the crew on that ship."

"Well, I'm not crew on that ship."

"You were once. And you weren't treated properly."

"There was... *is*... nothing wrong with me."

"Let me fix the wrongs of the past. You deserve that much. Don't you?"

Tom puts his hands on his head and turns to Mike. "You don't know the things I've done."

Mike watches Tom.

"I already go to AA. Isn't that enough torture?"

"Is it torture?"

"Have you *seen* the biscuits they put out? And the weak tea? It's torture."

Mike grins. "What if I promise to have strong black coffee and Penguins available?"

Tom huffs and sits. He hides his face in his hands. "Can you make it go away?"

"Make what go away?"

"All of it?"

"I can help you process it and live with it."

Tom rubs his face with his hands and leans back in the chair. "Proper coffee. None of that instant freeze dried shit."

"Done."

"And I prefer jaffa cakes."

"Can do."

"Fine."

———

TOM IS ON HIS FOURTH LAP AROUND THE ORTHOPAEDICS WARD when a nurse puts her hand on his arm. "Excuse me Sir?"

Tom looks at her and waits.

"Well, it's just… you've been wandering for the last fifteen minutes. Are you looking for someone?"

"No. Sorry. I'm waiting for…" He bites his lip. "I was just thinking and forgot I was on the wrong floor." *Could you sound any more pathetic?*

The nurse smiled as though he was an escapee from the psych ward. "I see. Well… if you need anything." She pats his arm and patters away.

Tom leans against the wall next to the lift. He shoves his hands in his pockets and tries to gather the strength to go back down to the girls. His exterior is stripped, and he can't hide anything. Facing two of the people that know him best right now wakes up the ball of angst in his gut.

His eyes travel up the doorframe of the room opposite the lift and he notices the heavy, bulky cast the patient has his leg inside. *Ouch.* He leans forward to see the patient watching the television suspended above his bed.

"Well, fuck me," Tom whispers. He looks to the nurses' station and they are chatting with their heads down looking at papers under a lamp. Tom pushes himself off the wall, walks across the corridor and leans against the doorframe. "What's on?"

Pike looks across the room. "Graeme Norton."

"I like him." Tom walks in, grabs a chair and straddles it.

"Yeah, today's guests aren't much cop." Pike presses a button on the remote and Graeme disappears mid question.

Tom gazes at the blank screen.

"Why are you here?"

"I was in the neighbourhood?"

Pike raises a brow and picks up his water. "Right."

"How's the leg?"

"In pieces. I've got more screws and wires than a suspension bridge."

"I bet."

"Seriously. Why are you here?"

"Commodore Matthew Lawrence took First Sea Lord Peter Moore hostage on *Arrochar*, and in the process of me and James trying to rescue him, Moore got dosed up on opiates, James was shot in the stomach and Lawrence was stabbed in the chest."

Pike glares at Tom. "You could've just said, passing through. No need to make shit up."

Tom shrugs as his phone sounds. He pulls it out. "Judith."

"Any word on James?"

"He's hanging on by a thread."

"I see. How are you?"

"I'm fine."

"I'd like you to pass some information on to Abigail if you would?"

"Of course. What is it?"

"Are you near a television?"

"Yeah."

"BBC news."

Tom dips the phone from his chin. "Can you put it on BBC?"

Pike rolls his eyes but flicks it on.

"… in an unusual twist today, Commodore Joshua Phillips was released from military prison where he was awaiting Court Martial, whilst the officer who accused him, Commodore Matthew Lawrence, was charged instead. Sources have made no comment about the suggestion Phillips will give evidence against his one-time accuser …"

Tom turns his attention back to the phone while Pike watches the rest of the news story as it recaps what Tom already told him. "Abbie will be happy about that."

"No doubt."

"Right... Well if that's it?"

"Did Mike find you?"

Tom swallows and doesn't answer.

"Don't get snippy. I was extremely concerned about you."

"You know I'm not sixteen anymore right?"

"A parent... guardian always worries, Tom."

A lump grows in Tom's throat, and he swallows again. "I'll call you later." He hangs up before any more emotion is allowed to surface. *I think that's enough for today.*

"Wow." Pike mutes the television and shakes his head. "You weren't having a go."

"Why would I bother?"

Pike shrugs and goes to speak before stopping.

"What is it?" Tom stands. "I need to go so…"

"If I could make it better I would."

"Make what better?"

"What I did to Hampshire. It's just… I was desperate and he was easy prey…" He shrugs. "I was the same at school… always stealing kid's lunch money. I'm the epitome of a stereo-typical schoolyard bully." He flops back against his pillows. "I'm a git."

Tom studies Pike a moment before sitting back down. "You want redemption?"

"Yeah. I mean… what have I got apart from the Royal Navy?"

"You tell me."

"Nothing. It's my life. *Was* my life. But once they look at everything I've been up to... I'm cooked, not to mention I might never walk properly again."

Tom runs his thumb across his bottom lip. "What if I could help you in some way?"

"What can you do?"

Tom grins. "I'm so glad you asked."

44

TOM

Tom walks into Martha's office as she's hanging up the phone. He sits on the sofa without saying anything.

Martha walks across the room and sits opposite him on the coffee table. "I was wrong."

Tom drags his eyes from the floor to meet hers.

"I should never have put you on that ship."

"If I couldn't do it, I would have said so at the start."

"You did. I didn't listen."

The silence stretches for too long before Tom shakes his head. "It's done."

"Exactly. And it can't be undone."

"James is awake."

"How is he?"

Tom nods. "They removed his spleen. He will be in for another ten days. I didn't speak to him."

"I'm sure we can cope without him for a time. Though it might be nice for you to go visit and… exchange actual words with him?"

"I waited at the hospital for half the day. What are you implying?"

"Nothing. Just… it might be nice for you to visit."

"Do I have to take flowers?"

Martha fixes him with her cat's bum face. "Now… what's this I hear of you striking a deal with Liam's solicitor?"

"Who told you that?"

"I have people."

Tom scoffs. "I didn't strike a deal with anyone."

"Is that right?"

"That's right. I simply said Pike may be able to assist in his defence. That's not striking a deal."

"What did you promise Pike?"

"That he wouldn't face dismissal with disgrace."

"You can't make that call."

"We saved Peter Moore's life. *He* can make that call."

"Isn't Pike's leg in a million pieces?"

"He can sit behind a desk… don't you have friends in recruitment?" Tom raises a brow.

"Don't drag me into your wheeling and dealing." Tom chuckles and Martha smiles. "What about Liam?"

Tom gut clenches. "What about him?"

"What are they going to ask for?"

"A suspended sentence. He knows he did wrong. But as far as he's concerned he was following orders of his superior."

"Is that defence going to work?"

"Haven't you seen A Few Good Men?"

"No. I never watch naval dramas… it's all bulldust."

"Fair. I read it if I'm being honest… the point is, their defence was that they were given a direct order."

"And what happened to them?"

"Dishonourably discharged."

"Oh."

"But… not guilty."

"I see."

"So let's test it in a real court martial." Tom shrugs. "Although, he'll more than likely be found guilty. And dismissed with disgrace."

"How do you feel about that?"

"He did the wrong thing. He knows it. Who cares what I think?"

"That wasn't my question. I asked how you *feel* about it."

Tom rolls his eyes. "You and Mike would make a good pair."

"He sounds like quite a lovely man—"

"Don't." Tom blanches.

A knock at the door catches both of their attention. Martha stands. "Yes?"

Isabella opens the door and peeks in. "Can I come in?"

"Of course, my dear."

The heaviness on Tom's shoulders lifts as he stands and pulls her into a hug against his chest. "Call me when you get there?"

She stands on tiptoes and kisses him. "Okay but stop stressing. All the baddies are locked away now, and I'll be home for good in two weeks." She winks and lets him go. Isabella turns to Martha and Tom hides a smile as she stiffens and gives Isabella a curt nod.

"For goodness sakes Martha. Hug me." Isabella smothers her in a hug and Martha gives her the usual pat on the back.

"Good luck for the rest of your training, my dear."

"I'll be back before you know it." She winks at Tom and blows him a kiss. "Keep me updated."

Tom nods. "I will."

She skips out the door and Tom sits; the heaviness lingers over his shoulders again.

Martha claps her hands together once. "Now. We need to discuss Abigail."

"Can I speak to her first?"

"You can. And I'd like you to mention something…"

———

Tom climbs the stairs to his flat, counting them as he goes. *Lucky thirteen.*

"Ah! Tom."

Tom looks up into the smiling face of Edward, standing at the top of the stairs with a black trash bag.

Tom nods. "Ed."

"Haven't seen you and Isabella around much of late."

"Working." *I'm really not in the mood...*

Tom leans against the wall and Edward makes no attempt to keep going down the stairs. "Well, if you're both free soon maybe we can have tea."

Tom rubs his face. "Sure. Great. It's a date." Tom trudges to his door, hoping Edward gets the message.

"When?"

Tom sighs and plonks his forehead against his door. "I'll get back to you."

"Lovely! Well… cheerio."

Tom opens his door as Edward's footsteps fade down the staircase. The chain on Lorna's door jingles and Tom slips inside before she gets it open. He leans against the closed door and takes a breath. "It's a minefield, that hallway."

Abbie sits up on the sofa and rubs her eyes. "Hey."

"Were you sleeping?" He sits in the armchair.

"Dozing."

Tom nods and fiddles with his hands.

"What's up, Tom?"

"What do you mean?"

"You're fiddling with your hands."

"So?"

"You obviously have things to say that aren't comfortable."

She tucks her feet under her backside and nurses a throw cushion. "So let me have it."

"It's annoying how well you know me sometimes."

Abbie grins. "Ditto."

Tom leans forward and rests his forearms on his knees. "You're going to be investigated for your part in Lawrence's actions."

Abbie bites her lip and picks at the corner of the cushion. "I figured I would."

"You just need to tell the truth, Abs."

Her eyes pierce his own. "I always have."

Tom holds up his hands in mock surrender. "I know. I'm saying… the truth doesn't change. So be honest and don't try and dance around any of it."

Abbie nods. "What do you think will happen?"

"I don't know. But… unless they can prove you knew what was in that envelope… or that you made deals with Amir over dinner…"

"I guess I'll have to roll with the punches."

"And they will have Liam's side of things… that'll bode well for you."

"What about Matt?"

"Do you care?"

Abbie shrugs. "Curious."

"He committed serious offences against the Commonwealth, the Royal Navy, and murdered his wife. I'm no expert but I figure he's going to be locked away for the rest of his miserable existence."

"Well, I guess I better start looking for shelf stacking jobs at Tesco or something. And a shoebox to live in."

"You can stay here as long as you need to."

Abbie smiles. "I know. But that's a big imposition."

"Martha would like you to meet with her at nine am on Monday morning."

Abbie sits up straighter and the cushion falls to the floor. "About?"

"No idea."

"Liar."

Tom stands up. "I'm offended." He opens the fridge. "Maybe it's secret girl's business."

"I can see straight through you, Grant."

Tom gulps milk from the bottle before putting it back in the fridge. "Goodnight, Abs."

"Grant!"

Tom laughs as he closes his bedroom door.

45

ABBIE

A bbie follows Penny through the warehouse towards Martha's office.

"She may have stepped out," Penny says as she opens the door to the empty office. "Take a seat. She won't be far away."

Abbie sits and squashes her hands under her legs. Her shoulders creep up under her ears as she looks around the room. Her eyes rest on the sofa. *Looks lumpy.*

"Ah! Ms Perkins." Martha sits behind her desk.

"Yes. Sorry. Penny told me to sit—"

"It's perfectly fine." Martha waves away Abbie's concern. She slaps papers in front of Abbie. "Have a read through these. If they work for you, please sign where indicated by the stickers."

"I… sorry what is this?"

"Employment contract. And training requirements." Abbie looks up from the papers and Martha smiles. "Training starts in three months."

EPILOGUE
TOM

Isabella knocks on the smart white door and Tom observes the hallway. "Are you sure this is the right place?" Tom frowns at the elegant Murano glass wall sconces and the gilded moulding around the cornice.

"Yes."

The door opens and Mischa smiles at them with Sylvie on her hip.

"Mish!" Isabella envelopes her and Sylvie in a hug. "I didn't know you'd be here."

"He will not cook for himself." She grins and pecks Tom on the cheek before handing Sylvie over as she clambers at him.

"Hey, Squirt." Tom holds her in the air as she giggles and kicks her legs. Tom pulls her in against him and follows Isabella into the flat.

"Hey." James is on the sofa with a pillow behind his back.

He clicks the television on mute as Isabella kisses his cheek and sits next to him.

"How are you feeling?"

"Fine. I'm bored to be honest."

Tom sits on the sofa across from James with Sylvie on his lap. "How long have you lived here?" Sylvie immediately tries to climb up Tom's chest and grab his nose. He takes her hand and blows a raspberry on it.

"About five years. My grandfather left it to me." James grins at Tom. "Too posh for me isn't it?"

"Well since you mention it—

"It's beautiful." Isabella accepts the tea Mischa holds out to her before looking at Tom. "Behave."

James shrugs. "It's just a two bedder but it does the job."

"How are you feeling?" Isabella sips her tea and shoots Tom a side eye warning.

Tom swallows a grunt and raises his eyebrow in response. "Yeah. When are you coming back?"

"Do you miss me?" James smirks as Mischa puts a plate of cake on the coffee table and sits next to Tom, relieving him of Sylvie.

"Like a hole in the head."

James laughs and winces, pushing his hand against his abdomen. "A couple of weeks, I reckon I'll be back."

Mischa tuts. "This is major injury. Stop trying to be hero." She gives him a warm smile.

Tom cringes before realising his thoughts are showing on his face and looks at the plush carpet. *Oh, this cannot be happening.*

"I'm lucky Mish has been around to cook for me. I'd be living off curry and Chinese."

Oh Jesus, it is happening.

Isabella bounces on the sofa and claps her hands. "Oh, I'm so happy for you both. You're adorable together."

James looks at Mischa and they both blush before Mischa busies herself with putting Sylvie on the floor to crawl around.

"You haven't moved in here have you, Mish?" Tom widens his eyes and looks between the pair of them. *Please say no.*

"No. I have not." She pats Tom's leg. "Relax."

"I'm relaxed."

"Is that why your voice is so high?"

Tom clears his throat and stares at the mute television. "Hey, turn it up… that's Joshua Phillips."

James clicks the mute off.

"… Commodore Phillips was reinstated at a meeting in the Secretary of Defence's office yesterday. It is believed he will be considered for promotion as early as the New Year… "

"Uncle Peter came by the day I came home."

Tom snorts. "I bet that was a barrel of laughs."

"He apologised to me."

"For which bit?"

"Everything. It's like he's learned some kind of lesson and decided to make amends. I didn't quite know what to say to him."

"That's great to hear James. Family is important." Isabella squeezes his shoulder.

"Thanks, Iz. But my dad still hasn't even called to say hi. So let's not get carried away."

Tom can't understand why this conversation makes him uncomfortable, but it does, and he looks back at the television.

"... she's the seventh teenage girl to go missing in the last six months from the area. The National Crime Agency has reached out to Interpol—"

"Tom?"

Tom snaps his face around and everyone is looking at him. "What?"

"I said it's great Abbie is starting up with us." James adjusts himself on the sofa and Mischa jumps up to fuss over him.

Isabella wrinkles her nose and smiles at them.

Dear God.

"I've kept all my notes and stuff for her," Isabella says. "She'll breeze through." She looks at the television and her face pales. "What's that about?"

"Nothing." Tom reaches across and snaps the television off. "Wanna hand me some cake, Iz?" His feeble attempt at distraction fails, as he knew it would.

She blinks, staring at the black screen. "What's happening to those girls?" The room is silent, and all eyes turn to Tom.

"Running away from home probably." He waves and gets Isabella's eyes on him. "Cake?"

She picks up the plate and holds it out to him. "They aren't running away from home, Tom."

"Carrot cake. My favourite." Tom narrows his eyes at Isabella and gives his head the smallest shake. "So James, what year was this block built anyway?"

ABOUT THE AUTHOR

Samantha Adair lives on the Northern Beaches of Sydney Australia with her family and golden retriever.

When she isn't writing, she can be found in her favourite coffee nook reading a good book or nattering with friends.

Find out more about Samantha by visiting the following:
www.samanthaadairauthor.com.au

Join Adair's Assassins Here:
https://www.facebook.com/groups/356574645452483/

Become part of the street team here:
ARC offers - https://booksprout.co/author/19790/samantha-adair

ALSO BY SAMANTHA ADAIR

Blood Orphan

Deadly Deceit

Motherland